Mountain Justice

Hope you enjoy it.
Jerry L. Haynes

Mountain Justice

A SEARCH FOR THE TRUTH
IN THE AFTERMATH OF THE CARROLL
COUNTY COURTHOUSE TRAGEDY

JERRY L. HAYNES

WORD ASSOCIATION PUBLISHERS
www.wordassociation.com
1.800.827.7903

Printed in the United States of America.

ISBN: 978-1-59571-769-6

Library of Congress Control Number: 2012931383

Designed and published by

Word Association Publishers
205 Fifth Avenue
Tarentum, Pennsylvania 15084

www.wordassociation.com
1.800.827.7903

I dedicate this book to the memory
of Deriek Wayne Crouse

Deriek grew up and played baseball in my hometown Fries, Virginia. He was the son of a high school friend Bonnie Arnold, and the nephew of my other friends and classmates, Linda, Anne, and David Arnold. He served as a soldier in Iraq defending the country I love. Shortly after noon, on December 8, 2011, Officer Crouse, at the age of 39, while serving as a VA Tech campus policeman, was shot and killed in an act of senseless violence while defending the University I love.

Acknowledgments

This book is a work of fiction. As an historical novel, I strived to weave an exciting tale from a series of actual events.

Often authors state they don't know where to begin in expressing their thanks, but as for me, it is very easy. If it were not for the hard work of Ron Hall in *The Carroll County Courthouse Tragedy,* I would never have ventured to write my novel. I have read almost every book written on the subject, and in this author's opinion, Hall's accounting is by far the most accurate, complete and unbiased. Not only did Ron take the time to introduce me to the fine volunteers of the Carroll County Historical Society, but he also took me on personal tours of pertinent sites. Although I was raised in Carroll County, I had never known these locations. Thank you Ron for your patience in answering my numerous inquiries, even interrupting your honeymoon to answer my e-mails.

Speaking of the Carroll County Historical Society, what a wonderful asset you were to me, and are to people throughout the state. I was amazed at the genealogical data base that you have compiled.

Kudos to two new friends, The Honorable Michael Valentine, retired Judge, and Tom Caceci, PhD, esteemed professor at the Virginia-Maryland Regional College of Veterinary Medicine, for their advice on the various firearms used in the tragedy. I extend my heartfelt appreciation to them for assembling models of the various weapons and allowing me to shoot them to get a first-hand experience of the characteristics of the different models. Further appreciation is given to the Honorable Judge for his critiquing of my legal dialogue and narrative.

Additional thanks to the staffs of The Public Library of Virginia, the Carroll County Historical Society, the Wythe County District Court, and the Carroll County District Court. I appreciate the editorial comments of

Shelby Puckett, Ron Hall, E. Gary Marshall, and most especially, my old classmate, Gail (Compton) Minter. As always I appreciate not only the proofreading of my good friend Diann Gardner, but also for her never-ending words of encouragement.

If you have not read Ron Hall's true account of the 1912 gun battle, "The Carroll County Courthouse Tragedy", I urge you to order it on-line by going to http://historicalsociety.chillsnet.org/ and clicking on book sales.

I do hope you enjoy this story. I have tried to capture the passion of the participants of the tragedy, but I do want to emphasize I do not want to trivialize or romanticize the event. It was a horrific example of the human frailty of needing to impose one's paradigm through violence. This violence has divided friends, families, and a community for more than a hundred years.

As a historical novel, there has to be antagonists and protagonists. In no way did I seek to pass judgment on either side, or to find fault, but for the purpose of the book, it was necessary for the main characters to have certain inherent perceptions as to where fault might lie. My apologies to any that feel my main character may have seemed harsh to some.

There were some lessons learned from the tragedy, but unfortunately, senseless violence still exists today. To witness, those recent events on the campus of VA Tech, my alma mater, where within a span of 42 months we have seen 34 innocent people die through violence. The most recent of these was the subject of my dedication.

I hope this novel will make you think. I'm sure you'll have some questions about what in the novel was based upon fact and with what I have taken literary license. I invite you to contact me at *handh_services@hotmail.com* about this book and my other books listed on the next page.

Fiction:

A Cottonmill Town Christmas

The Cotton Mill

The Saga of Caty Sage

Non-fiction:

The All New, and Improved, You

Introduction

Floyd Allen fidgeted on the edge of the holding cell cot, cleaning his fingernails with a broom straw. He ran his fingers through his hair. Of all the things he had missed being in prison, two were his pocket knife and his metal comb. He jerked his head upward, tilting it to listen to the footsteps echoing in the concrete hallway. A quick but heavy tap, tap, followed by a slight shuffling. That would be Clarence Jones, the jailer who walked with a limp. He then heard a livelier, but quieter footstep. That would be the Lutheran pastor Dr. John J. Scherer. His heart raced. Maybe the ruse had worked.

The jailer turned the corner, carrying the tray of food. Floyd's heart sank. Instead of the usual unknown meat, stale green beans, dry corn, and three-day old bread, he saw the large Porterhouse steak, cabbage and corn-beef, apple cobbler with ice cream, and fresh rolls.

The look on Dr. Scherer's face confirmed that Floyd Allen had been brought his last meal.

He tried to stand, but his leg, still crippled from the gun-shot wounds of a year earlier, failed to support him and he fell back to the bed. The cell door squeaked, and the jailer, a forlorn look masking his weathered face, carried the metal tray to the prison. The jailer quickly turned away, refusing to look at the inmate.

"Floyd, I'm so sorry..." the pastor said, then stopped without being able to continue.

"What happened?" Floyd asked weakly. "Did the lieutenant governor change his mind about going through with it?"

The week before renewed hope had been sprung. Encouraged by the 50,000 signatures of Virginians calling for a stay of execution for the Allens, and fueled further by his dislike of Governor Mann, Lieutenant

Governor J. Taylor Ellison had agreed to consider exercising a relatively unknown, and never before used state law. Governor Mann had scheduled a trip to Trenton, New Jersey for a speech. While he was away, the lt. governor would assume executive power. This authority extended to the stay of executions. Everything had supposedly been kept discrete. So as to not indicate any covert plans, Floyd, as scheduled late the night before, had chosen his final meal to be eaten on his day of electrocution, He had also been shaved to prep for the electrodes.

"I just don't know Floyd," the pastor said, as he wiped first his glasses, then his eyes with a cotton handkerchief. "Someone warned the governor when he stopped in Philadelphia. We think it might have been Attorney General Williams. So the governor jumped back on a private train and made it back to Alexandria early this morning. He wired that he was back on Virginia soil, and was again assuming authority, so the electrocution ..."

The pastor could not finish. He merely sat down on the cot next to Floyd and put his arm around him. Floyd Allen remained stoic, determined to not break down. He nodded understandingly.

"I guess that's the way it has to be then," Floyd Allen said, and then began to eat.

The cell was silent; the jailer looking out the bars into the hallway, the pastor with his head bent and resting on the open Bible on his lap and Floyd eating. After about ten minutes, Floyd laid the half eaten dinner down onto the floor.

"So when will it happen?" he asked.

"I'll be coming back to get you in about sixty minutes," the jailer said, not turning to face the condemned man. "The pastor can stay here with you until I come back."

"And Claude?" Floyd asked, his voice cracking at the speaking of his son.

"He's scheduled for about thirty minutes after you."

"Does he have someone with him?" Floyd asked the pastor.

"Yes, Pastor McDaniel is with him."

The jailer stepped back into the hallway. He turned. The jailer, and the condemned, looked into each other's eyes.

"Floyd, you know if I thought there was anyway you'd make it out of here, I'd leave this door wide open, don't you?"

"Yes, Clarence. I know you would. You've been a good friend. I appreciate all you've done."

The jailer slowly closed the door, turned the key, and walked away. Floyd listened until the footsteps had died away.

"Floyd, we'll spend the time anyway you want. You've already made it right with God. If you do have anything else you want to say, to confess..."

A flash of anger swept over Floyd's face, but then disappeared just as quickly. "No Pastor, I've said all that needs to be said about that day. Thinking back, I know I've done bad things, but I've made my heart right with God."

"I'm glad to hear that?" the pastor said. "What about your feelings though. I feel you still have hatred."

"I've forgiven those who committed trespasses against me. I will confess that I do still have hatred in my heart for some though, especially Deck Goad. So I guess we should pray about that."

All too soon the heavy tap-tap was heard coming down the hall. Floyd pulled several sheets of paper from the Bible that Pastor Scherer had left with him.

"Pastor," Floyd whispered, "Claude and me, we put down a few things, I guess you'd call it a...."

The pastor took the papers from the trembling hands and slipped them into his Bible.

"What would you like for me to do with them?" The pastor asked.

"Please see that they get to Jeremiah Haynes, that young journalist. He agreed to be a witness today, so you should be able to find him. After it's over."

The lock moaned. Clarence Jones, and another jailer whom Floyd did not know, entered. The second guard, who looked barely twenty years of age, pulled a set of shackles from a canvas bag.

"No, Jimmy, no chains."

"But you know that's procedure, Clarence."

"I'll take the blame, but no chains. Not yet."

Floyd gave an appreciative nod.

When they reached the end of the hallway, Clarence turned away from the exit, and started down the corridor. The second jailer looked puzzled, but followed.

They came to a cell containing a handsome man of about twenty-three years of age.

"Daddy," Claude said, springing from the cot that he was sharing with Pastor McDaniel. Clarence unlocked the door, and motioned for Floyd to enter.

"I'm sorry Floyd, I can only give you about three minutes, or they'll be sending someone to check on us. Come on, pastors, let's give them some time alone."

The group walked to the end of the corridor, while the father and son embraced, unable to overcome their emotions enough to even speak.

"Son, I'm sorry I got you into this mess," Floyd said, as his emotions choked him. "If I had known what was going to happen, I would never have had you in the courthouse that day."

"If I hadn't of been, they would have shot you down like a dog Daddy. I know they would've."

"Well, that would have been better than both of us dying today."

"Floyd, we have to go now," the voice came from the end of the corridor. The sound of shackles clanging echoed throughout the hall.

The father took one last look at his son.

"Stay strong, Claude. Remember, you're an Allen."

1

Find the truth

I turned the folded note over in my hand for at least the fifth time since sitting down. Mr. Allen had given it to me two days before, with the stern instructions not to read it until he had been executed. I looked around the room at the others, all called together for the same reason, to witness and authenticate the execution of Floyd Allen. Many were jurors from the original trials.

A commotion on the other side of the one-way glass commanded my attention. I watched a very frail, but still proud, Floyd Allen, hobbling to the center of the room.

Was the limp from the bullet still partially lodged in the old man's hip, or from the shackles around his ankles?

I watched as the 2-inch leather straps secured him to the thick wooden chair. I watched his body shudder as the electrodes were secured to his shaved arms. I grimaced as a hood was slipped over his head. Mr. Allen's fingers began tapping the arm of the chair, as if tapping out a tune. A familiar tune.

I saw his chest heave a few times.

Then the lights flickered, as 2000 volts surged through the man seated before me. Floyd Allen's fingers splayed, stretching as if trying to throw each knuckle out of its socket. I felt my own body jerk in response. His fingers twitched twice more. A puff of smoke gushed into the air. The body became flaccid, as if all essence had been drained. I felt light-headed as if I might actually faint, but then realized I had been holding my breath for several seconds. I tried to exhale, but the air caught in my lungs. My chest ached, burned.

My God, am I having a heart attack?

Finally, my breathing returned, in short, quick pants.

I tried to stand, afraid I was going to vomit. Instead I slumped back into my chair, trembling. I felt numb, as if the life forces had been burned also out of me. The others began departing, some laughing, joking, but most silent, dumbstruck, like I at the horrific sight we had served witness to. I watched as the prison doctor placed a stethoscope to the man's chest. He nodded his head, indifferently, looked up at the clock overhead, and apathetically signed the form that was placed in front of him.

"You need to leave now," a gruff voice interrupted me from my observations.

"What?" I said, with a start.

"You got to get out now," the prison guard said, "the other witnesses need to come in for the boy's execution."

I stood, took a step cautiously, praying my legs would carry my weight, and then I exited the room. After entering the hallway, a man approached me. I recognized him as being someone who had been ministering to Mr. Allen the last several months.

"Are you Jeremiah Haynes, the journalist?"

"Yes Sir, I am, and you're Mr. Allen's pastor, Dr. Scherer?"

"Yes, I am," he said, extending his hand. "I've offered Mr. Allen spiritual guidance since he's been here in Richmond."

He opened his Bible, removed several pages, and handed them to me.

"Floyd said to give these to you. He said you'd know what to do with them."

"Thank you sir," I said, slipping the papers into my coat pocket.

"After you read them, you might have some questions," the pastor said. "If so, I'll be glad to meet with you."

The journalist in me wanted to sit down and immediately read them, but all I could think about was getting back to the newspaper, where my life could return to a hectic normalcy. There I would be away from the most horrific experience of my life.

It was only then I remembered the folded note I still held. Slowly, I opened it. Scribbled in Floyd Allen's childish handwriting were three simple words, FIND THE TRUTH.

Little did I know that my life, as I knew it, would never again be the same.

2

In thirty minutes I was back at the offices of the Richmond Evening Journal. William Archer, chief editor of the newspaper, was pacing the floor in front of my desk, puffing on his ever-present cigar that always kept his head enshrouded with a brume of smoke.

"Where the hell have you been?" He said as he whirled on me. "The execution was finished nearly an hour ago. We can only hold those presses for another hour and half. I need something on my desk in sixty minutes."

I had learned years before that Mr. Archer was not happy unless he was stressed to the point of neurasthenia. I mumbled an excuse about being detained at the prison. Sitting at my desk, I pulled papers from several pockets, laid them to the side, and began furiously pounding the keys of my Underwood #5 typewriter.

My dream since graduating from Richmond College had been to be a world acclaimed journalist. I seemed to be on a fast track until two years ago, and was now working my way back to just being the best journalist at the second-best paper in Richmond. I had prayed for a story that would launch me on my way. This might just be the opportunity for which I had longed. Somehow though, I was going to have to put aside the emotions that were still churning inside me in order to report his death.

Why had I agreed to do this? I asked myself. I had grown close to the grizzled old man who had been called wild, villainous, and other much worse names. Why had he specifically asked me to serve as witness? I opened the note and read again. It was now so obvious. Mr. Allen had asked me to be a witness so that I would be committed to finding the truth, whatever that meant.

I did have to admit that I felt a sense of excitement that I had been one of only three journalists in the room, and the youngest by far. After all, I now had an exclusive for that night's edition. The press was even being held for my story. But the truth was I wasn't sure I could write about what I had just witnessed, or at least may not be able to do it creditably.

I had read reports of other executions by the electric chair. I had read the first execution, of a man named William Kemmler, had been botched, and had to be repeated. Many more had also malfunctioned. There were so many things that could go wrong, such as the flesh actually catching on fire. I knew Floyd Allen wasn't totally innocent, but no one deserved to go through some of the mistakes that could happen in that chair. I was very thankful that nothing had apparently gone wrong today.

My mind kept returning to the events from barely an hour before. Watching Floyd Allen hobble to the thick wooden chair. Those ten minutes had been surreal. I had read reports of "after-death" experiences where the people say they felt their spirits leave their bodies and watch from another point. That's how I felt. I knew my body was behind the window, but I felt like my spirit was in that room with him. We had been told that the glass was soundproof, so we would not be able to hear anything going on. But thinking back, I could feel those leather straps being drawn tight against his wrists. Once he jerked; I could have sworn I heard him moan. When the hood was slipped over his head, I could hear his rapid pants, either as a man suffocating, or as a man trying to take all the final breaths he could. And when the time had come, and Floyd Allen's body began to spasm, I had felt my own body convulsing. And when the smoke escaped from beneath the hood, my nostrils had repulsed from the offensive odor of burnt flesh. For a moment, I actually envied the man. All of his worries, all of his disappointments, now gone.

How I wish I could find such peace.

"Damnit Haynes," Archer roared. "I don't pay you top dollar to sit at your table and day-dream."

"You don't pay me top dollar," I mumbled.

"Uh? What was that?"

"I'm on it chief," I said as I returned to pounding the keys.

The roller squealed as I jerked the paper out of the typewriter five minutes before the deadline. I ran full speed to the editor's office. Mr. Archer by now had worn a groove in the floor. The typesetter stood waiting to rush my article to print.

RICHMOND EVENING DISPATCH

Floyd and Claude Allen Die in Electric Chair

Dateline: Richmond, VA.

Date: March 28, 1913

Earlier today, at a time most people are finishing their lunches, Floyd Allen, whom many considered to be the head of the Allen clan from Carroll County, Virginia was strapped into the electric chair at the Virginia State Penitentiary, and was electrocuted. His son Claude Swanson Allen, named for the highly respected former Virginia governor and Senator, followed him about ten minutes later. Little did the Allen family know, a mere one year and fifteen days ago, that today two of their members would be dead, and another four serving time in prison.

This journalist today served in the official capacity of witness, a role I swear I will never perform again.

I will not attempt to declare in this article as to the innocence, or the guilt, of either Floyd Allen, or his son Claude. This argument has raged for the better of five months among some of the most brilliant legal minds of our commonwealth. I will attempt, in my humble way, to present in as succinct manner as I can, a summary of the events.

As everyone in these United States knows, the two Allens were charged for murder following the events of March 14 of last year. For three weeks they dominated headlines across the nation until replaced by the sinking of the

Titanic. The men were eventually found guilty and sentenced to die. They arrived at the State Penitentiary on October 26, 1912. According to the guards I have spoken to, the Allens have been exemplary prisoners. It is reported that Claude was entrusted to do work throughout the prison and even for Prison Superintendent Wood personally.

The request for appeals began almost immediately upon arrival at the prison. Officially, a total of three requests were made which led to the sentencing being continued three times. During this time also, a petition was started by this newspaper for the actual wait of execution for the two men. Reportedly, over 50,000 signatures, including nearly all of the jurors who had originally cast the sentence, were collected. Much new information was presented to the current governor and the attorney general. In the end, it was all summarily rejected.

Thus ended the last chance of reprieve for Floyd Allen and Claude Swanson Allen. Following their last meal, the two men were led to the room housing the electric chair. I do not dare to even attempt to comprehend the horrific experience, the sight, the sound, the odor, of an electrocution. I will leave that to the reader's mind. Suffice it to say, Floyd Allen was declared dead at 1:26 PM, Claude Swanson Allen at 1:38 PM.

A reporter is not expected to lose his objectivity, but I would like at this time to lay my professionalism aside and express my sorrow to the Allen family. A journalist is not supposed to get close to his subjects, but I failed in my attempt to avoid this.

There will be several related articles in this paper over the next week.

The editor grabbed the copy and began reading. His frantic editing of the story, slashing a line here, adding a few words there, the whole while chomping on his cigar, combined with hair that stayed disheveled due to his incessant running of his fingers through it, gave him somewhat of a mad-man appearance.

"Gotta strike out that last paragraph about expressing sorrow to the family," he said.. "I'll do that tomorrow in an editorial. I do like how you mentioned the future articles. We want to keep the readers coming back for more."

He then wrote at the end of the article, 'We promise our readers an exclusive article, that will not be found in any other newspaper, each day for the next week'.

He handed the copy to the typesetter, who scurried off as fast as sixty year old legs could scurry.

The chief walked back to his desk, re-lit the soggy cigar, and sat down on the corner. I waited nervously. Finally I broke the silence.

"Well sir, how was it?"

"It was a good article, son. Damn good," the editor said, as he took a deep puff and exhaled the thick aromatic smoke. "Probably the best you've ever done. But what are we going to give them as exclusives?"

"For starters, I have the final statements of both Floyd and Claude," I said.

"You what!" The editor screamed, nearly biting the end off the cigar. "Why didn't you tell me? Why didn't you put that in the article?"

"It's complicated. Mr. Allen didn't actually tell me to print it. I needed some time to think about it. Also, I didn't have time to use it tonight, so that's why I said there would be some follow-up stories."

He resumed manducating the cigar, the tip looking like a see-saw bobbing up and down. By this time, my black suit was covered with gray ashes. I kept expecting some to fall into his overflowing trash can, starting a fire that would burn down the building, and the presses, before my story ever got printed.

"Does anyone else know about these statements?" He said.

"Only Pastor Scherer. He delivered them to me. Maybe Pastor McDaniel. I don't think they'll say anything, though."

"Believe me, the Richmond Times would pay most anything for this information. They'd steal it from the Pope himself. OK, this is what we're going to do. Spend tonight writing a follow-up and then show the statements. The lede is yours. Fill it up. And have it finished by 2 o'clock. We're going out with an early edition."

My eyes blinked in amazement. The lede? I had never had more than 200 lines before tonight, and those were usually buried on page six.

"What I thought, Sir, is that I could do a short story, and announce we'll be printing the final statements over a four day spread. They're pretty lengthy. Too much for one day."

"Yeah. Yeah. I like that. Good idea. Just keep the readers hooked."

"I'd also like to do an interview with the pastor, Dr. Scherer. I'll use this to lead in the release of the final statements."

The editor sat looking out the window at a pigeon cooing on the sill. He tapped the glass. The bird flew. For a moment I thought about repeating myself, thinking he had not heard me.

"That sounds like it might work," he said. I sensed a steeliness in his voice, as if he felt almost cocky over the articles.

"There's one more thing," I said. "I'd like to get all this written by tomorrow. Then while it's being run, I'd like to run down to Hillsville for the funeral and stay for five or so days. I think there's more there."

"You don't think we're trying to milk this cow too much?"

"No Sir I don't. I think this story has a life of its own. There's already talk by several religious organizations about bringing suit again the Commonwealth for wrongful executions. They've started calling it, 'judicial murder.'"

The editor walked back to the window, again scaring the pigeon away, and gazed down upon the street.

"So you think you can keep all this under wraps? We can scoop the Times on all this?" His voice had the anticipation of a child on Christmas morning.

"I think we can."

The editor pounded his fist into his hand. "Damn, what I'd give to have a couple of weeks out-scooping those guys. OK, you got it. Get me a week's worth of stories, then you can have five days, no more than seven, down with those hillbillies."

"Yes sir. I'll get started right now. Then I'll send you a couple of articles from the mountains."

I then witnessed an event that happens only occasionally more than a full eclipse of the sun. William Archer actually smiled. Not just a grin, a full, wide mouthed, cigar- falling-out-of-his-mouth, smile.

"Those bastards over at the Times," he said, "are going to crap in their pants when they see tomorrow's edition."

I never left the office that night. I made a fresh pot of coffee and raided the ice box. I took several big bites from a 3-day old meatloaf sandwich as I walked to my desk. I pounded away. It's times like this that I wondered why I do it. Is this all I will ever have to look forward to? Meeting one more deadline, just to find another. All for a second rate local? I only slipped away from my typewriter to take a quick nap between 4 AM and 7 AM.

When William Archer came into the office at eight I handed him the statements broken into installments, enough to last a week. I told him that I would get the last interview with Pastor John Jacob Scherer before I left town. I told him I'd send it to him by courier, because I'd have to rush to the train by five to have any chance of making it to Hillsville by the next morning.

3

After a couple of hours of sleep that morning, I grabbed the street car to Stewart Circle on Monument Avenue on the far western section of the city. After I had stepped to the street, I checked my watch. It was noon, hopefully the pastor would be in. For a few moments I just stared in awe at the mammoth stone structure before me. The church had only been built two years prior. The large towers at the corner reminded me of the Tower of London.

I approached a young boy pulling weeds from a flower bed at the front steps.

"Excuse me," I asked, "but can you tell me where I might find Dr. Scherer?"

"The pastor is in his study, at the back of the church," the boy said, never slowing down from his task, or looking up. "It has his name on the door., I'll show you if you want me to."

I watched the boy for a few moments, sensing something unusual about him.

"No, I'm sure I can find it," I said. "I hate pulling weeds. You actually look like you enjoy it."

"Yes sir," the boy said. "It's always fun doing God's work. The pastor said my weed pulling is just as important to God as his work is."

"Thank you very much for your time," I said.

I knelt and reached out may hand to shake his. He ignored my gesture. It was only then I realized the young boy was blind. For a moment, I realized my life wasn't as bleak as I thought it to be. I patted him on the head.

As directed, at the back corner were three steps leading down to a door. Above the door was a sign that read, "Dr. John J. Scherer, visitors always welcome." I tapped on the door.

"Please come in," a voice called from inside.

I entered and said, "Dr. Scherer, I'm Jeremiah Haynes. From the paper? You had told me I could come by if I had questions? I was hoping you might have a few moments."

The man stood and approached me, both his hands outstretched.

I couldn't help but notice that this man, who was not more than ten years older than me, seemed to have such a divine persona. Righteous, but not pious. Striking, but not handsome. Tall and slim, the pastor looked like what I though the Pope would look like, minus the vestments.

"Of course, of course. It's good to see you. Please have a seat."

"I met your young gardener; he is a fine young man."

"Oh, you mean Jason. Yes, he is a truly exceptional youngster. He came from a bad home that rejected him because of his disability. Anytime I can, I try to help young men find their footing. That's usually all it takes, a hand down, instead of a hand-out."

"I know everything that has happened has been arduous on you, but I was hoping you might offer some insight into what you think the real Floyd and Claude Allen were like."

The pastor pushed his six-foot frame back into the big leather chair, locked his hands in front of him, and raised his hands to his chin as if in prayer. His eyes took on a distant look, as he told his story of how, back in 1912, he and some of the other pastors had started a prison ministry. The Allens had been brought to Richmond on Saturday, October 26th. On the third or fourth day after they arrived he was given permission to speak with them. Dr. Scherer said both of them, at the beginning, were somewhat reserved. What mountain people would call 'stand offish'. He thought it was perhaps the shock of being in what people have begun to call "death row".

"But after a couple of weeks," he said, "they began to open up to me. I think it benefited me when they discovered I grew up near Hillsville."

"You're not from a big city?"

"No, not at all. I was born in Marion, only about 80 miles away from Hillsville. My father John J. Senior, was born in Rural Retreat, and was a college president. He opened Marion College. So, I think once they learned that, they felt I could understand them more than some of the other pastors, and they began to open up."

"If I might ask, what were the first things they talked about?"

"I'm sure you understand there are many things that were said in confidence that I cannot reveal."

"Yes sir, I certainly will respect that. Anything you might share will be appreciated. I'm sure you know, but I do want to be forthright with you, I am using this for future articles, and so I will be taking notes. If you wish, I will name you only as 'an unidentified witness'."

"I assumed that was why you are here, and I'll be glad to tell you what I know that doesn't fall within the realm of confidentially. I would like to help you find the truth."

My left eye twitched at the pastor's choice of words. He smiled and continued.

"To answer your question though, both men were more concerned about their loved ones than about themselves. Mr. Allen was especially concerned about his wife who was not in good health."

"Yes, I could see that reflected in his last statements. But I'm sorry, please continue."

"Claude was concerned about his mother and his girl friend Nellie Wisler. They were not allowed to write letters their first two weeks here, so they asked me to contact their loved ones saying I was their spiritual advisor, and to let them know they were adjusting, and to not worry."

"Miss Wisler was very active in trying to obtain a pardon for Claude, wasn't she?"

"Yes, very much. She was fervent in her defense of him. She was extremely articulate. A teacher I believe. I think I heard her father was also a clergyman. She had the tenacity of a bull dog though, and the governor had to respect her, even if he never fully supported her requests."

"How were their states of mind when they first arrived? The first couple of months?"

"Mr. Allen was still having a lot of problems with his hip, where he had been shot, and seemed to be in a great deal of pain. I don't think I ever heard him complain though. He would apologize because he couldn't kneel to pray. I told him that he need not worry, that God cared more for what came from man's heart, than what came from his knees."

"Dr. Scherer, ..."

"Please call me John, I couldn't be much older than you. May I call you Jeremiah?"

"Certainly John, Thank you." I said, then forgetting what I was asking, looked back down on my notepad. "Oh yes, Doctor, I mean, John, I have heard that you personally took the initiative in trying to get the Allens released. May I hear more about that?"

The pastor lowered his hands to the table and leaned forward.

"Yes, I think it is common knowledge that many worked diligently for some kind of reprieve, or at least to change the sentence to life, although I don't think either of the Allens would have wanted to spend their life in prison. I first began thinking about becoming involved beyond that of a spiritual leader about six weeks after they arrived. At that time, I ran into George Lafayette Carter..."

"You mean the millionaire?"

"Yes, Mr. Carter was from Hillsville. He is a very wealthy man, with coal mines, railroads, and real estate throughout Virginia, Tennessee and West Virginia. I knew him because he gave a very large endowment to Marion College."

"Marion College?"

"Yes, the college my father started. I met him while a student there, and he recognized me even fifteen years later. He asked me to go with him to meet with Governor Mann. It was my understanding that the two men were once close personal friends."

I continued to take notes as Pastor Scherer told his story. He explained how Mr. Carter had started out very cordial, telling how he had recited about twenty minutes of documented facts supporting his request, and then finalized his presentation by asking that the Allens' sentences be commuted. For the next thirty minutes Carter and the governor argued the merits of the case. Dr. Scherer said, even though Mr. Carter was not a lawyer, the businessman argued articulately. In the end though, the governor could not be swayed. It seemed the governor was mainly antagonistic toward Mr. Floyd Allen, so then Mr. Carter began pleading that Claude's life be spared. That was when the discussion got extremely hot. Mr. Carter wasn't used to not getting his way, and the governor was not used to having his authority questioned. Dr. Scherer said that after about two hours of the impasse, the governor told Mr. Carter that he had another appointment, wished him a safe trip home, and rose to shake his hand.

"That is when it really got testy," Dr. Scherer said.

"So it didn't end well?" I said.

"You are correct. Mr. Carter stood up, slammed his fist on the desk, and gave the governor one of the iciest stares I have ever seen. Then he said some words that I didn't fully comprehend, but I will never forget. I'll not forget because when he said them, Governor Mann turned a pale shade of which I have never seen on the most dreadful corpse."

By this time I was literally on the edge of my seat.

"And just what were those words?" I asked.

"He said, 'Well, Pontius Pilate, I don't care how many times you wash those filthy hands of yours, the blood of these men WILL be on you.' He then said, 'I can promise you, you'll never win another election'."

I let those words sink in. Everyone had been surprised when Mann was elected governor because of his almost fanatical temperance views. I had heard there had been some large contributors. But it was nearly impossible to believe a successful business man like George Lafayette Carter would support a staunch Democrat like Mann. After this investigation on the Allens was over, I definitely wanted to pursue a story. Apparently this businessman had layers of complexity most people had never imagined. I had heard some considered him even ruthless in his business dealings. I looked forward to meeting him one day.

"So is that when you started your campaign for commuting the sentences?" I asked.

"Yes, hearing the facts that Mr. Carter had presented, and witnessing the unreasonableness of the governor to even discuss the matter, filled me with the desire to do more myself."

"And that is when you came to our paper?"

"That's correct; that is when I approached The Evening Journal and gave them the evidence as I saw it. Your editor studied it for a few days, then phoned me that he felt they would change their original stand and take up a fight to commute the sentences. That's when the petitions began."

I remembered after the first editorial came out, we got a couple of threats, but then letters by the hundreds began pouring in wanting to know how to go about signing a petition for at least a new trial. Of course, it didn't hurt when now United States Senator, Claude Swanson came out in support of the young man who had taken his name as his own.

This was also about the time that Nellie Wisler began writing all newspapers throughout the state. She single-handedly won over at least a dozen papers on her own. We copied the letter she had sent to the governor, begging him to just talk to Claude, offering that she herself would stay in his death row cell until the meeting was over. After we reported that, we received a tidal wave of support.

"I had heard there were nearly a hundred thousand signatures on the petition at the end," I said and then added. "Is it true your brother Luther signed the petition, and he worked for Baldwin-Felts?"

"He did work for them, until he signed the petition and went before the governor with me. They then decided they no longer needed his services," the pastor said with a chuckle. "You do know that many, I think all except one of the jurors, who had sentenced them, signed."

"Yes, I remember that. It surprised me that information did not sway the attitude of the state."

"I just can't see how an elected official can deny the wishes of so many of his citizens," the pastor said, shaking his head with an unbelieving look.

"So how were the Allens in the final days before the execution?" I asked. "On the days that I interviewed them, they seemed to be holding up, but I'm sure the final days were rough."

"I believe they still had hope, all the way up until the end. The date just kept getting delayed. You know the first date was set for November 19th, then it was moved to December 13th. Then they decided they would let the state supreme court consider it, so they moved it to January 17th."

"That's when my editor let me come in. The reporter who had been covering it almost died from appendicitis. I was sent to cover the January 10th hearing when Mr. Byrd and Mr. Smith presented their case. When I left that hearing, I was certain there was no way the courts could refuse to retry the case."

"I agree," the pastor said, rubbing his temples as if he had a migraine, "the evidence proved beyond any doubt that there could not have been a conspiracy, and that is the biggest reason they were sentenced to death. I was so confident, and so were they."

"But they were once again disappointed?"

"Yes. Each time, two weeks prior to the scheduled dates, they would begin preparing for their deaths. Then it would be postponed. They were naturally relieved, but also the strain was weighing heavily upon them."

"I can only imagine how difficult that was."

"I can remember Mr. Allen's face when he read the first article you wrote, that the State's conspiracy charge had been shattered by new evidence, and if affidavits were to be believed, and they have always carried great weight in a court of law, it seemed more appropriate that the court officials should be charged with conspiracy."

I allowed a small smile.

"Yes, it was the next day that the editor got your phone call that Floyd Allen wanted to see me. I thought Mr. Allen was going to fall over when he saw how young I was."

"He told me that you had relatives in Carroll County."

"Yes, my grandfather's brother was a brother-in-law to Sidna's mother Elizabeth. I only found this out when I told an aunt that I had been asked to visit Floyd."

"So you saw as much of them as I did the last two months, up until March 24th when Justices White and Hughes refused to hear the case. After that they were placed in lock-down, and I wasn't even able to see them until the day of the 28th."

I hesitated for a few seconds, trying to form the sentence that I knew I had to ask. I knew there was no finesse way in asking, so I just blurted out.

"Just between you and me, were Floyd and Claude Allen guilty?"

"Guilty of murder? Probably. I do think they shot with the intent to kill. From what I understand, there was such bedlam, no one will ever know who shot whom. But one thing I will unequivocally say, there was absolutely no way there was a conspiracy to murder. Pure and simple."

"OK, John, as I said, I'm not going to use your name. Is there anything else you feel comfortable telling me? It was my understanding there were some, I don't know how to say it, some unusual activities the last night."

He walked to the door, and looked to see if anyone was within hearing distance. He returned, sat down on the sofa, and over the next fifteen minutes told me a story of espionage and intrigue of the last twenty-four hours of Floyd and Claude Allen's life.

After returning from my visit, a phone call to some old friends of mine in the governor's office substantiated the story I had been told.

RICHMOND EVENING JOURNAL

March 29, 1913

It has been learned, through unidentified sources, of a twelfth hour attempt to delay, if not commute the death sentence of Floyd and Claude Allen.

After the third continuance, a day of execution was set for March 28. The supporters of the Allens had one last hope. They researched the state code, and felt the lt. governor had the full authority of the office of governor in the absence of the governor. It was reported, by an unknown party, that when it was announced that Governor Mann would be leaving the state two days prior to the execution, that Lt. Governor James Taylor Ellyson was requested by Allen supporters to grant clemency to the prisoners. Prison Superintendent Wood agreed to schedule the electrocution later in the day on the 28th, rather than immediately after sunrise. It is expected that uncertain as to the legality, and possible accusations that might be brought against him, the lt. governor had contacted the state attorney general for clarification.

It was believed that early on the morning of the 27th, a wire was sent, possibly by his teenage son, to Governor Mann while he was in Pennsylvania. He expected later to continue his trip to Princeton University. The wire informed him of what was transpiring back in Richmond. He immediately cancelled his speaking engagement, boarded a train and returned to the Commonwealth. Upon arriving in Leesburg, he immediately sent a wire to the lt. governor that read, 'I am in Virginia and acting as governor, signed William Hodges Mann.'

He did in fact reach Richmond slightly before midnight, and immediately ordered the execution to continue the next day. Word was not delivered in time to the jurors who were serving as witnesses. They had been sent away earlier that morning and had to be quickly summoned to the prison.

As promised yesterday, we are giving you exclusives each day for the next week. Over those days we will be presenting the Last Statements as prepared by Floyd and Claude Allen, and given to this paper. We begin with that of Claude Allen.

THE LAST STATEMENT OF CLAUDE ALLEN

As I am now condemned to die and realize that all hope is gone, I thought it my duty to tell what I know of the trouble for which I have been tried, for which I must pay with my life. Before going further I will give a few things of my past life.

I was born June 11th, 1889, and from my earliest recollection and to the present time I have been taught to speak the truth in everything, and deal honestly with my fellow man, which I have tried to do. Our parents have tried to raise us to feel that we must be honorable and that under no circumstances must we speak falsehoods. When fourteen years old I started in at Fairview Academy, near Hillsville, Virginia, and was there a part of two years and afterwards attended business college at Raleigh, N.C. On account of my mother's health being very bad I decided to stay at home after leaving school and to be of what comfort I could to her, as my brother was married and I was the only child left at home. All my life I tried to live free from trouble with anyone and regardless of the relations between people and others I was never drawn into any of their troubles.

I have known sometime of my father and Dexter Goad being enemies but never thought of their ill feeling ending as it has. I went to Hillsville during my father's trial and heard some of the evidence and from what I heard I had no idea that he would even get a jail sentence and never thought for one moment of any trouble being there. The first I knew of it was when it began and what I did was without any premeditation whatever. There was no plot beforehand or any conspiracy, so far as I know, and I do not believe there was with any of the others. It was all so sudden and unexpected that I had no time to think and did on the spur of the moment something that I had never thought of doing. It is useless for me to repeat here what I have told on the witness stand, as that is known already, and I have no changes to make. Of course there may have been statements made by others very different from mine but if the whole world were against me I would tell all as I saw it just the same. What the other Allens and the Edwardses did and who they shot at I know nothing about. When I saw Dexter Goad shoot at my father I tried to shoot him and he is the only man I shot at.

Some probably think that I shot Judge Massie, but I did not nor did I fire the first shot in the court room. I always have believed and now believe that Judge Massie was a just man and a friend of ours. And I had no reason in the world to take his life or to harm him in any way. I have been accused of conspiring and planning to shoot up the court at Hillsville and other things which I am not guilty of. I had too much love and respect for my dear mother and my sweetheart, if there had been nothing else to keep me from planning a deed which would have separated me from them forever on this earth. No one could have persuaded me into trouble. This all came on so sudden and unexpected and I had no time to think of what was best. If the truth alone had been told I would not be where I am now. but if anyone knowingly testified falsely against me I forgive them and believe some have told such as they knew was false. There is a time coming when we will not be judged by what others say, but by Him who knoweth all things, even our thoughts; and then all will be made right. If I suffer here it will be made right in the great day when everyone must be judged according to their deeds.

The words you have read were transcribed directly from the statement. Neither this reporter, nor The Evening Journal, changed these words in any way. Continue to follow the printing of these statements over the next week.

4

By the time the Journal hit the streets that evening, I was on a southbound train, on my way for the first time in my life, to southwest Virginia. For the next eight hours I got the best sleep I had gotten in a week.

I arrived at Blair Station, near the newly named town of Galax, just after midnight. I was told there would be no transportation to Hillsville until early the next morning, so I checked into the Blair Inn. While there, I made friends with the telegraph operator. I have learned, in the newspaper business, you can never make too many friends.

At daybreak there was a knock on my door, and I was told a driver was waiting to take me to Hillsville. Two hours later I stepped down from his wagon and entered the Hillsville Mercantile.

"Hello. I'm here on business for a few days," I said to the young sales clerk behind the counter, "and I need a hotel for room and board."

"If it needs to be right here in Hillsville, we have a couple of hotels," the young man said, "but if you're wanting something outside of town, a lot of people seem to like Martha Guynn's boarding house. It's about half the price, and she's quite a cook. It's about five miles out, on Fancy Gap Road."

The mention of price reminded me that this was the first trip I had taken for the newspaper and I had not even asked Mr. Archer about travel expenses. Knowing him, I'd be lucky to get more than $2 a day per diem.

"The boarding house sounds good, how would I get there?"

"That will be easy enough. Mrs. Guynn's son is there in the back" he said, then turned and walked to the end of the counter, calling out. "Hey Jeff, come here."

A man in his late twenties lumbered up the narrow store aisle. He stood at least two inches taller than my 6 feet, and was probably thirty pounds heavier, probably around 210 pounds. His angular face looked stern at first glance, but as he got closer, I saw an almost mischievous glint.

"Jeff, this gentleman's from Richmond and is looking for room and board for a few days," the young man said, then turned to me. "Sir, this is Jeff Haynes."

I hesitated, making sure I had heard correctly. In the mean time, a smile stole the stern look from the man's face, as he extended his hand.

"Jeff, my name's Jeremiah Haynes," I said. "Are you related to John Haynes?

"I hope to shout I am. John was my grandfather. How did you know him?"

"My grandfather was a brother to John. He grew up with John and used to tell us about how, well, you know, how he died."

"Yeah, shot by Berry Combs, his wife's own brother, during the war. To beat it all, Uncle Berry was also married to my grandpa's sister. So what brings you to this neck of the woods?"

"I got to know Claude and Mr. Allen before they died."

I wasn't sure how much I should reveal to my newly discovered kin. I knew there were two categories of people in this area, those that loved the Allens, and those that hated them.

"I thought I recognized your name. You're that hot shot reporter that wrote the articles about the Allens. I wondered when I read them if you was some of my kin. So are you ready to go? I just need to pick up a few more things. I have the small wagon outside with the roan hitched to it."

As we started the drive out of Hillsville, I took notes in my reporter's pad on the lay of the land. Small but neat, white wooded two-story homes lined both sides of the hard-packed dirt street. Many rested a fixed distance behind whitewashed picket fences. Soon the street gave way to a narrow, amply rutted road. Farm houses, larger, but not as well kempt, sat in the midst of rolling spring-green pasture land.

"I understand you're related to Floyd's brother, Sidna?" I asked, laying my notebook down on the seat.

"Yep. My grandmother is a sister to Sidna's mom. It was their brother that killed my grandfather John."

"What do you think of the Allens?"

Jeff turned and eyed me skeptically. He turned back to the road ahead, and spoke with weighed words. "The Allens have always treated us kindly, as they do most folk. They're good with extending credit when it's needed. Although you best pay it when it's due."

"Really? Why's that?" I said.

"Sidna and Floyd have been known to send the Edwards' boys to collect. My mom does have a grudge against Sidna though."

"And that is because?"

At that point Jeff pulled the wagon to a stop. To the right sat a small store. To the left and on a slight knoll was a very impressive home in the Queen Anne style that would rival the nicest homes in Richmond. A turret on the left completed the wrap-around porch. A second turret accented the second floor roof. Unlike the mansions in Richmond though, instead of various colors, this house was simply white.

"That's the Sidna Allen home. Or at least it was before the state took it. The farm has over 100 acres. My Mom sold 63 of those acres to Sidna. She sold it to him for $810. He was to have paid $81, and the rest was for him to educate me at the Academy. She can't even sign her name, but she wanted more for me. She got the cash, but I sure as hell never got the learning."

"So you probably don't have much use for them, or at least Sidna?"

"No, I can't say I really have a problem.. All families have falling out now and then. And before you ask, no, I don't think they went into that courthouse aiming to shoot it out."

"Is that just a belief.?"

"No, I saw Sidna the day before, and he asked me if I'd deliver some goods to Galax for him the next day."

"Is that Sidna's store, I asked, "where Floyd took the Edwards' boys away from the deputies."

"Yep, but the state took it too. I don't see how they can do that, just take away everything a man's worked for all his life. Sidna was one of the richest men in these here parts, and now his wife and children are having to live off others."

We rode another fifteen minutes until we arrived at the boarding house. Mrs. Guynn sat rocking on the porch, darning a basket of socks. The woman carried the same stern, almost frozen, glare on her face, as Jeff did at times. I fully expected her to unleash a severe reprimand on her son at any moment.

"Momma, this here's Jeremiah Haynes. He's a reporter from Richmond. He wants to stay a few days. His grandpa was a brother to Grandpa?"

"Welcome, Jeremiah. Jeff, put him in the back room that has the fireplace in it. Make sure he has some wood and extra blankets. It's going to be nippy tonight."

Jeff picked up my valise, and started into the boarding house. Sitting at a table was a short, stout young woman. She had the long dark hair and high cheekbones of someone who might have Indian blood. Before her laid an assortment of pants and shirts which she was busy mending. Jeff introduced her to me as his wife, Annie. She looked up shyly. I only had time to offer a a hasty 'hello' as Jeff never slowed down, and was already bounding upstairs, his long legs covering two steps at once. I saw him enter a door, so I followed.

"Have they had the Allens' funeral yet?" I asked.

"No, it's actually in two hours. I had hoped to go to it. You want to go with me?"

"Yes, I think I would."

"We'll need to leave now. It's a harsh ride."

We started out traveling along a plateau but soon I found us traversing the steepest grade on which I've ever seen a road built. It was so sharply inclined that Jeff had to pull the wagon's hand brake every hundred yards or so to slow the wagon. I commented on the precipitous slope.

"Yeah, it's so bad that men hauling freight sometimes have to cut logs and tie them to the wagons to keep them from getting away."

'"Really?'

"Yeah, one city slicker was hauling some freight down one time, and didn't know to tie the logs off. That wagon got going too fast for the horses."

"So did they make it? To the bottom of the mountain I mean."

"They made it, but when the wagon got to the bottom, the horse was sitting in the seat, and the driver was hanging onto the back end of the wagon."

"Gosh, that's amazing?" I said.

When I glanced over at Jeff, I could see a small smile curling up around the Pall Mall cigarette.

About a third of the way down the mountain, Jeff pointed over to his left.

"That there's what they call Yankee Creek," he said. "Supposedly Floyd's father Jeremiah and the Combs killed themselves a Yankee soldier over there during the war. Some nights when you're traveling down, you can hear that Yankee screaming."

I reserved my response.

"So have you always lived in Richmond?" He asked.

"I have. My father grew up in Patrick County and went to Richmond College. He met my mother at the bank he worked at, and they married. so they've lived there ever since. Or at least until my mother died about eight years ago. Have your folks always been from Carroll County?"

"My mom's lived here all of her life. I don't know who my father was; that's why my last name is Haynes. That was momma's maiden name. She won't tell me or anybody, who my father is."

This made me feel more than a little uneasy. I guess Jeff could tell and knew he needed to lighten the tension, so he added.

"I am pretty sure though that she did name me after my father."

"Oh, you think his name was Jeff?"

"Actually Jeff's not my real name; it's Jefferson. And Jefferson is only one of my names." He smiled as he looked at me and then continued. "The given name my momma gave me is Sanders John Jefferson Joseph Colombus Emmitt Haynes, so I figure it's a real good chance that one of those name's my father's."

I looked over at him, and again saw the smirk. I risked a chuckle. It sounded almost foreign to me. It had been awhile since I had heard one escape my lips. To my right I saw a house with dozens, perhaps hundreds of people wandering around.

"Is that Floyd's house?" I asked.

"Sure is," Jeff said. "I heard there was a couple of thousand people went to the viewing last night."

"It's my understanding at the funeral home in Richmond, they estimated twenty-five thousand people filed through. They weren't supposed to have opened the caskets to the public, but there was such a crowd, the police thought there'd be a riot, so they ordered them to open the doors."

"Yeah, the family was mightily pissed at them for doing that. They didn't want a viewing up there."

By the time we were a half mile from Jones Cemetery, we began encountering buggies and horses tied off to trees. Many partially blocked the road, which was much more a trail than a road by now. The sides were lined with people standing three deep on the banks. When we reached the resting place, we saw a throng of people, maybe five thousand, wandering about.

"I guess Mr. Allen and Claude must have had a lot of friends."

"I'd say some are friends; some are enemies; and some just needed something to tell their grandkids."

Minutes later the cacophony began receding, like the surf washing away from the shore. Twisting, we saw a possession of two wagons, each carrying a casket, followed by a line of buggies and people on horseback slowly turning onto the road leading to the graveyard. Men began removing their hats as a solemn silence preceded the arrival. The wagons pulled along side the two freshly dug graves. Black suited pall bearers slowly removed the chestnut boxes from the wagons and, in unison, carried them to the open graves.

I felt myself torn between remaining reverent, and being observant. After all, I was here in Carroll County to file reports. I decided on a compromise that I would take no notes. I would just absorb all that happened around me. I'd then jot down observations on the way home, and write the article from memory.

I closed my eyes, as I so often did to allow all of my senses to heighten. The smell of fresh flowers in the wagons and around the grave. The crispness of the cold March wind as a slight mist stung my face. The voice of the country pastor sounding almost musical in its cadence, so unlike the stuffy Methodist pastors I was accustomed to hearing back home.

"You ok?" Jeff said, breaking my trance.

"Yes, I was taking in all that was happening," I whispered. "This is much different than the funerals we have back home."

As a second pastor began speaking, I noticed a buggy at the top of the crest near the church. A solitary figure, adorned in a black dress and veil, sat statuesque, facing the burial site.

"Who is that?" I asked, my mouth pressed to Jeff's ear.

"I'm not positive, but I think the buggy belongs to Reverend Wisler. This is his family's cemetery I believe that might be his daughter Nellie."

"Nellie Wisler? Claude's girlfriend?"

"Yes. She's really taking this hard. Everyone knew she would."

I found myself focused on her, oblivious to all around me. The preachers' voices interrupted my hearing only in snippets. She sat stoic, the only motion was the breeze flapping the folds of her black dress. Her hands gripped a black book that I took to be a Bible.

My contemplation of her was interrupted by the echo of the dirt clods being thrown onto the wooden coffins. I watched as the graves were filled. I began to ponder the fate of the Allens.

I almost envy them.

They also had lived difficult lives the last few years. But their heartache, their grief, was now over.

Would anyone notice, other than Jeff, if I jumped down into the grave and let the rocky soil finally bring me contentment?

Flowers were dropped into the hole as the crowd began dispersing. Low murmurs were again being heard.

How many would attend my funeral, if it were me? A dozen, maybe two at the most?

First the springs, then the wheels of the wagons, squeaked as the people climbed to their seats and started on their way. I watched as Pastor Wisler pulled his buggy down to the grave site. He helped the girl down from her seat. Enshrouded in black, from head to toes, she seemed to float to the grave site where Claude Swanson Allen had been laid.

I was mesmerized. Jeff was ready to pull the wagon out onto the road when I tugged on his arm.

"Could we stay? Just awhile longer?" I asked.

I wasn't able to tear my eyes from the sight before me.

Jeff pulled the reins taunt, and the wagon came to a stop. Even without seeing her face, I could empathize the grief she was feeling. I knew the knot she was feeling deep in her stomach. I wanted so much to go to her, to take her in my arms, to tell her that all would be ok. But then, I knew that was a lie. It would never be.

She pulled the veil from her face to kiss a bouquet of early-spring flowers before placing them on the fresh mound. My heart stopped. Even in her bereavement, I had never in my life seen a woman of such divine beauty. Her eyes, her lips, the contours of her cheekbones, each part as if God had personally selected the ideal feature. My Nancy had beyond fair beauty, but nothing like this woman. My heart began to thaw from its frozen state. I longed to take her face in my hands. To kiss away the tears that were streaming down her face. She fell to her knees, I thought distraught, but then she brought her clinched hands to her chin to pray. My heart began to ache anew at the sight of someone losing the person they loved. Then I felt flooded with guilt and shame for what I was feeling for another woman.

"Ok, let's go," I said softly. I was unable to watch any longer.

Within fifteen minutes we were starting up the mountain. I found myself very quiet, and sat writing notes while they were still fresh in my mind. Occasionally I would ask Jeff who certain speakers were for specific parts of the service. He gave me background on each of them. We topped the mountain and were within two miles of the boarding house just as the cinereal evening began turning black with night.

Ping!

Wood shivers flew from the right front buggy spoke. A second ping drew my attention to the wagon side not two feet behind where I sat. Jeff quickly pulled the horse up. Grabbing a rifle from behind the wagon seat, he jumped down behind the wagon.

"Grab that pistol quick from under the seat." he barked. "Then get over here."

I did as I was told and slumped beside the wagon next to my cousin. My ears pounded from the reverberation of my heart beat. We remained silent for a few minutes before either of us would speak.

"Was that a shot?" I asked.

"Yep. Sure was. I think we're ok though. It was probably just a warning."

"A warning? For what?"

"That someone don't want you down here writing stories."

After about ten minutes, no more shots were fired. Jeff cautiously took his seat on the wagon. I climbed up to join him, and extended the Colt revolver to him.

"I think you might hold onto that gun," he said. "Something tells me you're gonna be needing it."

RICHMOND EVENING JOURNAL

March 30, 1913

We continue with the exclusive printing of the Last Statement of Claude Allen.

Life is sweet and we would rather live if possible, but if death must come I am not afraid to die. Of course I am condemned to die a disgraceful death but I know I don't deserve it; although there is no way for me - only to take what other people give me. There are a great many things in this case which cannot be learned yet; but they will be known sometime, although too late to help me.

I wish to thank all who have tried to help me to get justice. While it is hard to die for a crime that you are innocent of and a death of this kind, at the same time, it is much better to die under these conditions, believing and knowing that God who knows all things will make all things right, than it would be to die knowing that we were guilty of the crime as charged.

We are charged with one of the worst crimes that almost could be committed and those who have asked by letters to the governor and through the papers for our lives and our blood do not seem to realize that we were not responsible for the trouble at Hillsville and that we are innocent of this crime and were not the cause of the trouble at Hillsville except in an indirect way. To be under the condition that we are under and to see and know how some who know nothing about the case whatever are keen set to abuse us not only to the governor but to the paper it is hard to understand why this is done. It is hard for us to realize why, after everything was practically settled, a minister of the gospel like Mr. Carter should write the letter that he did and why Dr. Cannon should take the time that he had to take and write the long column of untruthful abuse which could only hurt our people and take the advantage that was taken when we were confined in the penitentiary and soon had to pay with our lives. We cannot understand why Dr. Young should take the time which should be devoted in saving souls to hold us up before the people as outlaws and to say that we had got a just punishment. We cannot understand, yet all these things will come to light by the great Day of Judgment. I am sorry that this matter happened and am more than sorry that I felt it necessary to do what I did do. At the same time I feel that God, knowing all things, as he does, knows that I shot for the purpose of defending my father and saving his life, as I saw it.

And, therefore, I will be held guiltless of any wrong doing in connection with this trouble. I wrote Governor Mann some days back that I had told the truth and nothing but the truth and, regardless of whether I lived or died, my statements were true. It is of course, hard for one as young as I am to die and to die for a crime of which I am innocent. It is hard for me to leave my dear mother, sweetheart, and friends; but I feel that God has forgive me of all my sins and that I am saved and will soon meet my loved ones and many of my dear friends in heaven.

The words you have read were transcribed directly from the statement. Neither this reporter, nor The Evening Journal, changed these words in any way. Continue to follow the printing of these statements over the next week.

5

I climbed the steps to the boarding house, still trembling from what had happened on the road. Annie sat on the porch, reading her Bible.

"Everything go ok at the funeral?" she asked, without looking up. "Any problems?"

"Nah, none at all," Jeff said, as he kissed her on the cheek. "Everybody behaved himself."

"There's some fried onions and pork chops still warm on the stove, and the biscuits are in the warmer," she said.

We sat down to dinner and discussed the events of the day. Jeff gave me more background on some of the participants in the funeral, and added some anecdotes, or perhaps gossip, on others who attended. We ended with a whispered discussion of the shots fired.

"Any idea who might have fired them?" I asked.

"No, could be one of several people. The shootout was a year ago, and there's a lot of people that thinks it needs to be forgotten about. They feel like you're down here sticking your nose in our business."

"Is that what you think?"

"It doesn't really matter what I think, but if it makes any difference, I think if you have a job to do, you do it."

We ended the evening with a piece of pie and cup of coffee out on the porch. Mrs. Guynn sat in her rocker. Annie and Jeff shared the porch swing. The women kept both of us busy relating the details of the funeral service. With it still fresh in my mind, I went back to my room to write my article.

THE RICHMOND EVENING JOURNAL

March 30, 1913 Hillsville, VA

ALLENS LAID TO REST

On a dismal, chilling Sunday afternoon in Carroll County, Virginia, a father and son were laid to rest in adjoining graves. Thirteen months prior to March 30th, the father was a successful, if confrontational, businessman. The son, educated, polite, was known as a handsome, humorous young man liked by all. But now, they would be joined together in the annals of infamy.

It was a day of gray and black contrast. The contrast of a gray canvas funeral tent, flapping in strong gusts, and the black suits and dresses of the mourners, which numbered in the thousand, some say as many as ten thousand. The contrast of the colors were reflected when this reporter observed a line of ebony crows silhouetted against the gray sky. Perhaps the greatest contrast observed were two gray buggies, pulled by matching black horses. Each buggy contained black-clad figures. One carried the frail widow of Floyd Allen, the other the fiancé of Claude Swanson Allen.

Visitors had begun arriving as early as Friday when the coffins arrived in Mt. Airy by train from Richmond. They walked; they rode horses; they drove buggies; and they took trains. They came from Wytheville; they came from Winston-Salem; and they came from Richmond. They came out of reverence; they came out of curiosity; and yes, I'm sure, some even came out of reprisal.

On another day, perhaps later in the spring, this site would have been considered beautiful, breathtaking, idyllic. To the north, within sight, rose the rugged Blue Ridge Mountain range. To the south stretched the flat piedmont of North Carolina.

Local pastors conducted the funeral services. Reverend Rufus Monday led off by describing Floyd as a friend to the righteous, a good husband, father and provider. He then quoted John 15:13, No greater love hath no man than this, that a man lay down his life for his friends. With a quivering voice, he then asked what greater love could a son show than to lay down his life for his father. Elder Floyd W. Bunn then spoke of the many contributions Floyd had made for the benefits of his neighbors in need. He then led the assembly in several hymns, including Amazing Grace. This was only fitting, as I am certain that was the tune Floyd Allen tapped out on the arm of the electric chair prior to his execution.

At the conclusion of the service, the coffins were opened a final time. Victor Allen, brother to Claude and son to Floyd, was seen removing something from the coffin. He walked to the buggy where Nellie Wisler watched and handed the item to her. It was later discovered the item was a gold medal that read Presented to Claude Allen for Defending his father. It was reported that this gold medal had been given to Claude to wear during his execution, but state authorities had not allowed it.

The reporter could not help feeling that this marked not only the end of life for these two men, but also the end of a way of life. The Allens had been one of the last holdovers of pre-civil war Democrats. They were strong-willed and independent like so many of the Scots and Irish that came to settle the wilderness of Virginia. With the passing of Floyd Allen, those days are gone.

I had thought about adding some excitement to the piece by describing how Jeff and I had come under attach. How I had covered my cousin's body with my own, protecting him from certain death. How I had grabbed the rifle and standing heroic before the ambush, had single-handedly turned back the attack of a dozen Baldwin-Felts detectives. But I decided to leave that part out.

The next morning I rose early and found Jeff having his coffee. I had spent the night before preparing an interview list. I had sub-divided the list to include court officials, deputies, Allen Family, defense attorneys, prosecuting attorneys, jurors, witnesses, and other people of interest.

Over nearly an entire pot of coffee, I used my previous knowledge and Jeff's recollection to prepare a tabulation of about eighty possible informants.

Later that morning I rode into Hillsville with Jeff. He took me to the local telegraph office where I wired in the article. Afterwards, I went over to the mercantile where I found Jeff arguing prices with the clerk.

"Hell's fire, Jacob, just last month you were selling this feed for seventy-five cents, now it's eighty. Who can afford to keep chickens anymore?"

"That's the way it goes. Prices have to go up at times," Jacob said, then seeing me enter, added. "Tell him Mr. Haynes. Tell him how much feed costs in Richmond."

"There's not too many people raising chickens in Richmond," I answered.

This brought a chorus of laughter from everyone in the store. I had certainly not meant to be humorous.

Just then an older man, slight of build, entered the store. Jeff whispered to me,

"That there's John Farris. He was one of the jurors at Floyd's trial, and later testified at the murder trial."

"Think he might let me interview him?"

"I don't know, let me go give him a crack."

Jeff walked over to the man, shook hands. They laughed over something Jeff said. Then I could tell things got serious. Mr. Farris looked at me suspiciously a few times, then shook his head. Jeff put his arm around the man's shoulder, said a few more words, then began directing him over to me.

"John, this here's my cousin Jeremiah Haynes, from Richmond," Jeff said, then turned to me. "Jeremiah, we're going over to Miss Polly's diner for some coffee and fresh peach pie. Want to join us?"

Jeff gave one final perfunctory complaint, but paid his bill. The three of us walked two blocks to the diner. From the moment we entered, I began to salivate. The air hung thick with the smell of fresh brewed coffee, grease-laden ham and eggs and, best of all, a row of pies that lined the counter. We each got a cup of coffee, and a slice of fresh pie.

"Miss Polly, we've got a little horse-trading to do," Jeff said. "Mind if we use your back room."

"Sure Jeff, just tidy up after yourself."

Jeff opened the door to a small back room and we entered. A solitary table with four chairs was centered. The table top was marred by cigarette marks and stains.

"I'd sure like to have half the money back," Jeff sighed, "I've lost at this table."

The other man laughed nervously, and we all set down. Nothing was said for a while, so I broke the silence.

"So Mr. Farris", I said as I pulled my notepad discretely from my coat pocket to prepare to write, "I understand you sat on the jury in the Floyd Allen trial."

"Yes, that's right. The first one."

"Did you know him before the trial?"

"I'd seen him around town at times."

"Did you know the older Allens? Sidna, Floyd, Jack?"

"Yes."

"What did you think of the Allens? The older ones, I mean."

"I only had one problem with them myself. Over a horse."

"I think everyone in Carroll County had at least one problem with them," I said.

"Yeah, you got along with them better than their own brother Jack did," Jeff said.

This brought a short guffaw from the man. I watched him as he relaxed his shoulders, and began to take a bite of the pie. I mirrored his actions.

"Umm, this is a great pie," I said.

"Sure is," he said. "Miss Polly makes the best in the country. She says she makes it with a special lard."

"I always heard she adds a little brandy to the mix," Jeff said. I could tell he was trying to make the man feel more relaxed. I gave us a few minutes to eat half of the pie, then I continued.

"So Mr. Farris, who was the first person you saw pull a gun that day?"

The man took on an ashen countenance. His shoulders stiffened at the question. I could hear his fork tapping the table.

"I'm not sure I want to be talking about this."

"Mr. Farris, I don't even have to use your name," I said, as I put my pad and pencil back into my pocket. "I can just refer to you as an unidentified person."

"Yes, I think I want to be that. Un-identified," he said, then continued. "I changed my mind a lot after the murder trial. A lot of it had to do with the things The Evening Journal reported."

"Did you know that Jeremiah wrote most of those reports?" Jeff asked. "He's one hell of a reporter."

"Just for that, I'll pay for the pie," I said.

Everyone laughed.

"You sure opened my eyes, and a lot of other peoples," he said. "I think like most folks, I believed the evidence at the murder trial was the truth. But well, there were just too many things I found out afterwards."

"Really?" I asked. "Such as?"

He licked his lips, then sucked his lower lip between his teeth and chewed on it.

"I remember several things came out in our local paper about some of the testimony," Farris said. "Especially Dexter Goad's. It just wasn't the way I remembered it. Sure I was there, but everything just happened so fast."

"You mean about who fired the first shot, and if the Allens had planned it?" I said.

"Yeah," he said. "That had a lot to do with it. How the new guns had been bought. I mean I had never seen Lew Webb carry a gun, as long as he lived. And there he was the first to shoot..."

"You do think sheriff Webb fired the first shot?" I asked.

"I guess I shouldn't have said, 'fired the first shot.'" he said. "But I'm positive he pulled his gun first."

"Was there anything else?" I said. "I heard you signed the petition to commute the sentence."

"It just seemed the murder trial happened too quickly. The jurors had all that evidence thrown at them. I know how it is when they don't give us time to think."

"Yes, I can imagine that was a lot to comprehend, all so quickly." I said. "Go ahead, I think you were going to say more."

"Well, later, when I heard things about how Sidna had just deposited his money in the bank the day before, and some of them wasn't even going to be in court that day, but had been sent for. Well, it just didn't seem to add up."

"Who do you think fired the first shot?" I asked.

"I don't know. I don't think anybody knows. If they do, they're not a'saying. Maybe someday somebody will own up to it. I don't know."

"So what do you think started it?" I asked.

"I only know what I heard. I think something sparked it, maybe like Lew pulling his gun, and then all hell broke loose. I heard there was noise that sounded like a gunshot, but a lot of people are saying they're not sure that's what it was."

"Do you think it was the Allens or the court officials who killed Judge Massie, or Lew Webb?"

"Like I say, I think both sides fired enough shots; they both could have killed people."

"John, tell him about the hole in the judge's chair," Jeff said.

"When I went back into the courthouse," he said, "after all the shooting, I went up front to see if there was anything I could do for the judge. There was a big hole in his chair. On the side facing Deck Goad. In the trial they claimed it was just a chipped place, but I'm sure it was a bullet hole."

"Why do you think that?" I said.

"Cause it was a clean hole clear into the wood, and there was shivers on the floor. Wood was flying everywhere that day. A piece of wood fell out of my coat when I got home."

"Can you think of anything else?" I asked.

"No, that's about all. I'm not saying the Allens are saints, because they're surely not, but well, I think there was plenty of blame to go around. Not just on the Allens side."

I thanked him and Jeff led him to a back exit. I had a feeling it was an exit that Jeff and his poker buddies used a lot. We cleaned up the room, took our plates and forks back to the front, and left.

As if every corner of the town of Hillsville had probing ears waiting to hear loose talk, neither of us spoke until we were well back on Fancy Gap Road.

"Well," Jeff asked. "What do you think?"

"I think he feels bad that two men were sent to the electric chair. I would sure love to interview another one of the jurors. Especially one who would let me use his name, and had sat on the murder trials. Do you know of any who might?"

"No," Jeff said. "All the others, even though several signed the petition, have stayed pretty tight-lipped."

"Why do you think so? If they signed the petition, and the governor refused it, you'd think they'd want to make amends."

"There's a rumor that someone, probably Thomas Felts, has put pressure on them to keep their mouth's shut."

"What kind of pressure?"

"I'm not sure. I've heard some have come into money all of a sudden. They bought new horses they shouldn't be able to afford. Or bought up some land. Or built a new barn. But I also heard there were some threats."

"Against their lives?"

"More against their property, or maybe families. At least two have had sheds burn down for no reason on their property. A couple have had bullet shots fired through windows at night."

"But no body was hit?"

"No, everyone was upstairs in bed, and the shots came through the bottom windows. So I don't think they want to kill anybody, but they sure wanted them to keep their mouth shut."

"So how much luck do you think I'll have getting Dexter Goad himself to talk with me?" I said with a grin.

Jeff just looked at me like I had asked the most stupid question in the world.

"About as likely as a snow ball not melting in hell," he answered.

The next morning I rode back to town on a horse Jeff had loaned me for my stay. I had decided I needed to go straight to the source if I wanted information, in spite of Jeff's assurance I'd not have any luck.

I asked directions, and found myself at a office door bearing the sign 'Dexter Goad, Clerk of Court.' I entered expecting to find Goad but instead found a young man sitting behind a small desk.

"May I help you, sir?"

"My name is Jeremiah Haynes, and I'd like to speak to Mr. Goad, please."

"Certainly, one moment please."

The young man entered a door to his rear. I heard him announce my name, but then the voices became very agitated. After a couple of minutes, the young assistant, very red-faced, came back out the door.

"I'm sorry, eh, Mr. Haynes. Mr. Goad's schedule is very full today, and tomorrow he must go out of town. He said he'd be glad to make an appointment with you when his schedule clears up."

I have had many attempts to put off an undesired interview. I had found that there were usually two methods of confronting the situation. The first was to accept the delay, not wanting to antagonize the potential informant, and come back at another time. But the second was when I had no doubt the person merely wanted time to prepare himself. A person when contacted unexpectedly will either tell the truth, or it will be very obvious that he's lying. I felt this was time to consider Dexter Goad under the second category.

"Tell Mr. Goad that is ok," I said, loud enough to be heard in the rear office. "It's just that I've received some very interesting reports since I arrived. I was going to give him a chance to refute, or to clarify those facts, but the problem is I have to file my article by tomorrow. I'll just report that Mr. Goad refused to comment."

I turned to leave, but before my hand touched the doorknob, the inner door swung open and Dexter Goad walked out.

"Mr. Haynes, I think I can work you in. Umm, Jason, when the, umm, ten o'clock appointment gets here, reschedule him for ten-thirty."

The assistant got a very puzzled look on his face, and opened his mouth to reply.

"Just do it," Dexter said, then turned to me. "Come right in Mr. Haynes. I'm always happy to speak to the press."

I followed him into the room, my mind racing. I had mentally prepared a list of standard questions to ask, but now that I had bluffed my way in, I needed to hit him with some hard accusations if I was going to get any answers of substance.

"I'll get right to the point," I said. "I've had some reports made that, well, it troubles me. I just can't believe my source could be telling me the truth. I certainly don't want to report anything that isn't correct."

"No, no. You don't want to do that. There's too many innuendos, or just plain out lying , being spread around already. I'll be more than glad to correct any misconceptions you might have been given."

I knew I had to be very careful how I worded my questioning. I didn't want to come right out and falsify information, but I had not really been told anything since I had arrived in Hillsville that might be construed as incriminatory. But I had been told many things in Richmond. I turned to my notepad, looking intently at the blank page.

"I have been told that there were irregularities about the guns that were in the courthouse the day of the shooting."

"I don't think I know what you mean. Irregularities?" He said, tilting his head. The tight collar of his shirt suddenly appeared to be two sizes too small, making his Adam's apple bob. He tugged at the collar as if to free it.

"I've been told that Lew Webb never carried a gun, but yet he not only had a gun on that day, but he had a gun that was an automatic."

"You must know that Lew Webb was the sheriff of this county. Now we don't live in London, where I understand their policeman only carry a stick," he said with a slight chuckle, but he sounded more condescending than humorous. "He had every right to carry a pistol."

"Had he ever fired an automatic weapon before? Was he familiar with it?"

"I know for a fact that the sheriff, and all of his deputies, took regular shooting practice, and were up to date on the latest firearms."

"Isn't it true that the only persons who should have been armed that day were the sheriff and his deputies, mail carriers, and perhaps Floyd Allen himself, who at the time had been appointed a special officer by Judge Massie. Did you have the right to be armed that day?"

Goad gulped. I was afraid the tight starched collar was going to choke him. He again stuck his finger into the neckline to tug on the collar.

"I had discussed with the judge, that was Judge Massie, the one who was murdered by the Allens, that there might be trouble, and we agreed it would be advisable for us to arm ourselves."

"Judge Massie agreed to that?" I asked.

"Well, he didn't say we couldn't be armed."

"You stated the Allens murdered the judge. Do you have proof that it was their bullets that killed him?"

"Well, no. Not the actual bullets. But all indications, the position to which the judge fell, the angle of the bullet entry wounds, they all indicated they had to come from that side of the court."

"You referred to the angle of the entry wound; it was my understanding that there was no coroner's report."

Goad's face was taking on an alarming shade of red, clearly lineated by a slight white line along his neck just above the collar of his shirt.

"Mr. Allen, it's rather clear you've come into my office with a very biased agenda. I thought reporters were to be uninfluenced. Surely you've read the testimonies."

"I am unbiased, sir. I'm just asking you to explain some of the areas that have disturbed me."

"The courts have made their decisions, a jury of the Allens' peers have found them guilty, and they have, or are paying their dues. There's nothing that can be done now, so why don't you just head on back up to Richmond? I'm sure there's a lot of matters there that's much more important than what happens in little ole Carroll County."

"Sir, isn't it true that several of those peers who found the Allens guilty later signed a petition to..."

He leaped to his feet, opened a drawer, and for a moment, I thought was going to pull a gun from his desk and shoot me. Instead, he pulled a white handkerchief and began to mop his brow. He took several puffing breaths, his hands clinched.

"Mr. Haynes, I've given you all the information I have. Now if you will excuse me, I have pressing court business I must attend to."

I watched him for a few seconds as he put on his glasses, shifted some papers on his desk, and began making notations. Apparently this interview was over. I thanked him for his time, and departed.

The following is a continuation of the Last Statements of Claude Allen

THE RICHMOND EVENING JOURNAL

March 31, 1913

"My dear friend, Dr. J. J. Scherer, stayed with me almost constantly since my confinement, and has given me great comfort and support. I want to thank my attorneys' work, also to thank Dr. McDaniel for his words of comfort and cheer and the friends who have stood loyally by us undertaking to see that we got justice, especially Mr. Luther Scherer and the lawyers and the people who have given to our cause not only their money but their time and energy.

I want to thank the papers that have tried in every way to put our cause before the people. The [Richmond] Journal especially has made a wonderful fight and has helped us in every way that it possibly could. The Danville and the Clifton Forge papers have also endeavored to set the true facts before the people. I wish also to thank the penitentiary officials. All of them have shown me every possible kindness. We do not think our friends have taken the position that if the facts, as stated, were true that we should not die but that the facts and reports that have been stated and a great many statements made on the stand were untrue. I want every one to feel that we appreciate everything that has been done for us more than they can ever realize; and I hope that our giving up our lives, as we have had to give them up, will be in some way be a benefit to the public in general - to see that safe guards are thrown around the lives of innocent people in the future.

"My last words to the people of Virginia are, I knew absolutely nothing of any conspiracy and do not believe there was one. I did not fire the first shot and did not shoot until my father had been shot at. I did not kill Judge Massie. Those who have wronged me, I forgive and hope we shall meet in a better world where sorrow is never known. Pray God's blessing upon our dear old State, and to all her people I say farewell. I am with a clear conscience."

Claude Allen.

The words you have read were transcribed directly from the statement. Neither this reporter, nor The Evening Journal, changed these words in any way. In tomorrow's edition we will begin Floyd Allen's last statement.

On Tuesday, Jeff needed to patch the roof, so I took the wagon into town to pick up supplies. I checked for Mrs. Guynn's mail, and then stopped by for lunch at James Cochran's restaurant. While I stood at the counter, a tall, well-built man took a position adjacent to me and began studying the pocket knives in the display. He silently slid a folded piece of paper to me. I turned to speak, but he gave me a look that I knew demanded confidentiality. I cupped my hand over the note. As he walked away, I saw written on the outside of it, 'Read in private only'. I slipped the note into my pocket. I shifted my eye to watch him sit down at a corner table where he began studying the menu.

After paying, I turned to leave, just as the waitress said to the man, "Good morning Elmo, what for you today?"

Once out of town, I pulled the message from my pocket. I read the fine calligraphy, 'I understand you're wanting to know the truth of what happened. If you can assure me of your discretion, then meet me at the abandoned sawmill in the woods behind Mrs. Guynn's place tonight at 8 o'clock. Come alone'.

I felt some uneasiness about the missive and its need for secrecy, but it did intrigue me. If it was additional information, or for that matter, any information, it would be more than I had gotten to date. As soon as I arrived home, I helped Jeff unload the wagon and I then took a walk up to the edge of the woods. I soon found, deep in the woods, a building made from rough sawn lumber at the site of an abandoned saw mill. The logging road that led to it was completely overgrown with bushes.

I walked back to the boarding house and spent the rest of the day reviewing my notes. There were a lot of them, but nothing that remotely resembled an article. I also was bothered by the fact that Deck Goad was partially correct. Everything I had was biased toward the Allen's. I knew I really needed to talk to them, or to others who had proof instead of manipulated evidence. I just felt sensitive to their mourning period at this time though, I told myself.

THE RICHMOND EVENING JOURNAL

April 1, 1913

Floyd's final message: "Richmond penitentiary, March 27th, 1913.

By request of my father, I am writing a short statement of his past life as he states it to me. C. S. Allen (Dictated by Floyd Allen)

Knowing that I am to die and believing a great injustice has been done, I want to make a short and last statement of what occurred and, also as to a few happenings that have been referred to in the papers and by others that affect my past life.

I was born in Carroll County, Virginia, and am now fifty six years old. Lived all my life in Carroll country. My father was Jerry Allen. Most of my life has been spent in the Fancy Gap district. My father moved when I was fourteen or fifteen years old. I have had very few difficulties and cannot understand why I have been referred to" by some people and the papers and accused of so many things that I am not guilty of. The first difficulty I remember since I was a man was with Green Edwards. This was over political matters. I was a Democrat, he a Republican. This occurred at a public speaking. He called me a name that I would not stand for and I knocked him down for it. I have been much surprised and hurt by the statement of Judge Jackson. I had always considered Jackson my friend. He appointed me deputy sheriff and I would not accept it under a Republican sheriff and at one time he wrote and asked me to come to Hillsville and to be at court; and wanted me to protect him, or words amounting to about the same as this.

If I had been such a terrible man as he described, why would he appoint me deputy sheriff? Or permit me to be appointed? His statement, also, as to the Allens being Democrats; I voted in the first election after I was twenty one years old; voted the Democratic ticket and have been voting in all elections since and have been a very active worker in the Democratic party. I paid poll taxes of other men in order to keep them from being disfranchised. I have never voted the Republican ticket in any election, except in a few instances, in local matters.

When Dexter Goad first started out in politics I voted for him. as Isaac Webb was running against him. I did not know whether Webb was a Democrat or a Republican - he carrying water on both shoulders; and for that reason I voted for Dexter Goad. Webb later, in another election, came to my place and stated that he was a Democrat and I voted for him.

I first voted at Leonard precinct. I then moved to the Wisler precinct and to the best of my knowledge my father and I were the only two who voted the Democratic ticket. The precinct was solidly Republican. I have been voting at the Wisler precinct ever since, and do not think I have ever missed but one election, and that was when I was sick and could not go; and this was the only one I lost; and if I had been able to have been carried I would have gone there and voted at the last election when Goad and Sutherland ran. My recollection is that while it was close, it went Democratic by one or two votes.

The words you have read were transcribed directly from the statement. Neither this reporter, nor The Evening Journal, changed these words in any way. Continue to follow the printing of Floyd Allen's last statement over the next week.

After dinner, I told Jeff I was going for a walk. The path to the saw mill was even less accessible walking under a cloudy night sky. The door squeaked opened. I took a deep breath. I was not sure what was awaiting inside, but I entered. From the sparse moonlight shining through the window, I spotted a single lantern. It had oil, so I lit it. An eerie glow was cast throughout the room. It was a quarter before eight. The ghostly reflections from the lantern that flickered about the room took me back to my childhood, and the ghost tales my grandmother would tell me as we sat by the fireplace. I thought about building a fire, but hoped my appointment would be arriving too early for that. I sat down in a cane-bottomed chair. Minutes slipped into what seemed like an hour. I looked at my watch for the tenth time. I leaned back in the chair, almost dozing off, when a voice from outside the cabin startled me.

"Put out the lamp."

I did so quickly, nearly falling out of my chair in my haste. Through a side window slipped a figure dressed in black.

"So what do I call you?" I asked, not letting on I had heard the waitress call him 'Elmo'.

"No need for names quite yet," he answered. "We may not be here that long. I know I'm late, but I had to make sure no one followed you or me. Before we start, it is I who must ask the first question."

I could save the visitor time, because I knew the first question would be how much was I willing to pay for the information he was about to offer.

"Sure, what is it?" I said, playing along.

"My question to you is, do you know what you are getting yourself in to?"

I wondered if I had heard the man correctly. The question was not menacing. It sounded rhetorical. For a moment I considered if I should even answer, but when only silence followed I replied.

"I'm not sure I know what you mean."

"Everyone in this county knows that you, and your newspaper you report for, were very sympathetic to the Allens' cause. Naturally, they figure you're here to dig up information to prove their innocence. There are some people that wish to see that information remain buried, and would be willing to bury you to keep it that way."

I searched the darkness for some trace of the man's expression, but instead only saw a faceless profile. Sure I knew I would ruffle some feathers down here, but was this man threatening me? Was his sole purpose for this meeting to issue me a warning?

"I guess I never thought my presence was that disruptive."

"Well, you need to think about it now. If I'm going to risk my life giving you information, you need to consider if you are willing to risk your life using it. Also, you need to assure me that what I tell you will be kept in strictest confidence. If my name was ever associated with what you write, I'm as good as dead."

"I'd like to say that yes, I would be willing to risk my life," I said. "As for confidentiality, I'm always willing to offer that."

"You think about what I said for awhile," he said. "If you decide you're up to it, then we'll meet again here, same time, two days from now. If you don't show up, then I'll assume you've done the wise thing and returned to Richmond."

"That sounds fair," I said. "So what will you share with me?"

"I can provide information as to some of the background in both the works of the Baldwin-Felts agency, and perhaps some things you may not know concerning the court officials."

"I take it you are a friend of the Allens?"

"I know them well, but I don't consider myself a friend. I think they were guilty of at least attempted murder. But I also know beyond a shadow of doubt they were not guilty of a conspiracy, or at least, no more than the Court officials were."

I shivered as I heard the words. If this man was bona fide, this might be information that no newspaper had received to date. This could break the story.

"So, what are you asking for this information. I mean, I will need to get the money wired to me by the newspaper. I don't carry it with me. And keep in mind, we're just a small local."

There was a long silence. I guessed the man was trying to evaluate how much to ask for.

"I think you've misread me, Mr. Haynes. I don't want retribution for this. I don't want blood money. This is my penance."

"Why is it your penance?"

"Because in a small way, I was unintentionally responsible for the electrocution of two men."

This confession stunned me. Again I wished I could view his expression. I had always been good at reading a person's body language, especially the face. Now all I had to go on was the intonation of his voice. Although this man's articulation showed no emotions, I nevertheless felt he was sincere.

"Why do you say that?" I asked.

"Because Baldwin-Felts had a lot to do with it, and I worked for them. I wasn't a leader, but I was in a position to realize eventually what was happening. I should have come forth then, but didn't. I never dreamed the electrocutions would occur."

"And why did you think that?"

"Because I do know there was some information released that should have at least called for a re-trial. The state should have at least seen to that."

"And did you release that information?" I asked.

Just then a horse whinnied outside the front door.

"Who's in there?" a voice called out from the porch.

I instinctively looked toward the door, frozen, unable to move from my chair. When I turned back, the man who had stood five feet away had disappeared. I heard a squeak. Unable to speak, I glanced back to the door that was opening. I remembered the pistol. My hand started to reach into my pocket, but it was too late. In the doorway, silhouetted against the night sky, was a large man. I heard a click. I stared into the cocked twin barrels of a Remington shotgun.

6

Blinded by the lantern held by the man, I held my breath, awaiting the blast that would mark my demise. Would I hear it, or just see the flash?

"Jeremiah, what in the hell are you doing here? I just about shot you."

"Jeff? Is that you?"

"Yeah it's me. We've been having drunks come up here at night, and then they come down and rob momma's chicken coop after dark. I saw a light and came up to see who it was. But what are you doing here?"

"I, um. Well. I needed a quite place to come concentrate. I had seen this old cabin today and I thought it would be a good place to put together my thoughts."

"In the dark?"

"Well, yes. Sometimes I just need to focus. You know, the, um, darkness helps me do that."

"You just about put your thoughts to rest, for good. You gotta realize things are different here in the mountains. Sometimes we tend to shoot first and ask questions later."

The next morning Jeff and I sat at breakfast, neither wanting to bring up the night before. I think Jeff was slightly embarrassed, and I didn't want to have to further explain why I had been there.

"Do you know what the gift of sight is?" Jeff asked, breaking the silence.

I thought for awhile, then answered. "Doesn't it have something to do with fortune telling?"

"No," Jeff chuckled. "At least not like you see in one of those traveling circuses. It seems some of the Scot and Irish people that came to these mountains had a kind of knowing about them. I mean they know things before it happens. They also see things that the rest of us don't."

"What do you mean 'see things we don't'?" I asked.

"Haven't you ever seen, maybe around an old graveyard, some kind of a motion that you figured was just the wind blowing through the trees? Or maybe get a feeling someone was there?"

"Yes," I said. "I think everyone has felt that way before."

"Well, some people with the sight sees more than we do. They actually see the spirit of someone that has been left behind."

I stared at him incredulously. I wasn't sure if he was serious, or just pulling my leg as he had at other times. I finally realized he was serious.

"So you believe in this?" I asked. "I mean, about ghosts."

"Well, I didn't use to. Until I met Annie."

"Are you telling me she has this 'sight'?"

Jeff went on to tell me that it was Annie's sister Mary that has the sight. He told me they were direct descendants to Mary Ward, who was a famous Cherokee holy woman who had saved her tribe from many tragedies due to her "sight." He told me that women who have the Scot or the Irish on one side, and the Indians on the other side, have a stronger sense."

"So why are you telling me this?" I asked.

"Because Mary knows some things about Floyd Allen that I think you should hear."

"She knew him before he died?"

"Yes, she did. She used to go in his store. But that's not all." Jeff said, then gave me a very serious stare. "She also talked to Floyd Allen after he died."

I certainly didn't believe that it was possible for people to see, or to talk, to the dead. But then again when I was five years old, I never dreamed man would be able to fly, but just two years before I had seen the Wright

Brothers' plane fly into Richmond. So I wasn't about to turn away the possibility of a story. I asked Jeff to have his sister-in-law come over that night after dinner.

THE RICHMOND EVENING JOURNAL

April 2, 1913

The Last Statement of Floyd Allen (continued)

I realize that I will be in eternity when this paper is read, and I want to say that I believe that the attempt on my life was made for no other cause except for my active work for the Democratic party; and the bitter feeling that had gotten up between Dexter Goad and others on account of my work for the party. Dexter Goad and myself had been enemies for years. There never was an opportunity that Dexter had to do me a wrong that he did not do it. To show that this dated back for years, about ten years ago at Abingdon, Virginia, I was summoned there as a witness before the United States court. I had gotten my ticket and went to get my money for my attendance when I was stopped and taken before the United States marshal. I asked for an explanation, and they stated that Dexter Goad had told them that I had put in more mileage than I had traveled; that he came and looked over the tickets to find out what statements I had made. I did not charge for the extra miles. After being told that it was Dexter Goad who had tried to do me this way I told him that it was an unfair advantage to take and for a man selling blockade liquor in his office while he was United States commissioner. It was reported that the liquor he was selling came from his father's still, which was a blockade still. I was under the impression that Dexter Goad resigned after he was notified of the charges. I cannot say whether he resigned or was let out; but anyway, he was no longer United States Commissioner. We have been political enemies for years.

Now as to the trouble that led up to my trial at Hillsville, I never had any idea of taking the two Edwards boys away from the officer. I had a contract with the State's attorney to deliver them up at a certain time. I had been to Hillsville that day for the purpose of arranging this matter. As I was returning home, I met the boys with two officers. One of them was handcuffed and the other tied. I knew that the officers had brought them out of North

Carolina without any authority and without any right and one of the men was my enemy and I had trouble with him before. As I approached, he drew his gun on me and kept it one me for some time I had passed on beyond. As I passed the boys asked me to come to Hillsville and go on their bond. I told them I could not do so as I had been suffering with rheumatism and was not able to go back. However, as I passed by, knowing they had no father, I decided to go back and try to get Sidna to go on their bond. As I rode by the buggy the second time, the officer again drew his gun on me. I went on down and when near Sidna's got off my horse. When they drove by, the officer drew his gun on me a third time and I told him that if he did not take the gun off me I would take it away from him. He refused to do so and I took the gun away from him and broke it. I then told the officer to take the handcuffs off the boy and untie them and to take the boys on to court like gentlemen. In taking the gun away from the officer, we having a scuffle, I hit the officer. After the trouble was over I made the officer unlock the handcuffs and untie the other boy; and then the other officer, after I had turned around shot at me and hit me in the finger and ran off. I did not undertake to take the boys away from the officers, but on the other hand told them to get in the buggy and take the boys on like gentlemen; and they refused. After the officers refused to take the boys I later took them to Hillsville and delivered them on the day I had promised to and when they were sentenced to jail I told them to go on and serve their jail sentences like men and then go home and go to work. I had been an officer in that country for years and had arrested men for murder and other crimes and did not have to handcuff them and it was seldom seen in our county that men were handcuffed. I felt that these boys were being persecuted as they were tried in many different cases and were tried until Judge Massie told the court officers that he thought they had been tried enough and the court officers did not think that they had.

Judge Massie said he would not allow them to be tried so many times for the same offense. They had been indicted eight or ten times for the trouble at the church. After the judge had told them that they had been tried enough, later they took the boys before a magistrate and tried them several times. One of the boys and his father who were in the difficulty with the Edwards boys were never tried. Also, they were indicted at the same time that the Edwards boys were and it was proven at the magistrate's trial that they were both instrumental in the disturbance at the church. Their names were Thomas. One of them was summoned as a witness against me at Wytheville.

Editors Note: The words you have read were transcribed directly from the statement. Neither this reporter, nor The Evening Journal, changed these words in any way. Continue to follow the printing of these statements over the next week.

We were all sitting in the parlor that evening when Mary Tate arrived. Jeff led her in.

"Mary, this is my cousin Jeremiah. He's a reporter, but he's not like the others. He's really here to find the truth. I think you should tell him the things you know."

The young woman looked at Jeff with a disconcerting stare. She had a strong resemblance to her sister Annie, except the Indian features were even stronger in her.

"You know I never tell outsiders about what I see."

"I think you should do it this time," Annie said.

"Mrs. Tate, I promise I'll not use your name. I call you a "Confirmed, but unidentified, source."

"Mr. Haynes, do you believe in the sight?" she asked. Her eyes burned with intensity. I felt as if she were reading my mind, or maybe my soul. I shifted my weight uneasily. I was confident it would do no good to lie.

"I accept there are things in life that are beyond my understanding. Discoveries in the sky, under the oceans, and in our bodies. Besides, if Jeff said you have the gift of sight, that's good enough for me."

Mary twisted her hands until the color was bleached from them. Annie came over and placed her arm on her sister's shoulder. I felt sorry for her; it seemed she was in such anguish. I was ready to tell her to forget about telling me anything when she finally spoke.

"What do you want to know, Mr. Haynes?"

"Please call me Jeremiah, and I hope I can call you Mary. First of all, how long did you know Mr. Floyd Allen?"

"Our parents used to live at the foot of the mountain. That's when I got to know Mr. Floyd real good. When I was just between hay and grass, probably about 11 years old, I used to spend a lot of time there in the store."

"Oh, did you work for him?"

"Yes. Kinda. He didn't pay me. My momma had died by then and poppa had remarried. And, well, our step-mother, she didn't hold up to us much."

"So you spent time with Mr. Allen."

"Yes sir. He never paid no mind. He would always call me 'Little Mary', and give me candy. When I was grew up to about 15,Daddy, he decided we'd be better off living with our grandpa Morrison. He lived on top of the mountain."

"So you didn't get to see Mr. Allen any longer?"

"Not as much, but sometimes. Mr. Floyd, he would see me when he came to visit his brother Sidna. I could see Mr. Sidna's store from our house, and I'd beg grandma to let me go over there."

"What did you think of Mr. Allen? Mr. Floyd Allen." "Mr. Allen could be harsh. I've heard he's gotten angry toward several men. But he never showed me nothing but kindness. To me he was the nicest man I've ever known, other than my husband and my daddy and my granddaddy."

"Were you at the courthouse the day of the shooting?"

"I wasn't in the courthouse, but I was I town. I work for Mr. Hall at the Elliott Hotel. I still ret up for him, and the courthouse, and some other people. Doctors and such."

"Ret up?" I asked, glancing at Jeff.

"She cleans for them," he said.

"Wasn't that the hotel they brought Floyd to when he was shot?" I asked.

"Yes it was," Mary answered. "I watched them carry him in. He was as white as a sheet. Mr. Floyd was mighty spry for his age, but that day he looked like he had stared into the devil's eyes, and he had blinked first. I didn't think he'd live through the night."

"Did you get to talk to him?"

Mary stopped and looked over at Annie. A look of almost terror began to cover her face as she began striking her fists against her legs. Annie hugged her sister to her.

"It's ok, Mary," she said. "Just tell him what you know. It will be alright."

"I didn't talk to him that first night," Mary said softly, almost as if she was reciting a tale. "But he called for me the next day. After they took him over to the jail."

"He called for you?"

"Yes, he told his guards that I had nursed for him in the past, and that he needed me to give him a bath. I never had done no such thing, but I knew he had a reason for saying that, so I went and got a towel and a basin of hot water and a wash cloth, and took them over to the jail."

"And you gave him a bath?"

"Yes. They took off his shirt, and I bent over to begin washing him."

"Mary," I said, "there were people who claimed he had been wearing some kind of a bullet-proof vest, and that's why no more of the bullets hit him than they did. Did you seen any indication?"

"No sir. He just had his inner and outer shirt on. His sweater was all off when I got there. But no, I don't think he had been wearing any kind of steel vests or anything like that."

She stopped and looked over at Jeff, who just smiled and nodded his head.

"You're doing fine Mary," he said. Just keep going."

"As I bent over him, he began to whisper. He said to me, 'Little Mary', he still called me that, 'it's mighty important', he says. 'I gotta tell you some things, and we only have a few minutes. Then he commences to telling me that he had cut a slit in his piller, and he had slipped two half dollars into the slit."

"Did he say why he did that."

"He said he didn't want anyone to take the two half dollars. They were important to him. He said they were special because they were 1878 half dollars with an S on them. He said thirty years before Sidna had worked all week for their daddy, and he had given Sidna the two half dollars and told him he had them made just for him. That's why they had a "S" on them."

"So why did Mr. Allen have them on him?"

"He said that's why they were important. He said, once when they were kids, Deck Goad had knocked Sidna down and took the money from him. Well, Mr. Floyd, he said he just knocked old Deck down and took them right back from him."

"You mean all this happened, when they were still young?" I asked.

"Yes, when they were just kids. He said he always kept those half-dollars on him, and whenever he saw Deck out anywheres, he would pull them outta his pocket, and roll them over between his fingers. He said that was to remind Deck he had whipped him thirty years ago, and he could whip him now if he was a mind to."

"So he had them on him in the court."

"Yes sir. He said when they sentenced him, he was all set to go, but then he looked over and saw Deck Goad telling the sheriff to take him. He said Deck Goad had no right telling the sheriff what to do. He said he looked square in Deck Goad's eyes and said," You ain't a'taking me; I'm simply not going with ya.". He said he started to reach into his pocket to get those coins out to show to Deck Goad."

"You mean it was the coins he was reaching into his sweater for, not a gun?"

"Yes, he said it was just for the coins. His gun was on the other side."

"That's what they tried to tell the court, Jeremiah," Jeff said. "Floyd had his gun on the other side; he couldn't have been reaching for it. But they wouldn't listen."

"So why was he telling you about the coins? I would have thought he'd have a lot more on his mind at that time than two half dollars."

"Like I said, they seemed to be mighty important to him. He told me he had hid them in the slit in the piller, and when they took him away, I was to come into the room and take the coins."

"Who did he want you to give them to?"

"Nobody. He told me to save them, and one day I would know what to do with them."

I studied those words for a while.

"Mary, did Floyd know you had the gift of sight?"

"Yes, he did. There was a couple of times I saw Mr. Floyd having trouble, and I warned him. He said I had saved his life more'n once."

I tried hard to not be skeptical, but the words just seemed so unbelievable. I considered myself a good judge of character. I studied Mary's eyes for a few minutes, searching for a hint of chicanery, but I could not find any. She was either telling the truth, or she was fully convinced she had this special gift.

"Is there anything else you can tell me about that conversation?"

"Well, he did say he was a'going to come back to me, but before I could ask him anything, they came and made me leave."

"Tell him about him acting like he was trying to cut his throat." Jeff said.

"Oh yeah," Mary said. "He was almost laughing aloud because he said when they was a'taking him to the jail, they almost caught him cutting the slit in the piller with his case knife to hide the coins."

"You mean a Case pocket knife?" I asked, thinking she meant a knife made by the Case company.

"No, a case knife, you know, one of those knifes like you use to cut up your food. He said he had hid one from his breakfast tray that morning. That's what he used to cut the slit."

"But tell him about him pretending to cut his throat," Jeff said.

"Oh yeah, he said they almost caught him cutting the slit, so he stuck the blade up to this throat and pretended he was trying to kill himself. He said they believed it, but that old knife was so dull, he said he couldn't've cut butter with it."

Jeremiah then remembered what Jeff had told him at the breakfast table.

"Mary, Jeff said that you also saw Mr. Allen, just before the funeral."

"Yes sir," she said, lowering her eyes to study her hands. "I woke up in the middle of the night, and there he stood at the foot of my bed, as clear as you are in front of me right now."

"When was that?"

"The night that he was put in the electric chair that day."

"What did he say to you?"

"He called me Little Mary. He told me that he swore he did not fire the first shot, and there never was any kind of a 'spiracy. And he told me he would come back to me whenever I might need him. That I would know what to do, because he knew I had the gift. Then he was just gone."

"Anything else?" I asked.

"Well, nothing important. He did say he had sent you a note. That's why I'm a'helpin you."

I felt my heart race. Few people, and none in Carroll County, knew anything about the note.

"Did he tell you what the note said?" I asked.

"He said he had told you to find the truth."

THE RICHMOND EVENING JOURNAL

April 3, 1913

After I was indicted John Moore came to me and told me that Dexter Goad said that if I would support him for clerk that he would get a jury to acquit me. I told him I would not do this. While some of the jury that tried me and had trouble with Jack Allen and were friends of Dexter Goad's, there were some of them that I felt would give me justice. And I have since found out that they were my enemies and had been for some years. One man came to me and asked me not to cut off two men from the jury, that they were related to him and would give me a fair trial, but thinking that this man was my friend, I told my attorney. The attorneys stated that I had better not listen to him and had better cut these men off. But afterwards on account of so many being on the jury that we felt were friends of Dexter Goad's, we thought that we had better let these two men stay on. After the shooting at Hillsville the man who came to me took great part against me and I now think this was a put up job on me. The man who came to see me was Faddis, the revenue officer who swore he was at Hillsville at the time that Dexter Goad made the statement as to how the shooting occurred. I believe that Faddis knew that he was not there and was stating a falsehood. This evidence in my opinion was made up for the purpose of convicting my son, Claude, and was, of course, very damaging. I want to say that the threats that are reported that

I made about shooting up the court are untrue and as a general rule the men who testified as to these facts were men that I have had trouble with. One of them I helped to trace for stealing and one of them had been in the penitentiary and none of them lived near me.

If we had planned to shoot up the court house at Hillsville it seems that I would have talked to my friends and the people in my neighborhood, some of whom were summoned and testified that they had never heard me make any such statement. Charges as to such plans are absolutely false. A great injustice has been done me stating that I had sold or handled blockade whiskey. I have never run a blockade still in my life. There never has been a still operated on my land except one and that was a long time ago, which was there according to law. This still made brandy. I never sold whiskey and drank very little of it. The statements that have been made in regard to the shooting of the darkey have made a wrong impression. This happened while I was deputy sheriff when I was making an arrest of four darkies. I told them to throw up their hands and one of them drew a gun and I fired my gun to scare him but I saw he was going to shoot me and another was drawing his gun so I fired a second shot, which struck him and quickly drew my gun on the other one. I arrested the four and had them guarded until I got a magistrate. I asked the darkey if he wanted anything and he said he wanted to go to Mount Airy and I paid out of my own pocket the money to send him to Mount Airy and also told him to get a doctor to wait on him and I took care of him also. He did not bear any expense as he claimed he did not have any money to get any attendance with.

The words you have read were transcribed directly from the statement. Neither this reporter, nor The Evening Journal, changed these words in any way. Continue to follow the printing of these statements over the next week.

7

All day Thursday I was fidgety that the stranger would not return to the cabin that night after Jeff's interruption. It all seemed too good to be true. The information he promised exceeded any of my expectations. I knew there had to be a common link out there, someone who could connect all the aspects of this story. I had always thought that a former Baldwin-Felts detective could shed the light on a lot of things, but I never dreamed one would come forth, and especially not without the expectation of a big pay-off.

I had to wonder though if I were doing the right thing. I kept thinking about what the man had asked me. Was I willing to risk my life? When I had accepted Mr. Allen's charge to "find the truth", I didn't realize I might have to lose my life to find it.

By the end of dinner that night though, I had made up my mind.

"Jeff, I need to do some more thinking," I said, forcing a chuckle. "Reckon I could head up to the sawmill cabin without you emptying both barrels of that Remington into me?"

"Sure thing, cousin. I need to finish up some work in the barn anyway."

He removed a pistol and placed it in front of me on the table. "I would suggest you begin carrying this though. There's a lot of ornery varmints in the woods this time of night."

I slipped the gun into my coat pocket, and walked up the hill. It was almost eight by the time I opened the front door of the cabin and walked in. There was just enough moonlight for me to see the chair. I tentatively made my way to it.

"I'm somewhat surprised you showed up," the voice said from a dark corner.

I jumped, nearly tripping over the chair.

"I didn't expect you to be here already. I was afraid you wouldn't come at all after the last time. That was..."

"Yes, I know. It was your cousin Jeff . I recognized his voice, but you have to promise me you'll not reveal my identity to anyone, not even your kin."

"I'll be totally discrete, and before you ask, yes, I'm ready to risk my life. I'll be appreciative of anything you might tell me."

"So where do you want me to begin?"

"How about how you got the information you're going to share?"

"I'm from this area, but I have traveled a lot. I enjoy excitement and new experiences. When the shootings took place, I came up from Mt. Airy to offer my services to Mr. Felts. My official position was that of a courier, because I knew the area so well. I was also called to perform other duties. I will not reveal these, as they have no bearing to what you need to know."

"Fair enough. I take it as courier, you were privy to the exchange of information on a large scale."

"Yes, that's correct." The man grew silent for what seemed like minutes.

"Is there a problem?" Jeremiah asked.

"Mr. Haynes, I'm sure it's not illegal to reveal the information I'm passing to you, but I am very sure that it's unethical, or at least highly unprofessional. You must realize that I am a man of very high standards, both for myself and others. I do though, feel that some things must be made known in this case. It may prevent occurrences of this sort in the future."

"I can understand if it is an ethical dilemma, but you are right. The good may be greater than the wrong," I said. I hoped I sounded more convincing than I felt.

He looked at me intently. I could tell this man couldn't be coerced, and I made a promise to myself that I would be totally honest in my dealings with him. I was afraid I had totally alienated him, when he again began to speak.

"I don't wish to see anyone punished for the things I'm going to share with you, but I do want the truth to be known. I want you to be able to show that there were no innocent parties in this affair. Blame could not be placed singularly upon one side, but rather there was enough condemnation to go around for everyone."

"I think I would agree with you on that issue," I said. "I'm not here to lionize the Allens. I know they had flaws also."

"Yes, they had numerous flaws. That's certain. I would like, when all of this is done, that no layman will ever want to use violence to disrupt justice, and justice will never use violence to disrupt the layman of our land."

"I understand that, and appreciate the time you're spending with me. So tell me a little more about what you did."

"As a mountain courier," he continued, "I carried dispatches back and forth between the Baldwin-Felts camps. These messages usually coordinated the various raids that were carried out."

"Did you ever go on any of the forays?"

"Yes, if there were no replies for me to take back, I would participate in the ride until the officer in charge of the camp had a message to send."

"So you started work with the detectives soon after the shootout?"

"Yes. As I said, when I heard about the shootout, I thought it might be something I'd like to be in on, so I came up to Hillsville."

"And that's when you signed up with the Baldwin-Felts Detective agency?"

"No, actually they had not been brought in yet. Mr. Worrell, he was a newspaper editor from down in Radford, had come up that evening. He called a meeting, and the county deputized about thirty of us."

"Why did he feel that was necessary?" I asked.

"Everybody was sure the Allens would come roaring back into town, like the James Gang, and shoot everyone in sight and rescue Mr. Floyd Allen."

"So what was one of the first things you did?"

"The first thing they wanted was for volunteers to go to the Elliot House Hotel and arrest Mr. Allen. Norm Williams, a boy from over at Galax, and I made the arrest and brought him to jail."

"Did you have any problems?"

"No, there were just a couple of people with him. I believe I remember it was Cabe Strickland and one of Floyd's sons, I can't remember which one. Maybe Victor. We brought him back to the jail, and then about ten of the thirty deputies offered to stand guard. The others weren't of much use."

"What condition was Mr. Allen in?"

"He was in very bad shape. Doc Nuckolls didn't think he'd make it through the night."

"When did the detectives get there?"

"They didn't arrive until the next day. They had a heck of a time getting here, all the creeks were flooded. When they got here, they were sworn in as county officers, and I was sworn in with them."

"What did you do then?"

"The first thing we did, right around noon on that Friday, was to go looking for Sidna Allen. Once we got to within about a quarter of a mile from his house, we dismounted to split into three squads. We advanced on the house from different directions. I think we all felt certain there would be gunplay."

"Was there?"

"Surprisingly there wasn't any. We searched the house and all the buildings. All we found was a sweater with two bullet holes in it. So we headed back to Hillsville."

"What was your next action?" I asked.

"I guess it was later than evening, we got word the Edwards boys were at their mother's place. We went there at full gallop. At least those of us that knew how to ride did. It amazed me that some of the detectives could barely mount a horse."

"There were members of the posse who couldn't ride a horse?" I asked.

"That's right. They didn't even know how to mount. Again we were sure there would be gunplay, but found none. We did think we saw some movement up in the mountains, but by that time it was too dark to search anymore."

"During the raids, what were your orders?"

"What do you mean?"

"Were you ordered to take the Allens alive, or dead?"

The man thought for awhile, trying to formulate his words.

"Well," he finally said. "We were never told to kill them, but we were constantly reminded that the Allens had stated that they would never be taken alive, and would never serve a day in jail, so I think everyone in the group was probably ready to shoot first."

"What about the other raids? Weren't there several?"

"Yes, over the next week almost every day we went on two or three. We'd get a report that one of the Allens, or the Edwards boys, had been seen, and we'd take off to all corners of the county. It soon became apparent that the reports were untrue."

"Were you in on any of the captures?"

"Yes, on the 28th of March, I was reconnoitering with Mr. Payne in a densely wooded area about half way between Mr. Floyd Allen's house and Willis Gap. We thought we had Sidna Allen cornered, but it turned out to be one of our own men, Lucas. But Lucas then found Claude Allen."

"Was there gunplay?"

"No, we had him well-covered and he knew it. He was carrying a thirty-eight special Smith & Wesson, and a thirty-eight Smith and Wesson lemon squeezer."

"Lemon squeezer?" I asked.

"Yes, that's what they called them because you had to squeeze the handle before it would fire."

I made myself a mental note to find a local gun expert to instruct me as to the differences in hand guns. I hadn't had much opportunity to learn about them in Richmond.

"You were in on a lot of these incursions?" I asked.

"Yes, we all were. I kept a journal, and tried to figure it all up. The best I can estimate I rode about 1800 miles, walked about 200 miles, and rode on about 20 all-nighters."

"Were you in on any others that turned up any of the Allens?"

"No, by this time I was working as courier full time. It was just after this though, I think on the 29th, that Friel Allen, Jack's son, was arrested at his father's house. Then about the same time the Edwards boys were arrested. Then they brought bloodhounds in from the state."

"Did you ever consider yourself in danger?"

"I never got shot at, but I did have a couple of close calls, maybe not death, but potentially bad injuries. It seemed like it rained everyday. The roads were running like creeks, and many of the raids were at night, without light. One night it was so dark, I was having to lead my horse. I went head-first over a six foot ledge and just about broke my neck."

"So were you a typical Baldwin-Felts man?"

"I hope to God I wasn't," he said, not in a blasphemous but rather serious tone.

"There were really two types. The true professionals were former law enforcement men, even lawyers. These were known as 'opens'. You could always tell them by their leggings and black bowlers."

"But they weren't representative of the others?"

The man hesitated, weighing his words.

"Thomas Felts was one of the best organizers I have ever met. The 'opens' were the skin of the group, but the skeleton was a bunch of the most detestable, immoral, and unconscionable cretins I've ever had the misfortune to meet. They served as the eyes, ears, and fists of the group."

"So they didn't hesitate to 'break a few heads' if necessary?"

"I think many of them relished the chance to beat people."

"How about killing, murder?"

"Yes, several murdered."

"How did the agency keep from being charged with the action of these men?"

"They kept an 'arms-length distance'. There was no way to tie the agency to all of the activities. We didn't use names; we used numbers. Also there were no 'orders' to murder; the captains of the agency would give instructions that 'something had to be done' about certain individuals. If 'something' was done, then that person got a nice bonus out of it."

"Did you know any of the 'cretins'?"

"I did. One actually came from right here in the mountains. I understand he was once a preacher, but something went wrong that really screwed up his head. He was always quoting the Bible."

"That does sound unusual," I said. "Were there many like that?"

"No, actually I found most to be just the opposite. Many of them lied about their experience. They talked big, but the first time we got into the least amount of danger, they high-tailed it back home, or at least back to Hillsville."

"And you never felt your life was in danger, you know, of the Allens ambushing you?"

He studied the question, then answered.

"No, I knew the Allens enough to believe they'd not bushwhack you. If I cornered them, and was face to face, I think one of us would have had to die. But no, I was more afraid of being shot accidentally by one of the other agents."

The quality of the information was beginning to diminish. I knew this man knew a whole lot more than he was telling me. I decided to be direct.

"Did you find any information that you feel tied the Allens into a conspiracy to shoot the courthouse officials?"

"No. Actually to the contrary. There was much more information that showed there hadn't been a conspiracy. But most of that information was withheld."

"Do you have any documentation you'd share with me? You know, some directives that might implicate others, such as the court officials, with conspiracy?"

He looked at me as if he either hadn't heard me, or had not understood. He then began to grin. He stood up, and placed his hat on his head.

"I've told you enough to convince you that the Allens weren't totally at fault. I think that will be enough for me to get a good night's sleep now."

He shook my hands and walked out. I would never see him again.

Jeff had already gone to bed when I got back that night, so I didn't talk to him until the next day. I let him finish his second plate of biscuits and gravy and then tried to nonchalantly bring up a subject of interest to me.

"Do you know a guy by the first name of Elmo?" I asked. "I think he might have been with Baldwin- Felts."

"That would be Elmo Brim from down below the mountain, across the state line. Why?"

"I've just heard his name thrown around a few times. What can you tell me about him?"

"Don't too many people really know too much about him. He's a fellow that loves excitement. I hear he's worked out west in one of those wild west shows, you know, like Buffalo Bill had. I heard tell he had a close call with Floyd a few years back at the Flower Gap Church."

"And he works for Baldwin-Felts?"

"Yes, or at least he did. After they pulled out and headed out to the West Virginia coal fields, I don't think he went along."

This all fit in with the personality of the man I had been talking to. I wouldn't use his name in my stories, but it sure would be nice to know it.

"What does this guy look like?" I asked casually.

"Well," Jeff said in an exaggerated drawl, "he looks exactly like the man you've talked to those two nights up at the cabin."

THE RICHMOND EVENING JOURNAL

April 4, 1913

(Continued Last Statement of Floyd Allen)

Now in regard to my being such a terror in that section, I do not believe that I was a terror to any man who wanted to obey the law. As an officer I tried in every way possible to do my duty. If it is true that I violated the law, as charged in some of the letters coming from my enemies in an hour like this, it seems that with a clerk who was a bitter enemy and with the officers, mostly Republican, with the influence and methods used in Carroll county to procure evidence and vote and with a judge who, while at the time I felt was my friend and who since showed that he was not only not my friend but was my bitter enemy, I would have been arrested and convicted. I had no opportunity of selecting the jury and had no opportunity except what the court should give every man - the right to have my own witnesses and be heard. I was tried before judge Jackson for a difficulty with Combs and was fined one hundred dollars and one hour in jail. The jail sentence was remitted by Governor Montague. I also desire to state I had no idea that there would be any trouble at the court the day I was tried. I expected, and my lawyers told me that there would be nothing more than a small fine and certainly was not prepared in any way for trouble and went there expecting none. There was never any conspiracy and I have never talked to any of my people about anything of this kind. I had a good home, was well fixed and had a happy family. I tried in every way to do everything I could for my wife and family. I tried to raise my boys to lead an honorable and upright life. The statements that have been made as to my drinking and causing any trouble are untrue. My friends and any honorable man can testify to this as well as my family. The statements made on the stand that Claude came to me and felt my pulse and asked me how my pulse was, is untrue. The statement that I asked him whether the boys were ready is also untrue. I had no such conversation with him and after the verdict was announced we were arranging to ask for a new trial. I expected to go to jail that day and called Claude and asked him to ride my horse for a couple of witnesses. I know that I could prove by witnesses that Foster made statements which were untrue and would as I believe have caused the judge to set the verdict aside and give me a new trial. Another witness who had testified falsely, was

George Edwards. He was an enemy of mine and had been mad ever since I had trouble with his brother over politics.

Edwards swore at Hillsville that we were friends. Edwards also went to Wytheville and testified against me. Some of his testimony at Wytheville was not true. He stated at Wytheville that we were friends and the next day he was called back on the stand and admitted that we had been enemies for a year. This was done after we had witnesses to show we had been enemies. I fully expected to go to jail at Hillsville, and would have gone with the sheriff, but when I looked over and saw Dexter Goad drawing his gun, I told him that I was not going with him or it weren't him that I was going with, or words to that effect. I did not defy sheriff Webb and would have gone with the sheriff without any trouble if it had not been for Dexter Goad drawing his gun. I knew that Dexter Goad was my enemy. I knew that he had no business whatever in undertaking to have anything to do with me in my trouble. When Claude came over and I told him about the horse, I reached in my inside pocket for a subpoena. The sheriff did not summon my subpoena and I generally had a subpoena. The one I had was written on and I looked over towards Mr. Goad knowing he was the man to get a blank subpoena from and when I saw his gun and about this time I said Deck, I ain't a'goin with you,' or words to that effect. I looked towards the sheriff. Goad fired and struck me on the hip and the sheriff fired then.

The words you have read were transcribed directly from the statement. Neither this reporter, nor The Evening Journal, changed these words in any way. Continue to follow the printing of these statements over the next days

8

One day while Jeff and I were in Mt. Airy, he said he wanted me to meet someone who had a story about Peter Easter. I immediately recognized the name. Peter David Easter had been deputized to go with Deputy Samuels into North Carolina to bring back the two Edwards brothers. This is what had started the whole affair because, according to the Allens, and others agreed, although the county had not crossed the state line, having instead received the brothers from North Carolina authorities at the state line, they had acted illegally in extraditing without proper papers.

We entered a small shop on Main Street. A sign above the door read, Moore's Photography. An older man stood behind the counter. He smiled in recognition at Jeff.

"O.R., this is my cousin Jeremiah. How about telling him what you told me about Peter Easter."

"Well, Peter was in here a few months after the shootout. To have his picture made, you know. We started talking about the whole mess. He told me that he never had much use for the Allens, but he was standing just behind Deck Goad that morning."

"You mean the morning of the courthouse incident?"

"Yes, the shootout, you know. He said that after they announced the sentencing, that Floyd started fooling around with his sweater. He said that was when Deck Goad pulled his gun and shot at Floyd."

"Did Peter say if that was the first shot fired?" I asked excitedly. "Did he say if Deck then shot in the direction of Judge Massie?"

"He did say after Deck shot at Floyd, he whirled around..."

Just then a woman, whom I later found out was Mrs. Moore, stormed from the back. She called out sharply, "O.R. Moore, you need to learn to keep your mouth shut. Gentleman, you need to excuse us, we have work to do."

"Jeff, it was good seeing you. Give my regards to your wife and Miss Guynn. Now if you'll excuse me," he said sheepishly as he started to the back of the store. His demeanor reminded me of a dog, tail tucked between his legs, retreating in advance of a whipping.

On the ride home, Jeff had told me that Peter Easter came into the Elliott House restaurant almost every Tuesday night, so the next night I rode into town. When I entered I saw a man sitting by himself in the corner who matched the description that Jeff had given me. I approached him.

"Mr. Easter?" I asked.

"Yes. I'm Peter Easter," he answered, eying me suspiciously.

"Mr. Easter," I said, as I pulled out a chair. "I'm Jeremiah Haynes, and I was hoping I could ask you a few questions."

"About what?"

"About some of the events prior to, and on the day of March 14 of last year."

He took a couple of gulps of his coffee, using the time to consider me.

"You're that new reporter in town, aren't you?"

"Yes. I'm with the Richmond Evening Journal, I just wanted..."

"I've got nothing to say," he interrupted. "Not to you, or to anyone. That's all in the past and I, for one, plan on leaving it there."

"I was just hoping you might clear up a couple of items."

"I've already made several statements. You can go look those up."

"There's one bit of information I've not found in any of your statements though. Yesterday I was down in Mt. Airy, and Mr. O.R. Moore said that you stated that you saw Deck Goad fire the first shot."

"That man is either a liar, or is crazy in the head," Easter said as he jumped up, knocking his chair over. He smacked the table top, making the other diners jerk their heads around. "I've never told him anything of the kind. Mister, you'd best just stop trying to stir up trouble."

"Did Deck Goad fire the first shot that day?"

Peter Easter laid a dollar on the table, picked up his hat, and left.

I thought about following him. He couldn't get any more angry, and might actually let some things slip, but I chose not to. I started back to the livery to retrieve my horse, marking this up as a lost night. Win a few, lose a few. Such is a reporter's life.

"Hello Jake," I called as I entered the front door. "I'm here for the horse, how much do I owe you?"

When there was no answer, I started to the small room that the owner worked from. The door was ajar and a lamp burned. Just as I entered the room, I felt a hand wrap around my throat and a gun press against my temple.

"I don't have much money, but what I have is in my left coat pocket," I said.

"I don't care about your money, infidel," the voice snapped, "I'm here to give you some Christian brotherly advise."

"And what is that?"

"The rich ruleth over the poor and he that soweth sin shall reap death, for the rod of God's anger shall smite you."

"I don't know what you're talking about. Sure you don't have me mixed up with someone else, friend?"

"I have the right person, reporter. God has instructed me to warn you."

"Warn me about what?" I said.

"He says in Ezekiel, 'When I say unto the wicked, Thou shalt surely die; and thou givest him not warning, nor speakest to warn the wicked from his wicked way, to save his life; the same wicked man shall die in his iniquity; but his blood will I require at thine hand. Yet if thou warn the wicked, and he turn not from his wickedness, nor from his wicked way, he shall die in his iniquity; but thou hast delivered thy soul.' So consider this my warning."

I could tell I was dealing with an aberrant person.

"How have I been wicked?" was all the response I could think of.

"You've stuck your nose where it doesn't belong. You've got until tomorrow at sunset to get back on that train and go back to Richmond where you belong."

"And if I don't?"

"If you don't, you'll find yourself rubbing elbows with Floyd Allen down at bottom of the mountain," he said.

He used the gun barrel to plow a furrow from my temple to my mouth. The metal had a strange coldness to it, and I could smell the pungent aroma of spent powder. I tasted metal as he slipped the tip over my lips, pressing against my teeth.

I instinctively rolled my eyes to see the gun and noticed a peculiar thing. The man had his middle finger on the trigger. It was then that I noticed the end of his pointer finger was missing.

I contemplated what my next move should be. I felt quite certain this man meant business.

"I'm just here to visit my cousin, Jeff Haynes. Do you know him?"

He placed his mouth to my ear, close enough that when he began to speak, I felt spittle hit my face. He spoke through gritted teeth with an animosity that bordered on maniacal.

"The end is come, it watcheth for thee. The morning is come unto thee, O thou that dwellest in the land: the day of trouble is near, and not the sounding again of the mountains. Now will I shortly pour out my fury upon thee, and accomplish mine anger upon thee: and I will judge thee according to thy ways, and will recompense thee for all thine abominations..."

Just then there was a noise from the front.

The stranger momentarily dropped the gun from my face as he looked toward the doorway. Before I had a chance to consider the consequences, I grabbed his wrist and slammed it against the doorframe. He dropped the pistol. I recognized it as a gun like the one the Baldwin-Felts detectives carried. I dropped to my knees, seized the pistol and fired it, in one motion, at the stranger. For a moment I was looking into the darkest eyes I had ever seen.. There was no discernible pupil, as if I were gazing into a deep well. He kept coming. How could I have missed him? It was as if the shot had passed right through him. Then I realized I had pulled the trigger, but the gun hadn't fired. I raised it again. Before I could squeeze off another shot, he grabbed a pitch-fork handle and swung. I felt the crash to my head, just above my left ear. I felt a warm, oozing flow seep onto my cheek. I was sure he had ruptured my eyeball. My legs weakened; I struggled to stand.

My mind drifted back to when I was a reckless youth. I had taken a dare to jump off the old railroad trestle crossing the James River. I felt myself falling sixty feet down into the river. The warm waters engulfed me as I plummeted to the depth of the river. I felt my feet sink into the muck. I pushed up with my legs. They refused to free me from the silt, to escape the black shroud. I felt myself coughing and spitting water. Warm, red, water. I sunk deeper into the mire. I struggled to free myself. It was useless. I had no more strength. The muck welcomed me into its black-cloaked arms. I found myself becoming a part of the dark abyss, sinking into the River Styx.

THE RICHMOND EVENING JOURNAL

April 5, 1913

(Continued from the final statement of Floyd Allen)

The shot which struck me caused me to fall. The general shooting then began and a good many shots were fired at me while I was down. Judge Bolen was down in front of me and called to me to get away or they would kill him shooting at me. While I was not able to get up yet I tried to do so several times and after falling back several times I got up. After I was down I got my gun and as I was getting up and got about half way straight, Quesenberry shot me through the leg and I fired at him.

After I had gotten out of the court house Dexter Goad shot at me from the court house steps. and I turned and fired twice at him. I had only one gun on me that day. If we had intended to shoot up the court, knowing that the court was armed, would have taken both of my pistols which I had at home and would have been ready for this trouble. I want to say that I did not talk to Sidna Allen, Friel Allen, Victor Allen or Claude Allen, or Sidna and Wesley Edwards, in fact, no one about my trouble or about any shooting; and there was no plan or agreement between us or with any of us and such a thing was never thought of. I did not shoot till I had been shot at several times and I feel that under these conditions I was justified in doing what I did. When the true facts are known I am willing to leave the matter to the people as to whether I was justified in shooting or not. If we had intended to shoot up the court and resist arrest afterwards we would have prepared ourselves and had plenty of ammunition. After I had gotten out of the court-house I was struck in the knee and turned and saw Dexter Goad shooting at me from the courthouse steps and I fired at him twice. I did not shoot outside until I was shot.

As to Judge Massie: Judge Massie I felt was my friend; he had been good to me and good to us. When the Edwards boys were being persecuted he had it stopped. I had talked to him in his room. I believe that his death was an accident, he being unfortunately in the fire between Dexter Goad and others. It was some little time before I could see a lawyer. I could not write to my wife or anyone else. Everything I had was tied up by the courts. I did not have money to pay my witnesses and, of course, it was hard to get the witnesses there when they had to pay their own expenses in addition to railroad fare. I am told that in some of the cases some of the witnesses had to walk. When my trial was at Wytheville I was suffering most of the time and had to go carried from jail to conveyance and from the conveyance to the courthouse. It hurt me very much at different times. While I was in Wytheville my barn, wagon, buggy and harness and farming implements were all burned. It is, of course, hard for the public to understand or to feel as I feel on this, my great trouble. Why men should cry out for our blood I cannot understand, I know it is unjust. I have felt and hoped in some way the governor could and would know the facts and would spare our lives. Things seem to have been against me. I have not had a fair trial. Take the foreman of the jury that tried me, Mr. Nemis. Mr. Eiter, who I understand is a man of good standing, makes an affidavit that Mr. Nemis stated a few days before he was summoned on the jury that tried me at Wytheville that all the Allens ought to be electrocuted. Can a man feeling like this give a man justice? It seems to me that things of this kind coming up time after time would make people more careful about juries and about verdicts.

It, of course, is an awful thing to take a man's life and we feel that if we could have been tried at this time, when so many more facts have been learned, that the sentence would be different and that in the place of a conspiracy on the side of Allens that there was a conspiracy on the other side. We find Dexter Goad ordering a special gun to be there before the trial and things of this kind and other evidence leads me to believe that they intended to kill me in the court room. I feel very sorry that my boy, Claude, should have to give up his young life. I have tried in every way to do right by my family and I would rather have been shot to pieces in the courtroom than for Claude to have shot. I know that I did not lead Claude into this trouble. I have never lead him into any trouble and his record shows that he has been an exceptionally good child. This has been the first trouble that he has ever gotten into and this as he thought, to save the life of his father. This trouble, of course, is awfully hard on my wife. No man has ever had a better wife than I have. Her health has been bad and she has not been well for some time and I know that her suffering is something awful. And yet under these conditions people have not hesitated to hit me under the belt and hit in the dark.

I thank the Journal for the fight they have made to save our lives. I also want to thank the papers in the state who have helped us, who have tried to give the true facts to the people of this and other states. It has been a great comfort to see how many people believe in our innocence and have helped us as they have. I hope in some way our people will show their appreciation to our many friends who have stood by us loyally. The officers at the penitentiary have been kind to us, showing us every favor they could. We appreciated and no man who has not been in the shadow of death as we have for the last few months can realize what kindness of this kind means to anyone under these conditions.

I want to thank the lawyers who fought so nobly for us while fighting against great odds. They have stood loyally by us.

I want to the thank Mr. Luther Scherer and also all of my other friends who have stood so loyally by me. I am grateful to Mr. McDaniel for his visits and words of comfort and help. I thank my friend, Dr. J. J. Scherer, who has also given me words of comfort and cheer and been a great help to me. I forgive all my enemies; those who have testified falsely against me and those who have not dealt fairly with me. I forgive them and I hope God will also forgive them. Shortly we will have to stand before our God and each one will give an account of our treatment to each other. The true facts will all then be known. I say to my friends that I have told the truth. I am innocent of the charge of which I am convicted and I have no fear of meeting my God in connection with the crime for which I am dying, as I am innocent. Although I know it will be too late, yet I feel that the people will yet know the true facts in connection with this case and I believe the governor will see where we have been wronged. I pray God's blessing. I hope the lives of my family who I leave behind will show as far as possible to the world that we have been wronged and the true facts in connection with these cases, I hope by their lives they will contradict the statements and untruths that have been stated against us."

Floyd Allen.

This concludes the Last Statements of Floyd and Claude Allen. It does not end the exclusive reports that will be printed in the Evening Journal though.

9

I struggled to open my eyes, to gather my senses, but was unable. "Where am I," I thought. Or was I saying it aloud? I found myself rising from the opacity of the river that had consumed me. I heard myself being welcomed by an angelic voice.

"... and Heavenly Father, I beg you to let him escape from his Valley of Death, may your rod, and your staff deliver him back to us. I pray that it will be your will to bring healing to his body."

I felt my left hand clasped within soft, delicate fingers. A moan slipped from my parched lips. I felt the fingers squeeze tighter. I opened my eyes and was rewarded with a thousand pins of flashing light stabbing my eye balls. I quickly squeezed them.

"Just take it slowly, Mr. Haynes," my angel said. "You took a very nasty fall. Dr. Branscomb says you're lucky to be alive."

"What happened? My head feels like I've been kicked by a horse."

"That's about what happened. Papa and I found you by the side of the road on the way home from church service. You must have not cinched your saddle tight. It was loose, and you had been thrown to the ground. You took a really bad blow to the head when you fell on the rocks. You almost lost an eye."

I slowly opened my eyes, squinting, until the stabbing lights lessened. I found myself looking into the sweetest, most compassionate face I had ever viewed. Scant glimmers of happiness floated in a pool of despondency in the eyes looking down upon me. I took a deep breath, and inhaled her lilac fragrance. Instead of my angel being dressed in heavenly white though, she was draped entirely in black.

"You're Nellie Wisler, aren't you?"

"Yes, Mr. Haynes, how did you know?"

"I saw you at the funeral. You were in the buggy. Then by the grave site."

I stopped, realizing I had revealed that I had spent my time spying on her.

"Yes," she said, as her hand trembled on mine. "I couldn't bring myself to stand by the grave side. Not until everyone else was gone."

"I also saw you a few times at the prison."

"We all thank you for the things you and your paper did in trying to get a reprieve," she said

I suddenly felt a flush sweep over my face, and I began to sweat.

"Could you maybe open a window?" I asked. "The stove is too hot."

"No, Mr. Haynes. You are having the sweats. Doc said the first good sign would be you coming out of the unconsciousness. Then the second would be if you began to sweat, because that would mean your brain was trying to heal itself."

She turned loose of my hand, leaving me longing to feel her touch again. It had felt so comforting, so reassuring. I watched her pour some alcohol into a basin of water. She dropped a wash cloth into the basin, wrung it out, and began to mop my forehead.

"He said you'll fall back to sleep again. You may be away for a whole day."

"Will you, will you be here when I wake up?" I said, then wished I could take the words back. I saw a hint of a smile crack her stoic countenance.

"Yes. I'll be right here with you. I've gotten a substitute teacher to cover for me at the school. You're going to be alright, Mr. Haynes. God is watching over you."

I closed my eyes, and laid there for a few moments. The heat that had been coursing through my body cooled to a memory from my childhood of me taking a dare to break through the ice to go skinny-dipping. I took so many dares in those days, trying to convince my friends I wasn't some pampered rich kid. My body convulsed as I shivered. My mind became a whirlpool of reminisces, one flowing into another. I was back in grade school playing ball with my friends. Taking vacations with my parents. Sitting in the overstuffed leather chair in Judge Valentine's library. The joyous recollections began to metamorphose into a menagerie of fearsome beasts, terrifying me, taking me to the depth of every despair I had suffered through in the last twenty years, especially the last two. I then felt myself again leaving the murky waters, and walking back onto shore. I was at Virginia Beach. Father was laying in the sand. I was walking down the beach, my mother holding my hand, as we looked for sea dollars and splashed in the waves.

I opened my eyes and was again greeted with the smile of Nellie Wisler. I felt her warm fingers around my hand.

"Welcome back, Mr. Haynes. You slept for almost a day. I think the worse is over."

I tried to smile, but the flashing pinpoints again attacked my eyes.

"Now that I'm going to live, do you think you might call me Jeremiah?"

"Yes, Jeremiah, I think I can do that," she said, then asked. "During the worse of your sleep, you kept calling the name of 'Nancy". Is that your wife, or girlfriend?"

I felt my heart sink. I wasn't ready to tell her everything about my life. Not yet.

"No," I said. It was only a partial lie.

"Oh," she said, noting my discomfort.. "I am so sorry. Sometimes I am just too nosey."

"Oh no, don't worry, I don't find you nosy. I find you," I hesitated, knowing what I felt, but aware I shouldn't express it. After all, this was just a fleeting moment. "I find you very caring."

"Well, isn't that what God put us on earth for?"

I let my hand touch hers.

"I'm truly glad He put you on this earth," I said.

I looked at her for a moment. To have just met, it seemed we had known each other forever. I felt as if we could talk about anything.

"Do you think you'll ever love again?" I asked.

"I think I'll love again," she said, turning her head away from me. "It just won't be the same. In that grave went a part of my heart that I'll never have again. I'm not sure any man would want a woman who couldn't give him her complete heart."

I wanted to say that half of her heart would be sufficient for most any man, but I did not. It had been a long time since I had felt an attraction to another woman other than my wife, to be able to share my deepest thoughts with her. I wanted to say more, so much more. I knew she was not ready to hear some things though, so I contented myself to just lay there, listening to her humming another hymn, inhaling her fragrance, and feeling her fingertips as she continued to run the wash cloth over my forehead. I was feeling sleepy again. I tried to fight it, not wanting to sink into that darkness again. But it felt so peaceful, so satiating.

Perhaps the day will come to tell her, I thought. I then fell asleep.

"There's someone to see you," Nellie said, her hand gently shaking my shoulder.

I opened my eyes to see Jeff standing by my bed.

"Hey cousin, you look like death warmed over," he said.

"Death would have been the key word if it hadn't been for my Guardian Angel here," I said, nodding toward Nellie.

"It's amazing how powerful prayer can be," she said, as she smacked my arm playfully.

She did it so innocently, but the gesture to me had such intimacy. It was so familial, like a husband and wife at play.

"So do you think he's going to make it?" Jeff asked.

"Yes, the doctor said he's going to be fine. I'll leave you two alone. Tell Annie I said hello."

After she was gone Jeff came and sat down by the bed.

"I guess it's a good thing you've got the Haynes' thick skull," he said.

"Yeah, but even with a thick skull, it still leaves a heck of a headache. But I'm going to have to drag out of this bed and call my editor. I promised him I'd be back to Richmond on Sunday."

"Sunday? You do know this is Wednesday?"

"Wednesday? He is going to be furious. I promised him a phone call last Saturday, and that I'd be back at the paper on Monday to write the articles."

Jeff's expression turned more intent. He leaned over my bed and began to speak in a low tone.

"Do you have any inkling of what happened?"

"Well, I can remember going to town to meet Peter Easter It's kinda fuzzy after that. Nellie tells me my horse threw me on the way home."

Jeff squinted at me. I could tell he was about to get serious.

"Jake came over to the house last Saturday night. He said on that night he had received a message that his youngest boy was badly sick, so he had rushed home. Said when he got there, nobody was sick a'tall. And no one had sent a message to him."

"Yes, I remember now calling out for him, but he wasn't there." I said.

"He said when he got back to the livery stable, he found your horse gone. When he went into the office, he found it a mess. A window was knocked out, his pitch fork handle broken in two, and blood all over the place."

"Yeah, I'm remembering bits and pieces. Nellie said they found me on the road, and thought my horse had thrown me, and I had hit my head on a rock, but I thought I remembered something happening at the stables."

"It looks to me like someone tried to kill you, or at least make it clear you're not wanted here. Can you remember anything else?"

I closed my eyes, hoping that would restore the memory that was only a vague flicker of recollection.

"I remember coming into the stables. I called for Jake, but he didn't answer. I went back to his office thinking he might be there. When I walked in, I believe someone grabbed me. From behind. I remember that he stuck a gun to my head."

"So you were robbed?"

"No. I remember that I offered to give him my money, but he said something to the effect that I was sticking my nose in business where it didn't belong, and I was to be back in Richmond by sunset the next day."

"Sounds like you're rubbing someone the wrong way. I didn't realize you had dug up that much."

"Well, I've made some contacts," I said, "and I've gathered some information. But it's hard to believe it would be anything that someone would kill me for."

"I think there's a whole lot more to this story than has come out," Jeff said, "and someone wants to keep it that way. Can you think of anything else?"

"It's starting to come back. In small flashes. I remember, the horses neighed, like someone was coming in, and when he did, I turned around to look. We scuffled. I remember; he dropped his gun. I grabbed it and took a shot."

"Did you hit him?"

"I thought I had. I think he thought so too. I wasn't six feet away. But I guess I missed him. Or I'm not sure the gun even fired, although I pulled the trigger. But just trying to shoot him gave me a new insight into the Allen's reaction in the courthouse that day."

"What do you mean?"

"It always bothered me that Mr. Allen and Claude said that they didn't fire the first shot, but when someone did, they just began shooting to defend themselves. I couldn't accept that you'd just try to kill someone because a shot had been fired. But this man hadn't even fired at me, just threatened me, and I was so scared, I tried my best to kill him."

"Well a good dose of being scared, mixed with a good dose of being pissed off, will certainly make a fellow do things he never thought he'd do. So you did get a good look at him? Did you recognize him?"

"No, I hadn't seen him before. He was maybe an inch taller than me, maybe twenty pounds heavier. Had a beard. He wore one of those felt hats and dusters, like I saw some of the Baldwin-Felts detectives wear. I did see his gun. I think it was one of those thirty-eights I saw in a photograph, like the agents used."

"I don't think there's any of their men around. They've all left for the coal wars out in West Virginia. Might have been one that don't work for them no more. It wasn't Elmo Brim was it? Doesn't sound like something he'd do."

"No," I said. "It wasn't him. Oh, something else. He talked strange."

"You mean with an accent?"

"No, he talked with a mountain accent, but it sounded like he was talking, I don't know, Elizabethan."

"Elizabethan?"

"You know, like Shakespeare wrote. You know, with thee and thine."

"Oh yeah, I'd really know how *he* wrote," Jeff said with a laugh.

"No. Thinking back now I remember it was Bible scriptures. Yes, he said it was from the book of Ezekiel."

"Do you remember any of them?"

"Something about fearing the LORD lengthens our days: but the wicked's days will be shortened. Something else. Also when the man held the gun to my head, I noticed that his middle finger was on the trigger guard and his shooting finger was missing."

Jeff looked at me with a very perplexed expression.

"Did this guy have about a 3 inch scar across his cheek?"

"I'm not sure. It was pretty dark in there. Plus he had a beard? Why? Do you think you know him?"

"I would think I did. I would have thought you had a run-in with Preacher Lucas."

"Well, this guy sure didn't act like a preacher."

"The preacher part was left over from his younger days. He did some mighty fine preaching when he was a teenager. People came from fifty miles to hear him. But then something happened when he was about twenty. No one knows what. Then things changed."

"Changed how? I asked.

"He stopped preaching and started working for Baldwin and Felts. I heard he had traveled all over the country for them, and that he did some 'off the books' work for them."

"What does that mean?"

"He did some jobs that Tom Felts didn't want tied back to the agency. You know, bushwhacking jobs. Maybe even some torture. He would come back to town every few months, flashing large amounts of money. When people would ask where he got it from, he would answer, 'from doing God's work.'"

"Did he have a missing finger?"

"Yeah. I always heard Jack Allen, Floyd's brother, shot it off. I've seen with my own eyes old Jack shoot birds off a tree limb fifty feet away with a pistol. They say he and Lucas got in an argument. Lucas started for his pistol, but Jack pulled his and shot preacher's shooting finger off."

"That sounds like that might be him. Does he live around here?"

"You might say he is still around here. He just doesn't live around here."

"What do you mean?"

"I mean he's here, but he's in a cemetery out near Devil's Den. I know, because I went to the funeral."

"What happened?"

"About six months ago, right after Sidna and Wesley Edwards was caught out in Iowa, Preacher Lucas was blown up in a cabin out in the West Virginia coal fields. Those union organizers blew him to kingdom come. They couldn't even open his casket. The funeral home said they only found a few pieces of clothing and personal articles."

"So how did they know it was him?"

"They got signed papers from the other detectives swearing he was the only one in that cabin. I bet old man Jack Allen was mighty glad to see him go."

"Why's that?"

"Because Preacher Lucas had sworn to Jack he'd come back one day and shoot him dead."

"I'll just wait to see what happens," I said. "I tell you what I'm going to do though. I'm going to make two copies of all my notes. I'm going to leave one copy in the desk drawer in my bedroom. If anything should happen to me, I want you to send the notes to Mr. Archer at the Richmond Evening Journal."

"So what are you going to do now."

"I'm going to have to get back to Richmond. I'll probably come by the house, pick up some things, and head out tomorrow."

After breakfast the next day, I took my bag, swung it over my rented horse, waved goodbye to Jeff and Annie, and started toward the train station.

From a rhododendron thicket the man knelt. He lined the silhouette of Jeremiah Haynes' in the sights of the Springfield M1903.. He slowly squeezed the trigger. A low muffled ping of a dry fire was swallowed in the noise of the day. "Bang!" the stranger said, smiling as the journalist, his bag in hand, retreated back to the safety of Richmond.

"God's will be done," he said between clinched teeth.

As I waited at the Blair Station, an automobile pulled to the drop off. They were rather common place in Richmond, but I had only seen a dozen or so here in the mountains. The usual transportation was a single horse, a wagon, or a buggy. A well dressed man exited. A porter ran to the car and grabbed the suitcase. I recognized the man from photos I had seen. I approached him.

"Mr. Carter," I said, extending my hand. "My name is Jeremiah Haynes. I'm a journalist for the Richmond Evening Journal. I think we also share a common acquaintance, Dr. John Scherer."

George Lafayette Carter studied me for a moment. I could feel him sizing me up. I had heard what a shrewd businessman he was. Some even called him ruthless. Few had ever bested him in the business world. I then saw a slight smile crack his visage.

"How is the Most Reverend Dr. Scherer?"

"He's well. I just spoke to him two weeks ago."

"About the Allens? "

"Yes," I said. "How did you know?

"I recognized your name from your articles."

"I didn't know my articles were written here." I said.

"They weren't. I read about ten newspapers a day. What are you doing in the mountains? Does it have to do with the Allens?"

"Yes, it does. I'm here doing some research for future articles."

"If you're traveling in my direction, you're welcome to join me in a private car as far as Roanoke."

"Thank you. I'd like that very much."

The porter carried the polished leather valise with the brass snaps to the last passenger car and we entered from the rear door. The coach had been divided into a dining and sitting area. A dining table for six, two sofas, and two chairs were provided. A liquor cabinet made from teak stood in one corner. By the time we entered, a dinner setting for two had been placed, and a covered tray stood nearby.

"I hate to travel alone," Mr. Carter said. "I always order two dinners in case I can convince some wayward traveler to share the trip with me."

We sat down to a dinner of roasted chicken, potatoes, and green beans. Mr. Carter offered me liquor or wine, stating that he seldom drank. I declined, and he seemed pleased that I did so. After dinner Mr. Carter poured us a cup of coffee and cut a slice of apple pie for each of us.

"I understand you no longer live in Hillsville," I asked.

"No, I live in a new little town, just outside Bristol, called Johnson City. I still have business interests here in this area, and I also enjoy visiting my wife's family as often as possible."

"I understand you have several business interests now."

"Yes, I've been very fortunate since my days of working for fifty cents a day at the Wythe Lead Mines. I now have about a half dozen iron furnaces, and have started some coal mines in southwest Virginia and in southern West Virginia."

"And also some significant railroad lines."

"Jeremiah," he said with a grin, "I think you've done your research on me."

"I have found you to be somewhat fascinating," I answered. "You've accomplished so much, but still have maintained such a high reputation of being fair."

"Please Jeremiah, you're about to give me a big head."

For the last half an hour I had been anticipating about how to approach him about the Allen case. I took my pad and pen from my coat pocket. I had found this was a way to discretely ask permission without doing so verbally, which often was intimidating. When Mr. Carter made no protest, I began.

"Thank you sir for such a delicious meal. Could we discuss the Allen case?"

"I have seldom been as disappointed in mankind as I was with the Allen case."

"So do you think the Allens were innocent?"

"Heavens no. But a dozen people in that courtroom could have been charged with either second degree murder, or at least wanton endangerment. It was like teenage boys all throwing a match into a hay loft, then trying to say only a couple of them were guilty of burning the barn down."

"Do you think they were guilty of conspiracy?"

"I am absolutely positive that there were no grounds for conspiracy. I've known the Allen's for nearly four decades, since I went to work as a 16-year old at Johnson's General Store in Hillsville."

"So you don't think they are capable of murder?"

"Oh yes, they are capable of anything they put their mind to. But if they had conspired to have shot up the courthouse, there would not have been a single court official alive today. If they had gone in, all in one accord, Deck Goad and his bunch would not have gotten off a single shot."

"And Judge Massie?" I asked.

"I think he was unfortunately, what they call in war, collateral damage. I know for a fact that the Allens, especially Floyd, held the judge in high regards. There was a lot of talk that the Judge Massie could possibly become the next Democratic governor. Floyd would have loved that."

"Do you consider yourself a Democrat?" I asked.

For a moment I feared I had asked that question that was going to inevitably end the interview. Mr. Carter looked at me with a steeled look that I must admit intimidated me immensely. All I could think was that I would certainly hate to have to go tête-à-tête over a business table with this man.

"When it comes to politics, I like to paraphrase Shakespeare's Hamlet. 'Neither a democrat nor republican be'. I pride myself on voting for the man."

"I understand that you tried to convince Governor Mann to either reprieve the Allens, or at least commute the sentence."

"You certainly have been talking to Dr. Scherer," he said, with a grin. "Yes, I tried. It was one of the most monumental frustrations of my life. I considered Bill Mann a friend, and a reasonable man. I was wrong on both accounts."

"I understand it's because he feels so strongly about bringing the National Progressive Movement to Virginia."

"Perhaps so, but I don't see how anyone could be so morally fanatical to close a thousand bars in the state, but then send two men to their deaths when there were so many questions unanswered."

"Do you think his refusal will affect his political career?"

George Lafayette Carter looked at me, his eyes steely..

"I don't think William Hodges Mann could be elected dog catcher after this term is over."

By this time we were pulling into the Roanoke station, and I was going to have to switch trains.

"Sir, it has truly been a honor for me to share your car," I said. "Thank you, and do I have permission to quote you?"

"Jeremiah, I never say anything, that I don't expect to see in print the next day. Thank you for letting an old man rattle on with you."

10

I took a deep breath before entering William Archer's office. Although I had thought about phoning before coming, I knew if I did, I'd get chewed out on the phone, and then again at the office. I knocked on the doorframe. He looked up, glaring at me for a few seconds. I could feel my body pricking from the darts that his eyes were casting.

"I sure as hell hope you have a good excuse for being so late," he said.

"I don't know if it's much excuse," I said, hoping a little humor might save my job, "but I was mugged and beaten nearly to death."

A hint of an emotion that might have been construed to be solicitude crossed his face. A moment later his expression returned to stoic. He continued to stare at me. Only the chomping on his cigar showed any variation in his demeanor.

"I guess whoever did it saved me the trouble, because that was exactly what I had in mind of doing. So tell me what's happened."

I spent the next half-hour telling him of the events of the last ten days; the interviews, the threats, the mugging. I had never known the editor of the Evening Journal to let someone talk uninterrupted for such a long time. Only occasionally would he interject a question. I ended by telling him I had only gained consciousness a couple of days before, and had returned as soon as I could. When I stopped talking, I looked at him for a response. He eyed me for what seemed like minutes, but was probably more like fifteen seconds, and then replied.

"I think this story has run its course. Take the rest of the day off. I want you back at your desk tomorrow."

"Oh no, this story is far from over, there's some things going on that..."

"Jeremiah, this isn't open to discussion. We're through with this story. You can either show up here in the morning, or find yourself another job."

I looked at him in disbelief. From what I had told him, he could not have surmised this story was over. His eye twitched, then the look of apprehension swept across his face again. It could only be one thing. He was afraid of something happening to me. Or perhaps it was something, or someone, else.

"Mr. Archer, has someone gotten to you? Is that why you're ending this story?"

He stared in a way I had never seen from him. It was in my direction, but it wasn't at me, more like through me. I could usually read him like a book, but at this moment, I had no idea what he was thinking.

"I am the editor," he said, "and I do not have to explain my decisions. I will either see you at your desk tomorrow morning, or I'll be looking for a new reporter."

At that moment I knew there was something drawing me back to Carroll County. I wasn't sure it was the story, or my new found relatives, or a woman named Nellie Wisler. It may have even been a responsibility to fulfill the last wish of Floyd Allen. But I knew that I only had one choice. I extended my hand to the man sitting across the desk from me.

"Mr. Archer, I can't thank you enough for what you've done for me. Not many bosses would have stood behind a reporter during the rough times like you did for me. I'm not sure what is there in Carroll County, but I know I'd never forgive myself if I turned my back on it."

I spun and walked out the door, leaving a red-faced editor with a dropped cigar burning a streak on his desk.

I contemplated my future as I walked throughout downtown Richmond. I had some money saved, probably enough to support me for a few months. But not enough if I had to begin buying information. This could be problematic. It was common knowledge that most informants came with a price tag.

I remembered having met a rather renowned journalist, David Laurence, at the prison one day. Although we were the same age, he had certainly had a meteoric career, while mine may had just become a setting sun. Laurence had been the youngest journalist to report on the Courthouse tragedy, but its most creditable. Most reporters had come to town, camped out in the local hotels, and paid for reports, which was almost always erroneous. Laurence instead had rented a horse and ridden straight into the mountains, usually fresh on the heels of the detectives.

The difference was that David Laurence reported the facts; the others reported fiction. The local people, either just to get paid for juicy gossip, to aid the Allens in their escape, or to intentionally make the reporters look stupid, tended to bring outrageous claims to the journalist. Without taking time for checking sources, these fallacious reports inevitably found their way onto the headlines of papers around the nation.

The most egregious was probably the report filed by many papers, including the world renowned New York Times. The headlines, in bold print, read "SIDNA ALLEN'S WIFE KILLED IN SHOOTOUT: Allen captured." In truth the posse had gone to Mrs. Allen's home,;they had searched the house and found nothing; she had fed them dinner, and they had left. And Sidna was far from being in captivity. He was, in fact, hiding out in the county, and would soon be making good his escape to Des Moines, Iowa. To my knowledge, David Laurence never reported a single item that was not accurate.

Currently he was a leading journalist with the Associated Press in Washington, D.C. . I placed a phone call to the AP office hoping to talk with him. I was encouraged when I was told that David was actually at the Richmond office on that day, preparing to do an article on the recent death of General Robert E. Lee's son, Custis. I rushed over to the AP bureau, and luckily caught him as he was departing. After a few minutes of conversing, he agreed to consider purchasing free-lance articles from me on anything of interest, other than the Allen case, that might come out of the mountains of southwest Virginia. I was confident with what I could earn doing the freelance, complemented with some magazine work, I could probably stay in the mountains at least an additional six months. I would then sell my work as a series of articles, or perhaps even as a book.

During our discussion David Laurence had also given me some valuable advice. “Believe only half of what the locals tell you, and print only half of that.”

Over the next two days I settled some affairs, sold some personal items, and emptied my savings account from the bank.

After arriving back in Hillsville, I went to Cochran’s Restaurant for a late breakfast of fried catfish topped with over easy eggs. I had developed a fondness for this local cuisine. Afterwards I walked to the mercantile to pick up some supplies. As I stood at the counter, I felt a hand gently touch my arm..

“I must say, Mr. Haynes, you’re looking much better than the last time I saw you.”

I turned to look into those blue eyes that made my knees weak.

“Yes, Miss Wisler. I can’t express my appreciation enough for your kindness in taking care of me.”

“Well, that is the Christian thing to do. I’ve not seen you around for awhile. I thought that perhaps you had left the mountains without telling me goodbye.”

“I truly apologize for that. I just had to deliver some articles to the paper. I had hoped to only be gone a couple of days, but I had to take care of some additional business.”

“Jeremiah,” she said in a much quieter voice, her cheeks reddening. “If you are not doing anything Sunday, I would like to invite you to my father’s church for services. I have something I’d like to show you.”

“I would feel honored, Nellie.”

I felt my heart do a little butterfly flutter at the hopes that this was more than a casual invitation, but then she dashed those aspirations when she added, “My father and I will enjoy that. I, of course, will not be able to sit with you, but I do hope you'll join me afterwards outside as I will show you what I speak of."

The next morning I put on my best suit and bowler hat and rode the four miles to Pastor Wisler's church. As I entered, I saw Nellie turn her head to watch me. Even though the veil concealed her face, I sensed her smile. I sat down on the back pew.

After the service I started down the steps.

"It's a blessing to see you up and about," Pastor Wisler's said as he shook my hand.

"Yes, thanks to you and your daughter," I answered.

"I think our Heavenly Father also had more to do with it," the pastor said with a wink. "It was much more of a miracle than Nellie or I could have performed on our own."

From the corner of my eye, I caught a glimpse of black, and saw Nellie coming down the steps. She kissed her father, then walked to me.

"I'm so glad you came. I wanted so much to share this with someone, and you just seemed to be the perfect person."

Nellie led me to the cemetery. Lilies had been planted on the new ground of the twin graves. She knelt at the head of the graves, and placed a wildflower on an addition that had been made to the graves. It was a recently laid monument. I read to myself the carved lettering.

Sacred to the Memory of
Claude S. Allen
And his Father
Who was judicially murdered in
The Va. Penitentiary March 28, 1913
By order of the Governor of the State
Over the protest of 100,000
Citizens of the State of Va.
Placed here by a friend and citizen of Va.

Nellie had knelt and was tracing with her fingers each letter on the white stone.

"Do you have any idea who did this?" I asked.

"I think I know, but no one will confirm. It means so very much to me though. And to the family."

"I'm sure it does, Nellie." was all I could say. Once again I felt the overwhelming need to take her in my arms, to imbibe all the heartache she now felt. I would gladly do it. I could just mix it in with all the torment that swirled unceasingly throughout my soul. It began as just a whimper that quivered her lips, then, within seconds, she was sobbing uncontrollably. She swooned into my arms. I embraced her, unsure what to do, so I just held her close. The black silk of her dress was so smooth, so comforting to my hands. Her face pressed against my chest, I wondered if she could feel the racing of my heart.

"We had talked about getting married this past March, on Easter," she said, between weeps. "We thought that it would be so befitting, to get married on the day our Christ rose from the grave. Now…" She resumed her lamenting.

I was lost for words. I ached for her with my entire being. Just when I started to speak, Pastor Wisler appeared.

"Here, here Nellie. You just need to continue trusting in our Savior,." he said, taking his daughter into his arms. Over her shoulders, the Pastor mouthed a 'thank you' to me. I stood there for a few seconds, then patted her shoulder, and turned to go home.

All the way back to Mrs. Guynn's, all I could think about was how this woman, whom I hardly knew, had become the most important person in my life. How could I feel so blithe when I was around her, but yet feel so guilty?

The next afternoon I rode over to where Maude Iroler Marsh lived. The girlfriend of Wesley Edwards had married a Ken Marsh just months after Sidna Allen and Wesley were captured in Des Moines. I knew part of the story, but Jeff had filled me in with the rest. Apparently Wesley, who was around 22 years old at the time he and his uncle escaped from Carroll County, was quite smitten with the 16 year old Maude Iroler. The young girl seemed very anxious to get married and leave her home. Wesley was so infatuated with her that he risked capture by slipping back from Des Moines to see her. Reportedly he had given her $50 to come join him in Iowa. Apparently she did just that, except she also brought a half dozen Baldwin-Felts agents with her. She tearfully claimed the detectives had followed without her knowledge, but the rumors were strong she had sold her beau out for a couple of hundred dollars reward.

When I rode into the yard, a gaunt man of about my age sat on the porch, sharpening an axe. He looked up at me with dark, threatening eyes.

"Hello, my name is Jeremiah Haynes," I said, exuding camaraderie, "I'd like to speak to Mrs. Marsh."

"Are you from one of those newspapers?" He asked

I didn't quite know how to answer, since I technically did not work for a paper at this time.

"No, I'm not from a newspaper," I said. "I was hoping to ask her a few questions though."

He laid the axe down and lumbered into the small house, I presumed to get his wife.

I mentally rehearsed my first questions to the former Maude Iroler.

Mrs. Marsh, how did you account for the detectives knowing the whereabouts of Wesley Edwards and Sidna Allen?

Mrs. Marsh, just how much money did the detectives pay you to take them to Wesley Edwards?

Mrs. Marsh, if you loved Wesley Edwards so much, why did you marry someone else almost before the ink had dried on Wesley's sentencing papers?

But I didn't have the chance to ask these, or any questions. Instead of bringing out his wife, Ken Marsh introduced me to a double barrel Winchester shotgun.

"Now I told you, my wife don't answer no questions," he said "She's through with that Wesley Edwards, and she's my wife now. You get right back up on that horse, and get off my property. Or I might just blow a hole through you."

I studied the young man on the porch. I was fairly certain he had never killed anyone in his life. But I also saw how he was shaking uncontrollably. When I saw him place his thumb on the hammer, I decided the interview with Maude Iroler Marsh was not entirely necessary. Even if she had led the detectives to Iowa, she probably had scant other beneficial information.

"If Mrs. Marsh should like to tell her side of the story," I said, feeling I needed to show some kind of journalistic grittiness, "tell her I'm staying at Mrs. Guynn's boarding house."

I turned, praying I would not hear the clicking of that shotgun's hammers, and rode back to Jeff's.

I decided to attend that week's Wednesday night prayer meeting, this time sitting in the pew just behind Nellie. Afterwards, I chatted with her for a few minutes. I was feeling an emotion I had not known for three years. I promised myself I would not fall in love with this woman. I could not fall in love with her, or any other woman. Nancy had to be the only woman I could ever love. But I could not help from wanting to see Nellie, and I had to admit that our brief moments of conversation were the best parts of my week. They were the only moments that I didn't find myself swimming in my cesspool of despair.

On the third Sunday that I attended Pastor Wisler's church, Nellie was waiting on the outside steps. I thought I actually detected a sparkle in her eyes as I started up the steps.

"Mr. Haynes," she said in her formal, but playful tone, "you've been looking so lonesome sitting by yourself. I think it would only be expected that a visitor that has become such a regular visitor should sit with the pastor's family."

"I accept your invitation."

"You may withdraw your acceptance once all of my brothers and sisters begin crawling all over you. Since my mother died last year, I find I simply don't have enough hands to keep them in order."

True to Nellie's warning, by the end of the sermon, my coat, tie and hair were disheveled, but it was worth it to be able to steal glances over at that angelic face a dozen times during the service.

I decided that a good article for David Laurence would be Appalachian Mountain religions, so I began interviewing other pastors, gathering insight as to how their doctrine varied from that of the urban denominations. Over the next three weeks, I attended not only the services of Pastor Wisler, but was able to work in the services of most all the men of God in the area, including Reverend Rufus Monday and Elder Floyd Bunn who represented most every denomination known to mankind. I found them much different than the staunch Episcopalian, Lutheran, Methodist and Baptists churches in Richmond. I even took some overnight trips to the churches that handled snakes as part of their services. I gathered enough information to write a 3000 word article to David Laurence with the hopes he might find a purchaser for it. I hoped this article would earn enough to allow me to continue my investigating for an additional month. I now viewed my future in months, rather than years. This was an improvement over that of two years prior though, when my only expectation was to make it through that day.

The second Sunday after I was invited to sit with the family, Pastor Wisler invited me to dinner. It was a beautiful, sunny May day. The daffodils were in full bloom around the Wisler's modest home. Nellie had asked me to excuse her when we arrived. Fifteen minutes later, she returned. The black mourning dress had been replaced by a blue and gray floral print.

After dinner, Nellie asked me if I'd like to take a walk to a point from which the North Carolina Piedmont could be seen. As we walked, we both spoke in an overly-formal manner. It was as if we both felt we were treading on thin ice, and could fall through at any time.

"Your dinner was delicious," I said. "Best I've had in any of the fancy restaurants in Richmond."

"Now Jeremiah, I'm sure that is an extreme exaggeration. Dr. Scherer took me to a restaurant that was over top one of the big banks. It was so, elegant. I felt greatly out of place."

"Yes, they have fancy restaurants, but, well, your dinner, it seemed, how should I say it, was filled with love."

I could see her, from the corner of my eye, smiling.

"Oh, I just remembered," she said. "I have saved many of the newspaper articles that came out after the shootings. Even the bad ones, that were nothing but lies. Would you like to see them?"

"Yes, I would. That would be very helpful. Especially any that might be by David Laurence."

"When I get time I'll put them in a box and bring them by," she said softly, looking down as if she was counting her footsteps.

Her scent was natural, not contaminated with perfume. It took me back to walks with my mother through the Botanical Gardens of Richmond. She was so near; it was as if I could feel the heat from her body. I found myself beginning to take steps out of cadence just so the back of our hands would brush. I felt like a silly school boy. Once she stumbled, and I reflexively grabbed her arm. It was like an electric jolt passing through me. Finally, the forested canopy cleared to a vista. Nellie's description was unbiased. The view was magnificent. From amidst the giant oaks, maples, and poplars, I looked down to a piedmont that was at least 400 feet below our elevation. The view seemingly ran for a hundred miles..

"What is that strange mountain in the middle of all that flatland? It looks almost like one huge rock."

"It is a solid rock. It's called Pilot Mountain. It's a wonderful place to go to for a picnic, but usually takes all day to get there and back."

Even in the radiant sunlight, I felt frozen. This just might be the most romantic place I had ever stood on, or it just might be because of the shudders sweeping over my body because of the young woman standing beside me. I knew in a romance novel, the protagonist would take the woman in his arms, with Pilot Mountain in the back ground, and kiss her deeply. That's exactly what I wanted to do, but knew I couldn't, or at least shouldn't. But her words almost had an invitation to them. I took a deep breath.

"Perhaps we could go there sometime," I said, then realized what I had blurted and quickly added "I mean with your family of course."

Nellie smiled up at me. She shivered. The evening air had cooled. I placed my suit jacket around her. She turned, showing it was time to leave. I felt flushed. Embarrassed. Disappointed. Then she placed her hand on my arm.

"Or perhaps Jeff and Annie could act as our chaperones."

11

The first of May I made an expedited trip by train to nearby Wytheville to review the transcripts of the Floyd Allen murder trial. I only had a few hours, so I used my recently acquired speed reading skills to scan the four volumes. For some reason, one testimony jumped out at me, and I read it in more detail than the others. It was the testimony of Thomas Daniel. I already knew that others had testified that some of Judge Massie's dying words were "Sid Allen killedt me." I also knew that testimony showed that Judge Massie was shot three times; once in the right side and shoulder, once in the right arm, and once in the left leg. But Thomas Daniel testified that Judge Massie fell sideways to his RIGHT, on his right shoulder. It bothered me if he had been shot from the right, the direction the from which Sidna and Claude were standing, then why did he fall in the same direction, instead of the opposite. While there I made a list of the participating lawyers and jurors of the trial.

The next day Jeff and I left at sunrise on a clandestine mission to the town of Fries. It would take seven hours just for the ride, but we expected to be back by late evening.

As Jeff had promised , we did make it home in time for dinner. After washing up, I came to the table. Although we were both quizzed by Annie, neither of us would offer more in an explanation than we had "been hunting." In truth, the hunting we had been on was to find a house in Fries, because Jeff had been offered a job in the cotton mill built there on the banks of the New River.

"So Jeremiah, are you enjoying the newspaper clippings Nellie brought over?" Annie said after realizing she wasn't getting any information from either of us.

"What do you mean?" I asked. "I didn't see any clippings."

"Nellie brought them over this afternoon. I told her to lay them on your bed. Ain't they there?"

"No, but it did look like something had been laid, or someone had sat on the bed. I guess maybe instead she wanted to go over them with me," I said, liking this idea much better.

The next evening after dinner I rode over to Nellie's. As soon as Pastor Wisler opened the door, I could tell something was amiss.

"Jeremiah, my daughter doesn't wish to speak with you," the pastor said, after I had asked to speak to her. "Not now, or ever again."

"Doesn't want to speak to me? Why? I don't understand."

The pastor looked over his shoulder back into the house, then taking me by my arm, let me out into the yard.

"Young man, I know things are done differently in big cities than here in the mountains, but I am shocked that you feel like you can come down here, and trifle with the emotional state of a very fragile young woman."

"Trifle? Pastor, I swear. I have nothing but the most heartfelt respect for your daughter. I do care for her, very much. I have done nothing to show any disrespect toward her."

"A married man should not show anything at all toward another woman that is not his wife," he said, his face flushing with what was probably anger, but was so alien to his personality, I could not tell for sure.

"A married man? What do you mean?"

"Oh Mr. Haynes, do not make things worse by lying. When Nellie brought the clippings to you, she saw the wedding photograph, by your bed, of you and your wife."

Suddenly it all was all clear to me. I probably should have told her the whole story from the beginning. But I just felt so guilty.

"Pastor Wisler, you are absolutely right. I do owe you and Nellie an explanation. I beg you to go get her, and all of us sit down in the living room. Please let me make things right."

The pastor looked heavenward as if he sought divine guidance.

"Please don't upset her anymore than she already is," he said as he led me inside and went to get his daughter.

A few moments later Nellie walked into the room, again wearing her black mourning dress. Her face was a mask of hurt and disappointment. Her eyes, red and swollen. It shook me to my core to see her in such angst. I looked across at the two people who had become so dear to me.

"I, first of all, want to apologize that because I am such a coward, that I was not more forthright from the beginning," I said as I turned to look Nellie straight in the eye. "Yes, the photograph you saw was of me and my wife. We were married three years ago."

Nellie began to weep. Her father jumped up, his fists clinched as they shook by his sides. This time I had no doubt as to the level of his outrage. For a moment, I thought he might actually strike me. I held up a hand, pleading to be allowed to continue.

"We were very much in love. Within the year, she became with child. Then, while giving birth, there were complications. My wife, Nancy, died."

"Oh precious Father," Nellie wailed, as she rushed over to sit beside me. "That was the Nancy you kept calling for, when you were knocked out?"

"Yes, it was her."

"And the baby?" the pastor asked.

"The baby, a little girl, she died too," I said as I buried my head into my hands

The pastor came over and knelt before me, placing both hands on my shoulders.

"Jeremiah, I am so sorry. Why didn't you tell us this before?"

"Because I've not talked about his to anyone. Not for two years. I couldn't. Then, when I got where I could talk about it with you, I felt I needed to be here for Nellie. I knew if she knew, she'd think she had to console me. Instead of letting me be there to allay her grief."

Nellie hugged me, while her father took my hands in his.

"I know it must have been painful," Pastor Wisler said, "I know how I felt when I lost my wife last year. But I still had Nellie and the other children. I can't imagine how difficult it must be to lose both your wife and your only child.."

"I guess we both know how it feels to tragically lose the one we love," Nellie said. "Did you name the baby?"

I knew the time had arrived to talk about the tragedy. I had needed to for a long time. I had not shared my grief with anyone, not even my own father. Nancy's parents were definitely not someone I could talk to.

"Nancy and I had decided if it had been a little girl, we were going to name her 'Halley' because she was going to be born just after the time the comet passed over. If it had been a boy, we were going to name him Robert Lee, after The General."

"Those were wonderful names. You would have made a wonderful father," she said, as she added her hands to her father's, and stared into my eyes.

I now knew I had to unload myself fully. This was my chance to cleanse myself. The reason I had become estranged from my own father, and Nancy's family, was that I had locked it all in. I'm sure, to Nancy's family, it seemed that I felt no remorse. And I guess to my own father, it felt like I didn't need, or want his solace. They just didn't understand the shame I felt. I stood up, and walked to the window. My guilt was so great I did not deserve their compassion. I stared into the approaching darkness, praying for the right words. For the words that would free me from the shackles of culpability that bound my soul.

"I..., I was responsible for their death."

"What do you mean, son?" Pastor Wisler said.

"Nancy knew she was close to delivering. She had told me that morning. I promised her I'd be home by four o'clock. But that afternoon I found out the Wright brothers' plane was to be at the fairgrounds. I knew it would make a great story. Perhaps the story that would launch my career as a noted journalist. So I went to see it."

"But that still doesn't make it your fault," Nellie said, as she walked beside me and placed her hand on my arm.

"But Nancy started labor, and she kept putting off calling anyone. She thought I'd be getting home, as I had promised. I didn't get there until almost six. When I got there, she had had complications. We got her to the hospital. But it was too late."

I struggled to speak, but the words seemed to be all bottled up. I didn't think I could finish, so I spit out the final words in one exhaustive breath. "Her last words to me were, 'why weren't you here?' I killed her."

I had thus far fought back the feelings. I took such great pride in my ability to build a dam against the flood of emotions. But that floodgate broke. I began to weep uncontrollably. Pastor Wisler came over and helped me back to the sofa. They each took one of my hands.

"That's not ours to say," the pastor said. "Only God knows the time and day that we shall depart this earth. The important thing now is that you must live your life to their memory."

"After they died, I felt totally void, nothing to live for, or to care for. I began drinking. A lot. Looking back, I now know I had become an alcoholic. I should have lost my job, but my editor, William Archer, instead moved me down to a meaningless position because some weeks I'd not come to work at all."

"I've read your writing," Nellie said, laying her head against my shoulder. "You're a wonderful journalist. Your articles on Claude and his dad were some of the best I've read."

"Yes, that was because I had found something that was more overwhelming than my own torment. I cast myself into the plight of Floyd and Claude Allen. They became my new addiction."

""I could tell they cared for you. A lot," she said. "Mr. Allen's eyes used to brighten up when he talked about you; he'd say, 'that boy wrote this', or 'that boy wrote that.'"

"I would have lost my job if it hadn't been for them," I said, taking a deep breath. I looked at Nellie, to search her face for the reaction of what I was about to say. "So I'm here, without anyone to love, while they are gone, and I'm surrounded by the people who loved them so much."

"You have two people in this room right here that love you very much also," she said as she touched my face.

For the first time in two years, I felt I deserved to be alive and, perhaps, even happy.

Later that week I went to Hillsville to pick up Mrs. Guynn's mail. When I returned to my horse, I placed my foot in the stirrup and was ready to swing my leg over when I noticed a piece of paper peeking from the saddle bag. I removed it. It was a typed letter written on what appeared to be letterhead, but the top had been cut off.

It read "i have informashun you wont letters from Deck goad and sherff webb leave your horse behind the hotel tonight at 9 with 200 dollers in cash in the saddle bag and go to the bar don't come back for 30 minuts when you do your informashun will be in the saddle bag you'll be glad you did"

I reread the note three times. Other than the atrocious misspellings, I could feel my excitement growing. I trotted the horse toward the boarding house and found Jeff. I showed him the letter and asked him what he thought of it.

"Whoever wrote it spells worse than me. There's a lot of people in town that might have written it. Old Eli Cox is the handyman at the courthouse. It could be him. He might know stuff because he's been there forever, and he does work at Deck's and the sheriff's office both."

"So you think it could be legitimate?"

"It could be, although I wouldn't have thought Deck would be stupid enough to leave any letters laying around that would get him in trouble."

"This could be just what I need. That's not going to leave me much money though after I pay it."

That night after dinner I returned to town. As I rode, I had thought about the letter. I'd be stupid to just leave the money in the saddle bag. For one thing, someone else might find it and take it. I certainly couldn't afford that. Secondly, who was to say the informant would leave me the letters after taking the money? I stopped on the street, took a piece of paper from my notebook, and wrote in large letters 'Leave information in saddle bag. I have the money. I'll come back, get the information and then leave the money. I'll then go back to the bar for 30 minutes.'

I had never left the horse behind the hotel and was surprised how dark it was. The New Moon, or as the mountain people called it, the Lost Moon, offered little illumination. I was able to find a hitching rail though. I pulled my pocket watch and saw it was half way between eight and nine. I slipped my note into the saddle bag, then walked up the hill to Main Street, and entered the bar.

I only recognized a few people, mostly friends of Jeff's whomt he had introduced me to at various times. I eyed a solitary drinker. It was Jake from the stables. I approached him.

"Buy you a drink?" I said.

"Hey, Jeremiah. Good to see you," he said, then turning to the bartender. "Give me and my buddy Jeremiah here a beer."

"Just make mine a tonic," I said.

"I haven't seen anything of you since that night at the stables. Any idea who whacked you upside the head?"

"No idea. I'd sure like to find out though. Sometimes I get the inclination that some of your Carroll County citizens don't feel hospitable toward me."

"I think it's just the ones that have something to hide. Oh, I was about to forget. I found something in the stall that night. It might not mean anything. I don't even know if I saved it."

"What was it?"

"It was one of those Hard-core Baptist religious tracts. You know one of those 'the wages of sin is Hell-fire.' Was that yours?"

"No, it wasn't mine. The man, just before he whacked me though, was quoting Bible verses. I've had preachers try to drive the fear of God into me before, but never with a wooden handle."

"That sounds like something Preacher Lucas would have done, but I know he's dead."

"That's what Jeff said also."

"All kidding aside. I think there's some people here that want you out of here mighty bad. We don't talk about it much, but I think pretty much half the people in this county thinks there was a lot of things never brought out in the trials."

"I think you're right. I never got around to asking you what you thought of the Allens."

"I got along with them fine. They usually stabled with me when they came to town. They kept some of the best mounts in the county. Took care of them too. I always believed you can tell the character of a man by the way he takes care of his horse."

"Yes," I said, "I heard once, Sidna had been arrested down in North Carolina for counterfeiting some gold coins. Someone reported that the rest of the Allens had come down to free him, riding broken down mountain ponies and that the Allens took great offense to that. Not that they had come to free him, but that they were riding broken down mountain ponies."

"So what did you think of them?" He asked. "You got to know Mr. Floyd and Claude Swanson pretty good, I reckon."

"I found both to be admirable men. They remained strong up till the end. Both seemed to take their Christianity serious. That's why I do truly believe that they did not start the fight. I just can't believe anyone would lie in their final statements."

Just then a high pitched laugh broke through the nosiness of the bar. Turning and looking into a darkened corner, I saw Dexter Goad, sitting with someone I recognized as his clerk. There were several empty bottles on the table. I had found that most people develop loose tongues in direct proportion to the number of beers they have consumed. I checked my pocket watch. It was a quarter till nine. I excused myself from Jake and walked over to the table. When I was a few feet away, Deck looked up. It took a few seconds for his eyes to focus on me, but then he said.

"If it isn't the renowned Richmond journalist, Jeremiah Haynes. Come have a drink with us."

"I'd like that Mr. Goad. I haven't time right at this moment, but I'll be back in a few minutes. At that time, I'd like to present some information to you that I'd like for you to clarify."

The gray-blue of Dexter Goad's eyes gathered into storm clouds as I looked into them, taking on the color of gun steel.

"And just what kind of information might that be? I thought I made myself rather clear before that I've told you all I know."

"I just thought that I might be able to, let's say, refresh your memories on some points of interest," I said.

I hardened my eyes to match his. I know that it's usually better to use tact with most people whom I am trying to interview, but I had a gut feeling that if Dexter Goad could be pushed over an edge, that he would lose the seemingly iron-clad resolve that he appeared to personify.

"So do you think you'll be here in say, about fifteen minutes?" I added.

Goad stood up, adjusted his tie, buttoned his stiff-collared shirt, and slapped his bowler on his head.

"No, I was just leaving. You can call my secretary and make an appointment. I'm not sure when I can work you in though. I'm quite busy at this time."

"I'll be sure to do that," I said as I turned and walked away.

Many of the clouds had drifted into the distant sky, leaving a hint of visibility as I made my way to my horse. It seemed a little more skittish than usual. My heart was pounding as I opened the flap to the saddle bag. There were several pages. I pulled them, and quickly looked at the top, expecting to see some kind of County of Carroll letterhead. Instead, they carried a Texas House Hotel letterhead. Each page was also blank. Had I blown it, not leaving the money?

Then I felt the hardness of a blunt barrel, cold against the base of my skull.

"Don't do anything stupid," a squeaky voice ordered. "Just give me the money, and don't turn around, or I'll blow your head clean off. I swear to God I will."

12

I took a deep breath. It was becoming very tiresome feeling a gun stuck to my head.

"Yeah," I said. "Don't you do anything stupid either. I'm going to reach into my coat pocket, and take out the money. I have a gun in my right pocket, but I'm not going to pull it."

"Well, you better not, or I swear to God…"

Suddenly I felt the gun jerked away from my head, as my assailant's feet began to thrash against the back of my legs. I whirled to see Jeff holding a young boy of probably seventeen off the ground by his coat.

"Damn you Nicky Gardner, you little turd-brain. Don't you know you could get yourself killed pulling stunts like this?"

"Let me down Mr. Jeff, you're going to rip my coat and my momma'll tan my hide."

I was ready to duck as the gun swung wildly in an arc as Jeff shook the boy like you would shake out a rug.

"Jeez, Jeff. Be careful," I said, ducking and dodging. "That thing's going to go off and blow my head off."

Then the gun fell to the ground with a dull thud.

"I don't think he'd do much damage with a wooden gun," Jeff said as he dropped the boy to the ground.

"A wooden gun?" I asked. Bending over, I picked up a piece of whittled wood, blackened with shoe blacking.

"Yeah, Nicky's always carving something or other. So boy, care to tell us what in the world possessed you to do this?"

The youngster sprung up, dusting himself off. He couldn't have stood more than 5"3", and didn't look like he'd weigh more than a hundred pounds.

"I got tired of this here town. I'm might near eighteen now, but everybody wants to boss me around. Momma bosses me at home. Mr. Alderman bosses me at the hotel. I was wanting to get some money so I could go to Richmond and get me a real job." He then turned to me. "I'm sorry, Mr. Haynes. I wouldn't have hurt you bad."

I looked at Jeff and we both began laughing.

"I'll tell you what Nicky. You work for one more year, save all the money you can. And if your mother says it's ok, I'll buy you a train ticket to go back up to Richmond with me. I have a pastor friend there who I think will find you a job, um, worthy of your talents."

It didn't seem I had been getting much done in the way of obtaining information, so I thought I might take another approach. I had been bothered from the first day that, even with my limited knowledge of the law, several actions taken by the lawyers and the court simply did not seem right. I knew there was only one person I could trust to tell me the truth, so I set out for Richmond the next day.

Twenty-four hours later I was standing in front of 901 West Franklin Street. Before me was one the most impressive manses on the street, and West Franklin was considered to be the finest residential area in the city. I inhaled the fragrance of the magnolias that framed the front of the house, letting the memory of my youth waft through my conscience. The basement and first floor was of rust-colored brownstone. The second and third floors of rich red pressed brick. The roof was adorned with magenta Spanish tile .

This had always been my second home, and often, my safe harbor in a time of adolescent storms. My father and Judge Valentine were not only best friends, but also business partners. They single-handedly developed the area just beyond West Franklin that was now known as Monument Street. The judge anonymously contributed almost the entire cost of the Robert E. Lee monument that lent its name to the new street twenty years before. Because of this, my father had become very wealthy. This made it very difficult for a teenager to be just "one of the guys." As a consequence, I found myself having to fight my way out of a lot of misunderstandings. I always made my way to Judge Valentine's, who was there to clean my wounds. Although I never told who my transgressors were, I have a feeling Judge Valentine had a way of finding out, and must have made contacts, because the next time I'd see my tormentors, they were always extremely contrite.

After being received into the house by Robert, the man-servant, I was granted, as always, the privilege of walking the long hallway unescorted. I opened the mahogany French doors into the teak paneled office of The Honorable Michael James Valentine, retired judge of the Central Virginia Circuit Court. The ten-foot high ceiling of pressed brass was broken in the center by a large chandelier that I had always heard once hung in a French brothel. The back wall featured a huge bay window that was as big as many rooms in other areas of Richmond. On both sides of the bay window hung a collection of arms, everything from eighteenth century dueling pistols to Napoleonic sabers .

The two opposite walls featured floor to ceiling glass-fronted book cases. The left wall contained every legal book that could have possibly ever been written. The right wall contained Judge Valentine's rare-book collection. Many were leather bound. I know personally that one was a Guttenberg Bible. Other's were a first copy of Gulliver's Travels, The Adventures of Tom Sawyers, and of course, being a Richmonder, a first copy of every work that Edgar Allan Poe had ever written. As a child I would spend hours just reading the titles, and rubbing my fingers over the fine leather bindings. I had always felt so privileged, for I was the only child that I ever knew of who was allowed to enter alone the inner sanctum of Judge Michael Valentine.

His Honor sat behind a prodigious desk. When young, I often fell asleep under it, pretending I was in a tent on an African safari. Although now retired, he still did a lot of pro bono work for such groups as the Museum of the Confederacy and the State Library. He also sat on the board of a dozen prestigious corporations. I watched him, unannounced, for a few moments. Since I had seen him two years before, his salt and pepper hair color had progressed to silver. But still at 75 years of age, he struck an impressive figure. Of all my father's friends and associates, he had always been the man I admired the most. Almost to the point of worship.

I tapped gently on the door. The judge looked up over his wire-brimmed glasses, a scowl covering his face that Robert had allowed an interruption. The frown soon turned to a look that I can only describe as jubilation.

He leaped to his full six foot three inch stature and in five boundless steps reached me.

"Jeremiah, my lord how wonderful it is to see you. Where have you disappeared to the last two years? I've not seen you since Nancy's….." He hesitated, then lowered his head that he had so casually brought up the funeral.

"Yes sir. It took me a while to get over the shock. I don't think I would have made it through it if it hadn't been for the stories I did on the Allens."

"Your father tells me you've been down in Carroll County since the execution working on more articles."

I was speechless. There had not been any contact with my father for two years, and I thought he considered me estranged me from his life. I did not know how he would have known my recent activities. I finally recovered to the point of answering.

"Yes, your Honor, that's right. As a matter of fact, that's why I've come. Do you have a few moments?'

"Son, I'll always have time for you," he said as he draped his arm around my shoulder. The touch of his massive hands gripping my shoulders brought back wonderful memories. “Here, come sit in the chair and tell me what’s on your mind.”

I sat down in the mammoth leather chair that faced the front of his desk. I remembered being allowed to climb into it as a child, my feet barely reaching the edge of the seat.

“I just wanted to tell you about some things I’ve uncovered with the Allen Case,” I said. “Things that, well, just don’t seem right.”

“What kind of things?” He asked.

“Well, first of all, I thought to be convicted of first degree murder, the burden of proof is on the prosecution, and it has to be beyond reasonable doubt.”

“The standard of proof in any criminal case is always beyond a reasonable doubt. What do you think cast doubt?”

“There were several things,” I said. “I reviewed some of the transcripts of the murder case against Floyd Allen. There were a lot of witnesses who claimed they were friends of Mr. Allen who testified of statements made by him directly to them, but I think there was ample proof they were not confidants to the Allens.”

“Such as?”

“For one, a Sidney Towe, testified that Floyd Allen was a friend of his, and Floyd had told him that if he was convicted, he would leave the biggest hole in the courthouse that any man ever had.”

“What did Floyd Allen claim?”

“Mr. Allen claimed they had not been friends, and evidence showed Floyd had once rescued a government revenuer from Towe, and he had been sent to prison. but yet Towe’s testimony was accepted by the jury.”

“You said there were several.”

“There were others,” I said. “A man by the name of G. W. Edwards claimed he was friends with Floyd, and stated that Floyd had told him that Bill Foster would never give him a fair showing, and if he didn’t, that he, Floyd, would scatter them all with lead.”

“Edwards?” the judge asked. “Was he related to the Edwards’ boys?”

"Perhaps distantly, but more interesting, this man's son Bud was a deputy at that time, and was a participant in the fight at the church service that started the whole mess." Now do you think Floyd would be confiding things like that to him?"

"I'd concur that would be doubtful. I admit that I would not have found these witnesses creditable, but I'm sure Floyd's lawyers felt they did their best job. Anything else?"

"Yes, there was a statement from a man named Alph Thomas who swore that in the fall prior to the first trial, William Foster, the Commonwealth Attorney, took him into a private room and asked him if he had a gun on him. When Mr. Thomas answered that he didn't have one, Foster advised him to get one, and if Floyd Allen started anything, to shoot him down, and he would get him off."

"Was it possible Mr. Thomas was a friend of the Allens?" he asked.

"I don't know if he was a friend, but he had been called by the Commonwealth to testify against Wesley Edwards."

`"I see," the judge said, as he slowly rubbed his beard. "This is intriguing, do you have more?"

"Another deposition given by George W. McMillan claimed that Foster told him, the day before the shooting, that he was getting himself a good pistol, and if Floyd was convicted the next day, he expected he'd have to kill Floyd and Sidna Allen."

"Why wasn't any of this brought out in the murder trial?" He asked.

"That's what bothers me. There were nearly two dozen witnesses subpoenaed, and of all those, I don't think more than a couple were for the defense. All Mr. Allen's lawyers will say is that many of their witnesses could not pay their own way to Wytheville, and the courts did not require them to come."

"Couldn't the Allen's have paid the travel cost?"

"By this time, all of their assets had been confiscated by the state. They were impoverished."

"It certainly does seem the testimony, or at least some of it, was tainted," he said.

"I know how you enjoy reviewing trials, even ones that didn't come before you. Did you possibly review the transcripts from the murder trial?"

"As a matter of fact I did," he said as he pulled his Meerschaum pipe from his desk drawer, tamped a pinch of Dill's Best tobacco in the bowl, and lit it. "Both the misdemeanor trial for the obstruction and the felony charges. I found them, shall I say, disconcerting."

"In what ways?" I asked.

"As I said, I think the defense did the best they could under the circumstances. I don't believe they thought they had any chance of an acquittal, but I think they had great hopes to avoid the death penalty."

"Is there anything you would have done differently if you had the defense, say in the misdemeanor case?"

"I think I would have put more emphasis on the possibility that the arrests were illegal in NC and the extradition was a sham. Did you ever find any extradition orders? It would have been filed by the governor of Virginia, and the Edward boys would have had to sign off waiving extradition."

"I searched the court records in Hillsville and in Mt. Airy. I found no such orders"

"So what led to the apprehension?"

"The story I was told, by a creditable source, was that sheriff Blankenship, the Carroll County sheriff at that time, contacted sheriff Cape Haynes of Surry County..."

"How did the sheriff contact the other sheriff? Phone? Wire?"

"I'm not sure. Probably not by phone, or wire. There were no wires to the foot of the mountain. I'd guess the sheriff simply rode down."

"There are so many problems with that. I would have had a field day with that illegal seizure. In addition though, I would have shown the animosity between the families as an underlying reason that the rules were not followed"

"There was definitely bad blood," I said. "If I remember correctly, that one little ruckus there at the church service ended up with fourteen indictments against the Allens and the Edwards boys. But there was never the first charge against William Thomas and the others involved in the fight."

"In my learned opinion there was plenty of guilt to go around," he said. "But even though there were multitudes of people who were fed up with the Allens and felt they had never been held accountable, I feel there was no reason the judge had to give them a jail sentence on the obstruction or impeding charges."

"I don't think Floyd, or Sidna, thought there would ever be any convictions. As soon as they heard that Deputy Samuels had filed charges against them, Floyd & Sidna went to see Judge Massie and requested they be brought before a special grand jury."

"From what I have heard, that sounds like the Allens. They were certain of their innocence, but their enemies would say that was merely an indication of the Allens' insolence toward the law."

"Do you think they should have been held responsible for the shootings?"

"What you must remember," he said, "is the Allens had to a great degree lived immune from the laws that bind most of us. Judges had taken charges from juries, and dismissed them. The courts were determined to not let that happen again."

"So you do think they should be held accountable?" I said, my voice cracking with rising anger. "You think they deserved to be executed?"

"No son, I'm just trying to be fair," he said. "There was no excuse for Floyd Allen's thumbing his nose at the judicial system but Deck Goad bringing in three boxes of shells and two guns clearly showed that folks who had no law enforcement responsibility were ready to respond in spades if Allen carried out his reported promise to never be taken to jail."

"Anything else you would have done differently if you had been the judge, and not one of the lawyers?"

"I sure as hell wouldn't have allowed the guns to be brought in."

"Did you find anything that you might have judged differently. That might have given you pause, if you had been asked to review the case."

Judge Valentine eyed me, his head cocked to the side, his face phlegmatic. It was times like this when as a child I was ready to leap out of the big over-stuffed chair and run, for I was afraid he was going to chastise me for some terrible deed. But instead, he had always only given me fatherly advice. I hoped what I had asked him would not be deemed unethical or at least unprofessional.

"Your honor, I don't want to put you in an awkward position. I understand if you don't wish to answer."

He took two more deep puffs on his pipe. The clouds of smoke rising out of the carved dragon's head bowl always reminded me of the old James River Belle steam boat that I once saw on the river before it was sold for scrap. When I was a child, the judge used to puff hard and fast on the same pipe, and make it look like sparks were coming from the dragon's head.

"Jeremiah, can I be one of your "unidentified sources" you are always referring to?"

"Of course," I said.

"In that case, yes, there were some things that bothered the hell out of me."

"I can't wait to hear them," I said, as I leaned forward to the edge of my chair, my pencil in hand.

"If Virginia had a Court of Appeals, like some states, I think there may have been a more favorable ruling. But we have only the Circuit and then the Supreme Court of Virginia. Less than 1% of criminal appeals are ever reversed. In Floyd Allen's case, Gov. Mann had already made his "Judge Roy Bean" speech. Nothing would have made him back away from the stand he had taken."

"What about the thousands upon thousands of people who signed the petitions? Didn't they mean anything to him?"

"Republicans and democrats alike were heady with zeal to cast off the good old boy democratic politics and its domination of the legal system. The Allens were doomed. No post mortems meant no one had to know how many of the dead died from non-Allen guns. The Allens could pay for everything that happened. This was a fait accompli."

"What I don't understand is why the state made such a deal of trying to prove the shooting was premeditated."

"Because there was no statute making this specific type of killing, that is of public officials or of multiple homicides, a capital offense. So premeditated it had to be to get the penalty the governor wanted. In those days life in prison meant ten, fifteen years at the most. That wasn't going to be enough to the state. People thought this was a matter of Carroll County politics. It was really state politics."

"That explains a lot. So much of the transcripts weren't witnesses to the shooting, but people testifying of what they claim Floyd Allen had told them he was going to do. So do you think if the state had failed to prove premeditation, Floyd and Claude would only have gotten fifteen years."

"Well, maybe fifteen years on each count, but remember , they had several counts against them. I think at least Floyd would have died in prison, Claude would have been an old man before he wouldn't have gotten out. Of course, if a post-mortem had been performed, they probably would have found that one or two of the victims had died from shots which may have been fired by the court officials."

"They even had premeditated murder charges of Betty Ayres, and she was actually in court to testify in behalf of the Allens. I can't understand how they reached that conviction."

"The Common Law right of self help does not include breaching the peace, but premeditation was without a doubt the red herring in this case. If Floyd's carrying a gun into the courtroom was done anticipating shooting his way out if sentenced to jail, I have two questions: was carrying that gun that day, that place, something extraordinary for him?"

"I think anyone who had ever been around Floyd Allen would tell you it was not unusual for him . Maybe more so for Claude. But Mr. Allen, from what I understand, pretty much always had a pistol with him."

"If so then, how can it be a sign of premeditation? Secondly, if his carrying a gun that day indicated a nefarious plan, what was the nefarious plan of each of the others who would not have usually carried a gun into court that day?"

"Such as the court officials, the ones who weren't law enforcement?"

"Yes. Especially someone that might not usually carry a gun, but on that day carried two pistols, one recently purchased, and had three boxes of cartridges either on him or in his desk. Did he premeditate?"

"Another thing that bothers me," I said, "is that Floyd Allen had five months earlier, after his misdemeanor indictment, been appointed a Special Policeman by Judge Massie himself. Didn't that in itself authorize him to carry a firearm, same as the deputies who were in the courthouse at that time?"

"He probably had the right, but I still maintain that if I had been the judge that day, the only persons who would have been armed would have been the sheriff and his deputies."

"Some of the court officials said the ultimate responsibility for the shoot-out rested with Floyd Allen, since he was the person who had been charged. What do you think about that?"

"The real legal question has to do with the issue of connectivity," the judge said, "and whether a law breaker is reasonably held responsible for every tragedy that follows his illegal act. For example, a man storms into a bank armed with the intent to rob it. Should he be held responsible for the deaths of innocent bystanders who die in an exchange of shots between the bank guard and the robber?"

"I'm sure the law says the robber is responsible," I said.

"Not necessarily. What if the bank president had hired six untrained guards and equipped them with Gatlin guns?"

"Can I assume in this analogy," I said, smiling, "that Floyd Allen is the robber, and Deck Goad, or the court officials are the bank president?"

"If I remember from the transcripts, Floyd Allen had one gun on him. Deck Goad had two guns, one which was a new self-loader, and extra ammunition. I'm just saying I don't think the blame shouldn't have been considered to be so unilateral."

The judge picked up his pipe that he had placed in its ash tray, and began to again puff intently. I knew well enough that this meant he had said all he was going to. I stood to leave and extended my hand. Judge

Valentine instead pulled me to him, and gave me a bear hug, although not as back-breaking as they once were. He smiled as he stepped back.

"So aren't you going to ask me what I ask for in recompense for my "legal expertise"?"

"Of course," I said, startled, and not quite sure how I was going to pay what his time was certainly valued at. I knew, even though the Judge was my father's best friend, my father always paid him for his legal work.

"Your payment to me, is that you drive straight over to your father's, and settle whatever has come between you two for the last couple of years."

I knew it would do no good to protest. The judge had never lost an argument, and they were against much more proficient orators than I.

I don't know if the judge did it as a bribe, or if he generally wanted to treat the young man that he had always treated as a son that he never had, but he insisted I drive his new automobile, which he informed me was parked in the carriage house behind the main house.

The judge had been one of the first people in Richmond to own a motor car, an 1899 Marlboro Runabout. I was one of the first to get to ride that car. I can still remember the riders screaming oaths at the strange machine that spooked their horses, but then would recognize the judge behind the dust-covered goggles, and would profusely apologize.

I opened the garage doors, using some large rocks to prop them open. Before me, glistening in the sunlight, sat a machine like I had never seen. Totally unlike the judge, this car was, well, I guess I'd have to say, flamboyant. It shimmered with a lustrous color that I could only describe as St. Patrick's Irish Green. A luxurious leather seat for two sat behind a wood-panel holding a half dozen assortment of gauges, of which function I had no idea .

I climbed onto the running board, swung my leg over the levers, and settled into the seat. On the walnut panel was a brass plate that read "This 1913 Model-48 - Six Roadster was hand made for the Honorable Judge Michael Valentine. Peerless Motor Company of Cleveland, Ohio."

I just sat there, acquainting myself with the operational mechanisms. I had driven a few motor cars, but this one was more sophisticated than others. For a few moments I was totally lost in admiring this piece of industrial artistry. Then I remembered that I had made a promise to the judge. I fired up the engine, which roared like a train engine in the confined spaces of the building. After a few blunders, I was able to pull the machine onto the street to start on my way.

The trip by trolley would have normally taken thirty minutes, but today only took fifteen minutes. I would have liked to have had that extra time to contemplate what I was going to say to my father. All too soon, I was pulling to the side in front of 713 East Grace Street.

I was surprised that the house had changed so much in the last two years. It now looked so different, almost unkempt. Paint was peeling along eaves and the roses looked as if they had not been pruned or weeded in a year. But then again, Father had seemed to lose a lot of interest in the house after Mother died ten years before. I thought about entering unannounced as Father was often in the far library and would not hear the knock. Thinking that I did not deserve that privilege, I took a deep breath, and rang the clapper. Surprisingly I almost immediately heard footsteps. Before I had time to reconsider and run, the door opened.

My Father stood before me. I gasped, as he seemed to have aged ten years since I last saw him; so tenuous. We waited, surveying each other. I couldn't read his face, and for a moment I thought perhaps it had been a big mistake. It was apparent he did not wish to see me again. His lip quivered. Though, it was not like it used to just before he would lose his temper. It was more, vulnerable. A tear appeared on his cheek, then a second. With that, he took a feeble step on the porch and wrapped his arms around me.

"Son, I've missed you so much," he sobbed. "Thank you for coming."

Suddenly I wanted to fall to my knees and beg him to forgive me. I felt like the Prodigal Son, willing to eat with the pigs just to be near my father again. Without saying another word, we walked into the parlor and sat. Even though the day was quite warm, there were coals glowing in the fireplace.

"Father, I don't know exactly where to start. I know that I disappointed you greatly after…, after what happened."

He looked at me quizzically, his head seeming to barely be supported by his feeble neck.

"What do you mean, disappointed?"

"I know that my drinking and my failure at work was a source of embarrassment to a man in your position. I know that's why you didn't want to come around."

"What would make you think that? Do you not remember the times I came by? The times I found you passed out on your sofa, and bathed you. The times I changed your sheets and put you to bed?"

The words stirred up memories from a milky way of recognizance. Yet, I couldn't comprehend he was saying those things. I couldn't believe that I had not realized they had truly occurred, and thought they had not only been manifestations of my drunken stupors.

"I never knew," was all I could say.

"Then when you began to recover, you never came around."

"That's when I began burying myself into the paper, especially the Allens' Story."

"Yes, you showed great professionalism with those stories. I was very proud of you. I told everyone that it was my son writing those articles."

The words were a bombshell. I actually saw a sparkle come to my father's eyes. I could not imagine my work at the paper had ever been a source of pride for him. I thought he had always been disappointed I did not follow him into banking.

"I just wish things had worked out differently with the Allens," I said. "I was so sure we had uncovered things that would at least have produced a new trial."

"I understand you have spent the past several months in Carroll County. How have you found it? I've always wanted to go visit there, after hearing your grandfather speak of it."

I did not want to share everything that had happened since arriving in the mountains. There was no need to make him worry.

"Things are going wonderfully. I've ..." Suddenly I heard words spilling from my mouth, almost as the pouring of milk from a pitcher. "I've met someone. I care for her deeply, but I don't think there can be any relationship. If there was any possibility, I think I even know of a house I'd love to purchase."

"Really? A house? Tell me about it."

"I think you'd like it. It's rather Victorian, and very elegant, but with more of a rustic style. Instead of being built of masonry, it's all native wood, cut and timbered in Carroll County. It has a large wrap-around porch with a two-story turret."

"Is it for sale?"

"They say it will soon be. It's the house that Sidna Allen owned, the one who's in the prison. The State has seized it, and I understand it will be going up for auction. I detest the fact the state handled it that way, but someone must purchase it. Many consider it the most beautiful home in Carroll County."

"Son, you know if you wish to purchase it, the money is there waiting."

I was afraid he had misunderstood my reasons for telling him.

"Please don't think I was asking for money."

"I know Son, but it's your money. Your mother left it to you, and I was just waiting for the right time. I think this might be the right time. When you go back by Michael's to drop off his motor car, he will make the arrangements."

So that's why he answered the door so quickly. The judge had alerted him of my visit.

For the next two hours we caught up with the past years. It was so soothing knowing he would once again be someone I could come to when I needed a shoulder. He also filled me with renewed hope, not only that I might have a chance with Nellie, but also that I could support myself while investigating the story in Carroll County.

I promised him that I would return soon. As I left, he again took me in his arms. He held me for what seemed to be minutes, until I could feel his body begin to tremor. He loosened me, and sat down on the hall sofa. As I closed the door, I could hear him again begin to sob.

When I arrived back at the judge's, he already had the paperwork prepared to transfer the inheritance from my mother to me. I told the judge goodbye, but then he said words that struck me as aberrant.

"Jeremiah," he said, "your visit to your father was very important. I think it's imperative that you come see him again soon. You need to have him in your life."

I promised that as soon as I finished a few items in the mountains, I would return for a longer stay.

I came to Richmond filled with despair as to how I was going to be able to continue my story. I even had considered slinking back to Mr. Archer and begginh for my job back. I instead left for Carroll County with an account balance of $32,578 in the First National Bank of Richmond.

13

Once I returned to Hillsville, armed with Judge Valentine's insight on the case, I prepared for round two with the Carroll County Clerk of the Court.

"Hello, I need to speak with Mr. Goad," I said to the same young assistant.

"I'm sorry; he is busy and can't be interrupted," the boy said, red-faced.

"Oh I see." I said. "In that case, just tell him that I've returned from talking to a former judge of the Central Virginia Courts and he has problems also with several aspects of the trials. I'll just go forward with my story."

The door abruptly opened.

"You have five minutes," Goad said from his doorway "and not a minute more."

We walked into his office. I spent the next four minutes laying out the areas of concern that my "unidentified" retired judge had with the case. I looked at him, hoping he might show some angst at what I had just articulated.

"Mr. Haynes," he said calmly, "you have given me nothing but opinions expressed by some senile old man that are totally irrelevant to this case. Every bit of this has been presented before, and the state found it lacking in merit. You are not a citizen of this county, and I feel no duty to waste my time assisting you in your witch hunt."

"Mr. Goad, I have information and ..."

"You have nothing, and this *will* be our last meeting."

I didn't know if it were the frustration of him not reacting as I had hoped to my accusations, or the aspersion he had cast upon the man I revered. Whatever it was, I totally lost my composure. I clinched my into fists. One more disparaging comment and I had no doubt I would strike him.

"Have it your way," I spat. "But I assure you I can bury you with the information I already have."

He glared for a few seconds. Then I saw the anger in his eyes slowly dissipating and be replaced with an almost buoyant glint. I could see how charismatic he could be. I had to hand it to him. He was the kind of man who could get others to do his bidding.

"Maybe I've been too hasty," he said. "Please forgive me. I think we both just need to start over. Let me go back through my files. Come back after lunch, say 2 o'clock?"

I smiled to myself. I guess being more forceful than usual was the correct move.

I pushed the outer door to leave the office, but it almost instantly stopped with a thud. I heard on the other side a shuffling of feet. Then the door was slammed back into my face, knocking me almost to my back.

"You alright," Goad said.

"Yes, I guess I must have hit someone with the door, and they didn't like it."

By the time I gathered myself and exited, there was no one in sight.

I returned to the courthouse at five minutes before the appointed time and started up the steps. A drunk staggered against me, grabbing my coat to avoid falling to the ground.

"Buddy, can you give me a quarter to buy milk for my little ones?" he asked.

I pushed him aside. Although he could barely walk, I surprisingly found no signs indicative of a drunk like those I had encountered in Richmond, no smell of body odor or urine, no overwhelming smell of alcohol that seemed to escape through every pore of an alcoholic's body.

As I entered Deck Goad's office, the sheriff denied me entry by placing his hand against my chest. Without a word, he began searching my coat pockets.

"What are you doing? You have no right..." I started to say.

To my surprise, he pulled a small hand gun from my pocket . A gun I had never seen.

"I have no idea where that came from," I said dumbfounded.

He just pointed up at a sign reading "absolutely no guns allowed on premises."

"Jeremiah Haynes," he says as he cuffed me, "you're under arrest for attempted murder of an officer of the court.."

Within the hour, Jeff stormed in, Annie attempting to keep up with him, with her 12-inch shorter legs churning.

"What the hell's this all about? What's he done?" My cousin shouted to, and at, anyone within hearing.

"The warrant's for threatening the life of a court official," the sheriff said, not looking up from his desk.

"And just who might that official be, because I'm about this close to threatening the life of a county sheriff myself?"

By this time Annie had caught up with Jeff, and had grabbed his arm, pulling him back.

"Jeff, our quarrel's not with the sheriff; he's just doing his job," Annie said, then turned to the officer. "Jeff didn't mean anything by what he said. Will you be so kind as to tell us why Jeremiah was charged?."

"Well Annie, we received an anonymous tip that Jeremiah had threatened Deck this morning, and he was going to come back with a gun this afternoon at two to bury him."

"Was that anonymous tip from the Clerk of the Court?" I demanded.

"No, it wasn't," the sheriff said. "It was a note that had been left on my desk when I got back from lunch. Mr. Goad said he knew nothing of it."

"So how do you get threatening the life of a court official out of all this?" Jeff asked.

"When I saw Jeremiah coming into the building, I searched him and sure enough, he had a gun on him."

Jeff looked questioningly at me.

"I stopped by to see Deck," I said, "and yes we had words, but I said that I had 'information' that would bury him. He was just so condescending. He told me to come back at 2 o'clock, and he'd share some information with me."

"Are you listening to this sheriff?" Jeff asked.

"Yes, he's told me all of that. That's not the way Mr. Goad remembers it though. Besides, this is about him carrying a gun into the courthouse."

"What about that?" Jeff asked, turning back to me.

"The only thing I can think of is, just as I was coming up the steps, some drunk, or at least some guy pretending to be drunk, bumped into me," I said. "He must have slipped a gun into my coat pocket. I've never seen it before."

"Can I see the gun, sheriff?"

The sheriff pulled out a Remington derringer. It was so small, it could fit easily in a man's hand.

"Hell's Fire, this thing wouldn't kill a bird," Jeff said. "You know that. I gave Jeremiah a thirty-two Colt to carry. If he was going to do any shooting, he would have used it and not this pea shooter."

"Jeff, the sign says no guns. It doesn't limit them to size."

"When can we have bail set?" Jeff said.

"Judge ain't going to set any bail for this."

"Jeff," I said. "Here's a phone number. Go call Judge Michael Valentine in Richmond. Tell him what's happened."

An hour later I was led into the Commonwealth Attorney's office and handcuffed to a chair. He shuffled through some paperwork with all the solemnity of a judge ready to pass sentence. Finally looking up at me, he took his glasses off, laid them on his desk, and flashed me what had to be the most insincere smile I've ever seen.

"Jeremiah, I hope you realize the seriousness of your offense. I realize you're not from our county, but certainly you must understand the consequences of carrying a loaded gun into the court offices."

"You know, as well as I do, that was not my gun. This is a sham."

"No Jeremiah, I can't say that I do know that. But whether it is yours, or not, it was on your person, and I must act upon the facts that were presented to me."

"You mean the lies that were presented to you."

"Call it what you may, but between you and me, I think it was just an oversight. I don't think for a moment you would use that gun."

"I'm glad you acknowledge that."

"I think I can probably talk to the other party and get them to agree to a reduced charge of threatening an officer. That should only carry a small fine, and maybe a month in jail."

"And why should I agree to that, when I'm innocent of any crime. This is a bunch of bull, and you know it as well as I do."

"As I said, we just can't be too careful. So you think that you are innocent of all crimes?"

"Absolutely."

"Then I'm sure we can reach a mutual agreement."

I felt quite certain that this 'agreement" was going to be more one-sided than mutual..

"What is the 'agreement'?" I asked.

"I think, based upon the complaint, that your presence itself constitutes a perceived threat. But if you agree to leave the county within twenty-four hours, with the promise not to return for a period of five years, I think I can make all of this go away."

He actually stood and extended his hand, certain I was going to accept. I didn't know if he wanted me to shake his hand, or to kiss it for his magnanimous act of kindness and compassion. I must admit, for a few minutes, I considered both. But then I remembered my promise to Floyd

Allen; I remembered my ethics as a journalist, and yes, I remembered the blue-eyed angel from Fancy Gap who had stolen my heart, so I said the only thing I could think of to say.

"You, and Deck Goad, can go straight to Hell with that agreement."

Instead of to Hell, the Commonwealth Attorney went straight to the guard. In five minutes I was back in the cell. No one seemed extremely concerned that when the lights had been turned out for the night, I had never been brought anything to eat.

About four o'clock the next morning I was awakened by the sound of footsteps echoing in the hallway. I rose to see a guard, followed by a very red-faced, half-asleep commonwealth attorney. Behind the two walked a man dressed in a three-piece suit, who was wide awake. The guard unlocked my door and swung it open.

"The charges have been dropped, "the commonwealth attorney mumbled.

"What else do you have to say?" the third man asked.

"I, we, apologize for any inconvenience we may had caused you, Mr. Haynes," the court official said, his head and shoulders drooping like a school boy being made to stand in the corner.

The stranger waited until the others had departed. When they were out of hearing, he turned to me.

"I'm Congressman Branscomb. I represent the fifth congressional district. Judge Valentine sends his regards and says that he hopes you slept better than the time you spent the night in the tent in his backyard."

He smiled, shook my hand, and walked away into the morning.

Newspaper reporters like to think they have a wide range of knowledge, but after this event, I had to admit I had no idea what the difference was between the "pea-shooter" that had been planted on me, and a thirty-eight automatic that I had been told many of the court officials had carried. I did believe though there was a tie between the types of guns and who used them. On the way home that morning, I asked Jeff who he considered the most knowledgeable person in the area on the subject of hand guns. Without hesitation, he told me that even though he was young, probably the best gun expert around was E. C. Brant in Woodlawn.

"You'll have no problem getting E.C. to talk," Jeff said. "Getting him to stop might be a mite hard to do though."

That afternoon I went to visit E. C. Brant and found him in a small shed behind the main house. The rough-sawn timber building was approximately 14 feet by 20 feet with one door, and several windows. A counter ran the distance of a long wall. There was probably not ten square feet of the entire work top, or the walls behind it, that wasn't covered with some component of a handgun or rifle.

I found him bent over a piece of wood clamped in a vice. Jeff was correct. He looked no older than a teenager. I tapped gently on the door, and he turned.

"Mr. Brant, my name's Jeremiah Haynes. My cousin, Jeff Haynes, said you might teach me a few things about guns, specifically handguns, like the ones that were used in the Courthouse shoot-out."

He eyed me for a few minutes, then turned to spit tobacco into a nail keg that was half filled with wood shavings. He missed, and from observing the sides of the keg, and the floor around it, his expectorations missed much more than they hit.

"What'cha want to know for?"

"I'm writing a story about the shootout. I don't know how you felt about Floyd Allen, but I got to know him while he was in prison."

"I never had no problems with Mister Floyd, or any of the rest of the Allens. Did business with them, now and then. Carved old Floyd a set of grips for his gun. Heard he broke the other ones on somebody's head. So what do you want from me?"

"I, well, I'm just trying to find out more about what happened that day. I know a lot had to do with the guns that were used. I'm from Richmond. I know very little about hand guns"

"I need to finish this stock before the end of the day," he said, "so fire away, and I'll answer what I can while I'm working on it."

I came to his side and looked at the stock he was carving from a block.

"That's a beautiful piece of wood. What is it?"

"Wild cherry. It'll make a beautiful stock on Mr. Canterbury's twelve gauge."

"I've fired shot-guns and rifles before, but the stock looks different than anything I've seen. It's, I don't know, bent strangely."

As soon as I said the words, I regretted them, afraid I had insulted the young man.

"It is different," Brant answered, obviously taking no offense, "Mr. Canterbury's a rich coal mine owner from over in West Virginia. He lost an arm as a young kid, so I have to replace his stocks so that it's easier for him to balance the gun with his stub and one good arm."

"That's quiet ingenious," I said. "Where did you get your gun smith training?"

He looked at me with a puzzled look. I was sure he had no idea of what "ingenious" meant.

"If you mean where did I get my book learnin', I aint' got none. It's my believe you can accomplish more with "doin'" than "learnin'".

"You know, you're probably right." I said, thinking that I had plenty of 'learnin', but I had to come here to ask him about guns.

"So what do you want to know?" he said, never taking his eyes from the stock as he deftly ran the wood rasp over the curves. Minute ribbons of wood slivered to the floor.

"First of all, are you familiar with the various types of pistols that were used in the shootout?" I asked.

"I'm pretty familiar with most every gun that's come out in the last twenty years. I probably either sold, or repaired, most every gun that was in the courthouse that day. What do you want to know?"

I scanned the list I had prepared since arriving from various sources who claimed to have inside information on the shoot-out, and the weapons used..

"It looks like the thirty-eight caliber pistol was a popular gun." I said.

The young man made one last pass over the stock, unclamped it, and laid it on the counter. He went to a drawer and withdrew a wooden case, about three foot square. He lifted the lid. The inside was lined with what appeared to be a small velvet quilt. A dozen or so pistols, of various shapes and sizes, laid in the box. He withdrew one and held it in front of me.

"This here's a thirty-eight caliber. Lot of people call it a lemon-squeezer because you have to squeeze the grip before it'll fire," he said as he demonstrated. "The real name is The New Departure."

"Isn't that rather awkward? I asked. "I mean, having to squeeze the handle?"

"Not after you get used to it. Oh, and I know how accurate you reporters like to be. Usually pistol means a single-shot handgun. The ones in the courthouse were revolvers."

`I looked at him, wondering if he was being frivolous, but I nevertheless added this detail, determined that my readers were going to believe I was a handgun aficionado.

"Can you tell me other things about the gun?" I asked. "Like, why it is popular? What's good, and what's bad about it?"

"I guess it's popular because it's big enough to kill what you're shooting at. I don't mean always a man. There's a lot of wild dogs in these parts. A good size dog's just not going to be killed with a twenty-two or even a twenty-five."

"Where's the hammer?"

"Guns just have firing hammers in those wild west movie films they show down at the picture show. So they can rapid fire using their hands. Cowboys call that 'fanning' the hammer. People don't do that in real life. You ever been to one of those things. Those picture shows? They're the darndest things. I went to see one one time..."

"Yes, I've been to the theaters in Richmond. But what were you telling me about the hammer?

"Oh yeah. Most people carry guns in their coat pockets, not in those fancy leather holsters. Having no hammer makes it easier to pull them out without catching on your clothes. I remember one time, old man Wingo pulled his gun from his pocket, the hammer caught, and it might near ..."

"So they can conceal guns, you're saying?" I asked. By this time I had realized Jeff was very accurate in his assessment of Mr. Brant's verbosity.

"Not so much to hide them. Like I said, we ain't the wild west. People in these parts ain't gunslingers. It's just that people feel safer with a gun; it's easy to just slip one in their pocket. It's no more than carrying a pocket knife. You ever had a Case Brother's pocket knife? Now there's a knife. I remember once your cousin Jeff and me, we was a' playin' mumbley-peg with a sharp knife and..."

"So what's the bad things about these pistols? I mean, revolvers," I said as I turned the piece over and over, examining it. I tried to appear as if I knew what I was examining.

"Well, they costs a couple dollars more than say the owl-head thirty-two. And they only have five shots."

"It seemed the court officials liked the automatics," I said, hoping to get a response from the man to see toward which side of the conflict he had proclivity. "Is that because the automatics shoot more shots, and shoot them faster?"

"Like I said before, I know you want to be precise in your reporting, so let me tell you. The guns they used weren't automatics. Automatics are guns like machine guns, and I don't think anybody had those in the courthouse that day. Automatics, you squeeze the trigger and they keep a'firing until you turn loose of the trigger, or they run out of cartridges two or three hundred shots later."

"I see," I said. "So what were the guns they, the court officials, were shooting?"

"They're called semi-automatics, or a better name for them is self-loading. You have to pull the trigger each time you want to fire a shot. Speaking of machine guns, did you ever see one of those Gatlin guns? I remembered seeing a picture of one in one of those magazines that..."

"What did you call that one gun? Something about an owl?"

He picked up a small revolver and held it in his hand.

"Yeah, this here's a thirty-two Owl-head. It's a little cheaper than the thirty-eight, a tad lighter, but it shoots a decent load"

"So what were some of the semi-automatics that were used by the court officials?"

He picked up a gun that looked much different than the revolvers.

"This here's a 1903 Colt pocket thirty-eight, like Deck Goad was using. Instead of having to reload like you do with a revolver, you just load the shells into this magazine, then jam it into the grip. It holds seven, but if you go ahead and load one into the chamber, you can then add another bullet into the magazine, making eight shots ready to be fired."

"If you were wanting to be in a gunfight then, would you say you'd have a big advantage with a self-loading gun?"

"There'd be some. You can squeeze eight shots off with this one in about 5 seconds. If you're fast, you can get about five off with the lemon-squeezer in a couple of seconds longer than that. Now you do know that at least one of the Allens had a self-loader, don't you?"

"No, I did not know that."

"Yeah, I think it might have been Claude. It had those handmade wooden handles on it."

"So there are strong advantages to using the new semi-automatics?" I said, hoping he'd tell me something that would overwhelm me.

"They can also be a big disadvantage if you don't know what'cha doing. A revolver, you just load, pull the trigger, and shoot. With most self-loaders, you have to work the slide," he said as he demonstrated, "to load the shot into the barrel. If not, the gun's not going to fire."

"Do you think that ever happens?"

He reached down and pulled another semi-automatic from the box.

"This here's a Colt 1903 thirty-two. This is like what sheriff Webb had borrowed from Church Alderman I weren't there, but from what I heard, Lew may have been the first to pull his gun, but he had trouble firing. I'll betcha money, he hadn't loaded a round into the barrel."

"And that got him killed?"

"I'm guessing so. There's a rule of the land in the mountains, if you pull your gun, you'd better be ready to use it. Commonwealth Attorney Foster was using this same model," he said, then asked. "Have you ever fired a pistol?"

"No. I've shot skeet with shotguns, and shot a few cans with a twenty-two rifle, but I've never shot a pistol."

"Do you want to give it a try?" he asked. "It's a whole lot easier hitting something with a rifle than a handgun because of the difference in the distances between the rear and front sights."

"Yes, I would."

He slipped the guns back into the case and we walked out back to a small wooden outbuilding. Twenty feet away hung a Coca Cola sign, made from heavy metal and about three feet in diameter. It was pock-marked with rusted holes. Off to the side of the building was a wooden fence with slabs of wood with red painted circles. There were hundreds of holes in it.

"So you do a lot of shooting?" I asked.

"I sure do, but we also have a lot of people come here to shoot, try out guns I have for sale. Things like that. Deck Goad and some of his buddies was here a few days before the trial."

"Really?"

"Yeah. Old Deck started off couldn't hit a can at twenty feet. By the time he finished, he was hitting Bromo bottles at thirty."

I made a very quick note of that fact.

"I'm ready to try shooting now," I said.

"Hold out your shooting hand, palm up," he said.

I did as he asked and he placed a small revolver into my hands. I could have almost clamped my left hand over top my right hand, and totally concealed the gun.

"That's small," I said.

"Yep. It's supposed to be. It's a twenty-five self-loader. This is the model Woodrow Quesenberry was carrying that day. I'm not sure he fired the first shot, but I'll always believe he was the first to shoot Floyd."

"Why do you think that?"

"Shoot that gun you're holding. Shoot at the first "C" on the sign. Be careful, it's already got a round in the chamber."

I brought the gun up to my eye level, took steady aim, and fired. There was a meager explosion, much like I heard when I shot my twenty-two rifle at Prince Albert cans when I was a kid. All I heard was a light 'pling'.

"Didn't seem to do much damage, that must be heavy steel," I said.

Without saying a word, E. C. led me back until we were about thirty feet from the sign.

"Ok, now take this 1903 thirty-eight Colt Pocket like Deck Goad was using. Fire a shot at the same 'C'," he said as he walked about ten feet away from me. But before you fire, I want you to run over to me, looking at the sign, then aim and fire as soon as you get to me."

I smiled as I realized what he was asking me to do. I would be re-enacting what it was like to have been at the courthouse. I trotted toward him, never taking my eye off the sign. I slightly tripped over an exposed root, regained my balance, and continued until I was near him. I raised the gun. For some reason, my hand was shaking so badly I wondered if I could even hit the sign. Even though it was a short distance, and I was in good shape, I was breathing hard. I sensed how difficult this would be to hit a human target, in a room filled with smoke, when that human target was moving, and was also firing back at me. I inhaled, attempting to steady my panting, and pulled the trigger.

Bam! The gun nearly deafened me with its detonation. Shocked not only by the reverberation, but also from a strong kick, the gun flew up in the air, nearly breaking my nose, and slipped out of my hand. I almost dove to the ground expecting a second shot to ring out. E.C. Brant bent over, hands on knees, roaring with laughter.

"Sorry," he finally said. "I guess I should have warned you, but that wouldn't have left as much of an impression. OK, now go up and look at the sign."

I did as he said. Just off the first C was a small dimple. He pointed at it.

"That's what you did with that twenty-five. Floyd Allen told me himself that he was shot one time in the chest with a twenty-five. In was winter, and he was wearing a pair of long-johns, a wool shirt, and a heavy jacket. The shot never even broke the skin."

"I can see that wouldn't have done much damage," I said as I rubbed my fingers over the indentation.

"Now look at this hole," he said as he pointed to a clean drilled hole, not quite a half inch in diameter.

"Is that what the thirty-eight did?" I asked.

"Sure is. And I bet you were aiming at the same place you did with the twenty-five but look how far to the upper left you shot."

He was right, even from just about twenty feet away, I missed the target by more than a foot.

"Is that common, to miss that badly?" I asked.

"Yep. The bigger guns, thirty-eights and up, they pack a big load, which results in a strong kick. It takes an experienced shooter to know how to allow for it. But also, you was moving before you shot."

"Yes, and the target wasn't moving, like the targets in the courthouse that day," I said, then asked, "So what makes you think Quesenberry was the first to shoot Floyd?"

"Now take you a look at that little ping that the twenty-five made from twenty feet away. That's about how far Quesenberry was from Floyd. Now look at the clean hole made from thirty-feet made by the thirty-eight. That's the distance Deck was shooting from."

"So what are you getting at?" I asked..

"Remember," he said. "Mr. Allen was hit in the hip, but it wasn't so bad he couldn't make his escape to the outside. If it had been Deck's thirty-eight, it probably would have shattered the bone. Like the shot outside did."

I nodded.

"Speaking of Woodson Quesenberry," I said, "I understand he resigned from the court just four months after the shoot-out. Even though he was still a young man. Why do you think he did?"

"I'd say because his wife told him she wasn't going to wash his pants and long-johns out again." he said as he began to chuckle. "I understand he messed in them something fierce."

"I heard that Deck Goad had two guns, and plenty of rounds. Do you believe that."

"Yeah, Deck always carried that little thirty-two with him, but he ordered the thirty-eight from me a couple months back , along with about five boxes of shells."

"Did he tell you why he was ordering it?" I said.

"If I recollect, he said something to the effect that his smaller gun would only kill rabbits, he needed something to kill skunks."

"Yeah, I can imagine what skunks he was speaking of," I said. "So who was carrying other gun?"

"The deputies, Edwards and Jett, they probably carried thirty-eight self-loaders. I believe Gillaspie had a thirty-eight lemon squeezer. Fowler, now he usually carried a thirty-eight special revolver with a six-inch barrel. Big sucker."

"What about Peter Easter?" I said. "The guy who went down to North Carolina with Deputy Samuels to pick up the boys?"

"Yeah, he was there, but not as a deputy. He was probably carrying his thirty-eight long barrel too. The same's true for Gurvis Hall."

"So it wasn't that unusual for people to carry guns, even into the courthouse?"

"That's what I'm saying. Probably half the men in the courthouse that day had a gun on them. Like I said, carrying a gun in this here parts not more than carrying a pocket knife."

"What about the other Allens?"

"Wesley Edwards was probably carrying a New Police Model thirty-two Colt revolver and Friel Allen was probably carrying his thirty-two Owl-head revolver."

"What about Sidna Edwards?"

"According to witnesses, Sidna either didn't have a gun, or at least, didn't pull it. I think his momma got hold of him as soon as the trouble started. He did buy a little twenty-five from me a couple of years ago."

I looked down at almost four full pages of notes I had scribbled. E. C. had not only told me who carried which guns, but had also described the pros and the cons of each. He had let me fire each of the models. While shooting them, I tried to imagine why the individual had chosen to carry that specific gun. Why did Mr. Floyd Allen use the Smith & Wesson thirty-eight revolver 'lemon squeezer'? He was a wealthy man, he could have afforded a better piece, such as the larger bore self-loaders, if he had thought he needed it. The same was true of Sidna Allen. I had heard he was the third wealthiest man in the county; he certainly could have afforded a better gun. Why had Woodson Quesenberry come in with a gun as in-effective as a twenty-five? If there had been a conspiracy, either by the Allens or the court officials, it apparently did not include all the parties.

I thanked E.C. Brant for his time. I was leaving with a lot of answers, but I still had a lot of questions.

14

I knew I had to eventually interview members of the Allens. I discussed with Jeff who would be the best candidate. He felt Mrs. Floyd Allen was definitely too ill to talk and he was equally sure that neither Mrs. Sidna Allen nor Mrs. Edwards would talk. He suggested Jasper, whom most people called Jack. My cousin opined Jack 'would either agree to talk with me, or shoot me between the eyes.' Either way, Jeff said it should make for a good story. Lot of writers aren't appreciated until they were dead, he advised, so either result might get me the fame I longed for. So I rode down the mountain to Cana to visit Jasper 'Jack' Allen.

Jack's house wasn't nearly impressive as Sidna's, but compared to other Cana homes, was still quite imposing. Unlike Sidna and Floyd though, he had not been forced to sell his property. Jack escaped the ramifications by the simple fact that he had not been present. Some charges had tried to surface that he had "harbored" some of the group. Probably closer to the truth was that he had actually talked his son Friel into surrendering because he had bargained with the Baldwin-Felt's agency that if he assisted them, Friel would get a shortened jail-sentence. I'm sure Jack felt this was better than having his son shot down by a rabid posse.

The stories were voluminous about the confrontations Jack had had with others. These affrays did not exclude his own family, especially his brother Floyd. It was common knowledge that the two men had attempted to shoot each other on more than one occasion, even to the point of murder, but had always managed to only wound the other. Part of the friction between the two was that Floyd was a staunch Democrat, and Jack was a 'when to his advantage' Republican.

I've never been fearsome of, or even intimidated by, most people that I have interviewed, but I must be forthright in saying I was going to be very cautious how I worded the questions to the oldest surviving brother of the Allen clan. I found him in his work shop, sharpening some cross saws for the timber business he ran. Jack Allen didn't look like any of the other brothers. He was stockier. The others also dressed more like trades people, as both Floyd and Sidna had run stores before their convictions, but Jack usually wore work clothes, which represented his timber and farm work better. One of the few times he dressed above this was when he visited one of the several saloons he operated across the county. The greatest similarity he shared with his brothers though were enthralling blue eyes. When Floyd Allen laughed, those eyes would sparkle like ocean waves breaking in the surf. I certainly hoped I could see Jack's eyes sparkle, rather than take on the dull hue of a gun barrel.

To my surprise, Jack instantly agreed to an interview. His wife brought us a pitcher of tea, and we sat on the porch to talk. I sat erect in my chair, my legs crossed, trying to illude confidence. I relocated my note pad to my knee to support the trembling hand I seemed to have developed. Contrastly, Mr. Jack Allen sat across from me, slouched down in his chair, his arm slung over the back, with an almost amused grin twisting his mouth. His eyes shone brightly in the mid day sun, and I felt somewhat akin to the moth that is drawn to the lamp, hopefully not to be scorched.

"Mr. Allen," I started, "it's my understanding that your son, Friel, who surrendered to the Baldwin-Felts agency, was promised an agreement."

"I reckon that happens very often, in this day and time. If someone is wanted, and they surrender, they usually can expect to receive a shorter sentence. There's nothing peculiar about that."

"Would you share with me the agreement to that effect?"

"I don't have it in my hands, but it is my recollection there is one written out."

"I don't question that you love your brothers, and please don't take offense, but I understand that you and Floyd often had, um, unpleasantries with each other. Sometimes even to the point of shooting each other."

I watched as the corner of his mouth twitched. I couldn't tell if I had struck a nerve, or if he had actually almost laughed. I was relieved to see his eyes take on a sparkle.

"Floyd and me were both hot-tempered. I can't recall in my mind where we got that from. Poppa and Momma weren't that way at all. Sometimes we'd let our anger get the best of us, and if we had a pick handle, or a gun handy, then we'd more than apt not use it. I think it would have grieved us deeply if we had actually killed each other though."

"Did you ever have any problems with Deck Goad, or any of the other court officials?"

"I disremember having much dealings with any of them, not as much as Floyd. He just thought everyone should hate Republicans. That was carried over from the Civil War. He thought we betrayed our father's fighting for the south if we didn't vote Democrat. I just didn't see it that way."

"So you never had any problems to speak of, with them, the courts officials I mean?"

"Can't recall in my mind that I did. They sometime tried to say I was selling blockade liquor. But all I sold was bonded. They minded their business. I tried to tend to mine."

"Have you received any threats after the trial?"

He looked out over his corn field, his eyes reflecting the mid-day sun. I, for a moment, thought he hadn't heard me, and was just ready to re-ask the question when his attention returned to me.

"Everyone here in the mountains, at some time or another, has a burr in their saddle. There's probably not been a month go by that I don't get word someone's looking for me. If they are, they know where to find me."

"I hope you won't get angry with me on this one, and I'll certainly understand if you don't want to answer, but was there a conspiracy? I'll even name you as an unidentified source if you'd like."

"No, I won't tell you anything I'm ashamed, or afraid, of you writing. No, there absolutely was no conspiracy. Not by my brothers, anyway. Any one would be stupid to even say so."

"Why do you say that?"

"Just look at the facts, boy. I know for certitude that Sidna put all of his business account into the bank the day before, more than a hundred dollars. Think he'd do that if he was going to have to make a fast get away?"

For some reason, Jack Allen was making me feel at ease. Sure he had some rough edges, but the way he looked at me, almost made him appear fatherly. I felt like I could increase the intensity of my questions.

"I've heard some say that your kin was spread around the courthouse in strategic areas. So they could have a good line of fire when they started shooting."

"Where they were seated in that courtroom only had to do with when they walked into that courtroom. They got there at totally different times. The courthouse was full, so they had to go wherever there was to set. Besides, if they'd wanted to do the most damage, they would have chosen better locations."

"What would you have considered a better location?"

"Spread along the north east wall, right there where Sidna was. And they would have already decided who was going to shoot who. Not just firing willy-nilly. They could have picked off those court officials like crows off a split rail fence."

"Why were they even carrying guns, if they didn't expect trouble?"

"I didn't say they didn't expect trouble. I think they did. They knew how bad the court hated them. If there was going to be shooting, they expected to be ready. And they was right, the court came armed to the teeth."

"More so than your relatives?"

"Hell yes. My kin had old pistols. Guns they carried every day. But those court people had new automatics they had just been bought. Lew Webb never carried a gun in his life, until that day. You mean to tell me they weren't itching for a fight?"

"Who do you think fired the first shot?"

"I truthfully don't know. I promise you it wasn't Floyd. He was shot and laying on the floor before he got off the first shot."

"Any other proof you can give me that there wasn't a conspiracy?"

"Yeah, I can give you final proof."

"What's that?"

"Because I was at home that day, thinking I was dying of the grip. But if there had been a conspiracy, I would have been there, armed to the teeth, and I would have personally shot the first son-of-a-bitch that drew a bead on any of my kin."

15

That Sunday after church I again had dinner at the Wisler home. The pastor wasn't there, having left after church for a week-long revival in Wytheville. I could tell Nellie was unusually quiet during the meal, and I assumed it was because she felt uncomfortable not having her father there, although we were well chaperoned by all of her siblings.

When she walked me to the wagon just at dusk, she looked at me with doe-ish eyes. She had again began wearing print dresses rather than the black mourning dresses.

"There's no school tomorrow," she said, casting her eyes down. "Annie said she'd come over and keep the children, if you'd like to take a ride down to Pilot Mountain for a picnic."

I stood speechless for a few seconds.

"I'm sorry," she said, her cheeks flushing red, "That was extremely forward. Please forgive me."

"Oh no," I said. "It wasn't forward. I don't have any plans at all. I'd love to go. What can I bring?"

She looked up, a sparkle back in her eyes.

"You just bring Annie and the wagon. I'll have the food ready."

The next morning Annie and I left ,by moonlight, for the Wisler's farm. We arrived just before 7:15. Before the dust had settled, Nellie was on her way to the wagon, carrying a large picnic basket with both hands. She placed it in the middle of the seat, and before I could step down to help her up, was seated.

"How many people are you planning on feeding?" Annie said with a chuckle.

"You forget, I've seen him eat." Nellie laughed. "The children are still asleep. Thank you so much for doing this."

"I'm glad to," Annie said. "You two enjoy your day."

The four and half hour trip to the base of the mountain was quiet almost to the point of being discomforting. Each of us would break the silence with small, insignificant observations: a bird chirping in a tree, the sound of the wind whistling through the trees, the beauty of a rhododendron bush. Much of our time was also spent just staring in awe at the distant solid rock formation that sat on top of the wooded mound, rising more than a thousand feet above the flat lands of the piedmont. The horse labored to pull the wagon up the steep road that climbed the wooded area until we were at the very base of the rock itself.

"This is as far as we can go with the wagon," Nellie said. "But if you feel up to walking, there's a wonderful hiking path that takes us to a breathtaking overlook."

It took us another hour to reach the view, but amazing it was. By that time I would have sworn the picnic basket weighed fifty pounds. From there we could see all the way back to the top of Fancy Gap Mountain, and I'm sure almost all the way south to Greensboro, or at least Winston-Salem, in North Carolina.

For the next two hours I devoured a mouth-watering meal of fried chicken, potato cakes, corn-on-the-cob, and tea. We laid on the ground, the grass tickling our arms and necks. A thousand various forms of flora and fauna blended into a bouquet of fragrances. We picked out images formed by the clouds, never agreeing on what the shapes looked like.

We laughed at each other's interpretation of the shapes. This was as close to utopia as I could ever remember. I ached for it to last forever. But then Nellie said we should start back if we were to make it before dark.

We walked back to the wagon, where the horse grazed in the fresh knee-high pasture. I helped Nellie into the wagon. She placed the basket at the end of the seat, and she sat down in the middle.

"I hope I'm not crowding you," she said, her cheeks flushing. "I can put the basket back in the middle, if you'd like."

"No. You're not crowding me. Not at all." I suspect my cheeks were flushing also.

We arrived at the top of Fancy Gap Mountain, but still four miles from the Wisler home, when a thunderstorm swept down. Large hailstones began pounding us and the horse, but of greater concern were the lightning bolts splitting the sky. Although it was mid-evening, it had turned as dark as nightfall. Just then we heard a loud clap, and a large oak in front of us split, and half crashed to the ground.

"There's an old coon hunters' cabin just up in those woods," Nellie said, her voice cracking with panic. "We can wait out the storm there."

I galloped the horse where she had directed.

"Ok, you run up to the cabin," I said. "I'll get the horse tied off here in the clearing, and I'll be right up."

By the time I had cinched the horse, grabbed our belongings, and made it into the shack, Nellie had lit a kerosene lamp, and was trying to start a fire. Her hands shook so she could barely hold the flame to the kindling.

"Here, let me help," I said, taking the matches. "You take your cloak off. I see some blankets on the bed, wrap up before you catch a chill."

Soon I had a fire blazing . Nellie stood before the flame, still trembling. I pulled a small feather tick from the cot and dragged it in front of the fire.

"Nellie, please don't take offense, but we both need to get out of these wet clothes. I'll turn my head, and you slip out of yours, and wrap the blanket around you. I'll hang your clothes up to dry. Then I'll do the same with mine."

The steam wafted from our wet clothes. The staccato of water drips to the wood floor broke the silence as we laid, inches apart, on the feather tick, I on my back, Nellie on her side, facing the fire. The hail beat a steady rhythm on the tin roof. The lightning left a coppery taste in our mouths. The smell of charred wood drifted about the room.

"So how did you know about this cabin?" I asked, more to break the silence, than for information. "It sure was a God-sent."

"My uncle Eli loved to coon hunt. He used to bring me here," Nellie said, her teeth clattering slightly less than before. "Everyone that uses it has a responsibility to leave matches, and kindling for a fire."

Rolling to my side, I could see her silhouetted against the blazing fire. The steam from her hair shrouded her head like a halo. Taking an anxious breath, I slid behind her. Although we were both wrapped in our own blankets, this was the closest contact I had had with her, since the day at her house when I told her and Pastor Wisler about Nancy. I laid my arm over her side. I waited for her to resist, or at least tense, but instead, she took my hand in hers. "Your hands are like ice; let me rub them," I whispered.

My one hand was nearly as large as both of hers. I began kneading them, massaging blood back into her fingers. I could feel her side and stomach rise and fall with her breathing. I could hear the melody of her heart beat. I sensed her inhaling growing quicker, deeper. How easy it would be to tell her how much I loved her. How I worshiped her. I wasn't sure I could ever say those words though, and I was even more sure she'd not want to hear them.

"You're very quiet, Jeremiah Haynes. Did the hail freeze your tongue?"

"I've always been better at writing words I felt than saying them," I said.

I brushed her hair with my nose. I breathed in her pureness, and it made me feel a better man. I closed my eyes, capturing every moment, and prayed it would not end.

She shifted her body. I quickly released her hands, and started to apologize, when she rolled over on her back. Her blue eyes sparkled in the firelight. She had a distant, confused look on her face.

"Wouldn't it be nice if we could reach into a big pot of words, and select the right ones we want to say?" she said. "The words that describes the way we think, but we can't say. Then we could just hand them to the person, and not be afraid they'd throw them back at us?"

"I think they call that pot a dictionary, and that's what a writer does," I laughed. "And I do mean a writer, not a reporter."

"Have you ever thought about being a writer?"

"Yes, I think all reporters secretly want to be writers. I've thought about taking all the articles and the stories I've written the last year, I don't just mean about the Allens, I mean about the mountains, and its people, and write a book about it."

"Will I be in it?" she teased.

"You'll be in it. You'll be the angel who flew down from heaven to save me." I said, then I began to think how literal, and figuratively, that was true.

I partially sat up, resting my head on my bent arm, and looked down into her face. I didn't speak. I was afraid to, or the moment might be lost forever. Or that I would wake up from a dream. I was close enough that I could count the small freckles across her nose. I saw the small birthmark on her neck, just below her right ear. She smelled of lilacs after a spring rain.

At that moment, I knew she was the most beautiful woman I had ever known, and I knew I loved her desperately. Slowly I leaned down, stopping when my mouth was inches from hers, and looked into her eyes. I had once seen a fawn, lost from its mother. Nellie's eyes looked much like that fawn's. Slowly her hand came from the blanket, and wrapped behind my neck.

She didn't pull me to her. She just barely touched me but it was like an elastic band had been stretched between the two of us, and was now tugging us together. My lips touched hers, and in that instant, all the sorrow, all the latent grief, was lifted from my heart. For the first time in years, I felt truly alive, with no guilt for feeling happy. She sighed. My heart soared. I kissed her softly, as if her lips were morning dew on a rose. My heart flooded my mouth with declarations I dared not speak. I wanted to tell her the heights of happiness she had lifted me to. I wanted to tell her how she had illumined the black emptiness that had for the last two years sunk me into an abyss of despair. I wanted to tell her that I wanted to marry her, to have children with her, and to grow old with her.

But I didn't get the chance.

"Oh Jeremiah, what am I doing?", she cried as she rolled away from me. "I'm sorry I've behaved so badly."

"Nellie, we've done nothing wrong," I said, reaching to take her hand. "I love you. I truly do. We will not do anything that you don't want to. But I do want you to free your heart to me. It's been dormant long enough."

She sat there by the fire, just gazing into it, as if studying every flicker, every ember.

"I'm just so confused. I was so sure after Claude died, that I'd never allow myself, I'd never be able to, love another man. You kissed me in a way that I've never been kissed before. And I feel so guilty, because I know how much I enjoyed it, and how much more I wanted."

She began to weep.

"Will you promise me that you will follow your heart though. That you won't put a lock and key on it?"

"Yes. I will promise you that." she said, rolling back to face me, as she placed her hand upon my cheek. "Please don't be disappointed in me."

"I think the storm is over," I said, smiling to ensure her I could never be disappointed in her, "and our clothes are about dry. I'll hand you yours to put on and I'll take mine outside to change.

The man watched from the trees. The rain dripping from his slouch hat and slicker. He had been sure all had been innocent. But then, when the reporter had come out on the porch, dropped the blanket, and began dressing, he knew it hadn't been totally innocent. But he knew Miss Wisler would never do anything sinful. But what if the reporter had defiled her? If he had his rifle, that reporter would be laying in his own blood right now. But there's no way he'd reach him with his pistol, just scare him. No, the day would come. It needed to be more than a gun shot. Even a gut shot only carried a limited amount of agony. No, it would be something special. He would study The Word. God would give him the answer.

As I drove toward her home, I wasn't sure how to process what had just transpired. My greatest fear was my impetuousness had ended any possibility I might ever have with Nellie. But that anxiety was relieved when she slipped her arm through mine as I held the reins.

"I hope you understand," she said, her voice strained.

I turned to her; I'm sure the relief evident on my face.

"Of course I understand, I just hope you'll not hold it against me. I was just so caught up in the moment."

"Yes, I know that men get caught up in the moment very easily," she giggled. "Claude often did, but if it makes you feel better, we never went 'beyond the moment' either."

Since Pastor Wisler was still in Wytheville for the revival, we did not have to offer a reason for our still damp, and very wrinkled, clothing we wore. Who was there though was Jeff. As soon as I pulled into the yard, he leapt off the porch. His face carried a distraught look as he handed a telegram to me.

"I'm sorry," he said, "it was loose, and I read it. Let me know if there's anything I can do."

I took the wire, and read to myself,

*JEREMIAH*stop* COME HOME TODAY*stop* YOUR FATHER HAS PASSED*stop**

Signed; M. Valentine

16

As the train rocked northward through the Shenandoah Valley toward Richmond, I was able to reminisce about growing up as the son of Archibald Marcellus Haynes. As a child, I was never spoiled. My father had been self-made and he wanted me to be the same. At the time I thought I was deprived, not receiving the material possessions that so many of my friends received from their fathers who were not nearly as influential as my father.

For example, he would not purchase a new Schwinn bike for me although all my friends had gotten one. Instead, he said, if I wanted one, he'd make me a loan. I'd then get a paper route, and pay him back, with interest, for the loan. While rolling up the papers, I'd become mesmerized by the front page articles. It was then I became convinced I wanted to be a journalist.

Now I realized that he never failed to give me the things that were important. He gave me some things that money couldn't buy, such as integrity, perseverance, and discipline. I had pretty much lived my life to these virtues, other than the months I spent as an alcoholic. The other items, like the Schwinn bike, all taught me a vital lesson that had always made me a better person.

How I wished I could just go back and reclaim the time I had lost. In many ways it seemed the train ride back to the city of my youth took forever, but when it did pull into Richmond, I found myself not ready to accept the reality that my father was gone, and I would never see him again.

As soon as I entered the station overlooking the canal, I saw Judge Valentine waving. He opened his arms to me.

"I'm sorry son. I'm so sorry."

"What happened? Heart attack?" I asked.

"No. He had pancreatic cancer. He had it when you were here, but covered it up well. That was one of his good days. I think seeing you brought out the absolute best in him."

I suddenly felt anger, extreme red-faced, behind-the-eyeball-flashing-light anger.

"My father had cancer," I screamed, "and you did not think it important enough to tell me?"

The judge stiffened, and drew back. His face slowly changed from shock to compassion though.

"Your father made me promise not to. I thought once he got bad enough, I'd have time. But it seemed like he rallied everything he had into that one day with you. For the last few months, he deteriorated quickly. I still thought he had another month or two, and had already decided to defy my best friend in the world, and wire you next week."

It was then I remembered my promise to Judge Valentine on my last visit that I would come back for a longer stay. It was a visit I never made.

The next two days were spent in a daze. Most details had already been arranged by my father, and the Judge carried them out. My father was buried in the Hollywood Cemetery, within a hundred feet of the grave of Fitzhugh Lee, whom he had fought under during the War of Northern Aggression. After leaving the graveside service, the judge asked me to travel home with him.

"Son, I hope what I'm going to tell you doesn't make you think less of your father. He did what he thought was best."

I looked at him quizzically, and just nodded my head.

"Your father's will calls for me to sell his real estate," the judge said. "It's valued at an estimated $150,000. He instructed the proceeds to go to several charities; the Daughters of the Confederacy, his church, and many of the museums in the city."

"I see," was all I could say.

"Son, believe me, your father loved you very much, but he did want you to make it on your own. He does leave a trust account that I am to oversee in the amount of $35,000 that is to be released at that time that I feel will be of most benefit to you."

"So I guess I should feel confirmation of my lifelong belief that he was disappointed in me."

Without answering the judge walked to a table in the corner of his office and picked up a two foot by two foot chest. I recognized it as being the one my father carried during the war. I hadn't seen it in twenty years. He kept it locked and had always forbade me looking in it. Thejudge pulled a key from his watch fob and released the brass lock.

"Your father kept this chest locked in the bottom of his desk. In it he kept the most important items in his life: the Bible he carried throughout the war, the Southern Cross of Honor, his marriage license. I've not opened it before this moment, but I know what's in it because many times in the last year I came into his office and saw him going through it, always looking at the same items."

He turned the trunk to show me the contents. On top was a finely-crafted leather bound book. It was about 12 inches by 18 inches. I withdrew it, and laid it upon the desk. I opened the first page and read in my father's very descriptive calligraphy "Jeremiah's articles". I leafed through the pages. The first displayed an article I wrote while I was at Richmond College. It was more a letter to the editor objecting to President Boatwright's curfew on upperclassmen. I smiled to myself.

"I thought Father was going to yank me out of school over that article."

"He told you that. But he loved it. He told me that it showed you had a lot of spunk. He liked it so much, he convinced me to go have a chat with Frederic Boatwright. That's why the next year he dropped the curfew."

I continued through the rest of the book; every page was filled with articles, some no more than ten lines. I even found some magazine shorts.

"I never dreamed he had saved these," I said.

"They are all there. Everything you ever had published. He had his secretary at the bank check the Evening Journal and magazines just to see if she could find anything new."

My heart swelled. I never imagined that he found anything but abhorrence to my career as a writer.

I finally closed the book and placed it back into the chest.

"May I have this? The whole chest?"

"Certainly. It was in your father's will for you to receive it."

As I started to leave, I realized that I had been so preoccupied with the funeral, I had forgotten the simplest of civility.

"Oh, by the way Judge, thank you very much for getting me out of jail in Hillsville."

He just gave me his fatherly smile.

I felt an overwhelming desire to drink, but I knew I had to resist. I had learned one way to escape grief was by plunging myself into my work, so while in Richmond, I thought it would be a good time to go to the prison and talk to Sidna Allen.

Fortunately, I had not burned any bridges behind me with the warden, so he agreed to see me without an appointment. Sidna was willing to meet with me and I was led down to the prison workshop. There I found him working on an ornate table top. I knew little of woodwork, but I could tell by the various grains and colors that the table was being constructed of different species. He wore glasses, which I had not seen in his previous newspaper pictures, so I wondered if it was just for the minute work he was doing. He looked much more like an accountant than a sentenced murderer. He also appeared to have aged five years since his incarceration a year before.

He stopped the planing of the wood and wiped his hands on the apron he wore. He approached me, his hand extended.

"Hello, I'm Sidna Allen. I understand you want to interview me. I usually don't like to talk to reporters, but, if I remember correctly, you were friends with my brother and nephew."

"Yes sir, I was. I'm doing some follow up on the case, and was just hoping you might be willing to share some things with me."

"Perhaps. Let's see what you want to know, and I'll see if I can help."

"First of all, how are you spending your time in prison? I understand you're an exemplary prisoner."

"I've always felt that what ever circumstance life has presented us with, we must do our best to maximize our output. I'd always enjoyed doing wood work, but never seemed to have the time. Now I spend as many hours as they will allow here in the shop."

"You do beautiful work. That piece has a lot of different wood pieces, doesn't it?"

"Yes, when I'm finished it will have about a dozen different species of wood, and over a thousand pieces."

"Does that make it stronger, or are you just doing that for looks?"

"It does add to the beauty, by adding a unique pattern, but the truth is I don't have the money to purchase wood. I salvage any scraps from the trash, shave them down to uniform size, and find a place to work them into the pattern. Rather like working a jigsaw puzzle."

"Mr. Allen, I do appreciate you letting me see you. I've had several interviews, but you are the only person who is currently doing time. I'll come straight to the point. Was there a conspiracy?"

"Not by us. I still think there was some kind of understanding between some of the members of the court. Just too much preparation for them. They had multiple guns on them, they had guns hid. They had boxes of shells stored in desks. And they weren't just every-day guns, they were automatics. I think that's where the conspiracy was."

"Jack also gave me many of the facts also, such as you putting your money into the bank the week of the trial."

"Yes, that money would have come in handy while we were on the run."

"Did you fire the first shot?"

"Not the first. I saw Lew Webb try to shoot his gun. I think he was reacting to my brother reaching into his sweater, but that's not where Floyd kept his gun. I then heard a shot, and I saw Floyd drop to the floor. That's when I began shooting."

"You said Floyd was reaching for something other than a gun. In his sweater pocket? Was it two coins?"

"You've been talking to Mary Tate, haven't you?" he said with a smile.

I nodded.

"Yes, it was those two coins. Floyd sure knew how to rile Deck Goad with them. I think Deck would prefer having Floyd rubbing his nose in sheep poop than to roll those coins in front of him."

"Why didn't this come out in the trials?"

"We did think about it, but it was obvious to us that it would not make any difference. Between the county and the state, nothing would have gotten Floyd and Claude off. The verdict was locked in from the beginning."

"Do you think Maude Iroler turned you and Wesley in for the reward?"

Sidna allowed himself a slight smile, as he took on a contemplative stare.

"I think," he said, trying his words as cautiously as a person dipping his finger in water to see how hot it is, "that if Victor had not gone home and contacted her, we'd probably still be free. But actually, I'm glad we were captured."

"You are? Why is that?"

"I never left my wife and daughters behind to spend the rest of my life on the run. I just knew that with the blood boiling like it was back there, we'd probably be shot dead on the spot, or receive the death sentence like Floyd and Claude if we had turned ourselves in just after the shoot out."

"But you eventually planned on surrendering?"

"Yes, I believe I would have by now, but I would have preferred it to be on my own terms, not dragged handcuffed out of a boarding house in Des Moines."

"Do you think there will be any chance of an early release?"

"There are still a lot of debates over the executions, and a lot of people are upset. A lot of evidence is still being presented," he said, looking at me intently. "Maybe you can come up with enough that would lead to an early release."

I smiled at his suggestion.

"If you had it to do over," I asked, "would you have done the same? I mean, in the courthouse?"

"I'm not sure. When it happened, all I could think about was saving my family, especially Floyd. I know they were intent upon killing him. Knowing what I do now, that Floyd, and Claude, were "murdered" by the state instead of by the members of the court, maybe I would have not pulled my gun. But then again, I think I would have."

"Would you have stayed at home?"

"Well, I had to be there at the beginning. I was a called witness. No, I felt like I had to be there, for Floyd. Besides, if I had been unarmed, they probably would have shot me down."

"How filled with hatred are you? How badly do you want revenge?"

"Honestly, my days of hatred are gone. Revenge is mine, sayeth the Lord. I'm ready for Him to judge those that wronged us. So, no, I feel no revenge," he said, then with a wry smile, "feel free to tell the parole board I said that."

"Sidna, your family and friends seem to be religious. Did they ever hand out the Bible tracts that you see around?"

"No. Half of the people in the mountains, and in our church can't even read, so I never saw the good in them. Why do you ask?"

"Oh, I don't know. I had seen some around the county and wondered where they came from."

"Those sound like the type of things some of the revival preachers would carry that come through now and then. I've seen them. I know what they look like."

I thanked Sidna, wished him luck, and told him I hoped to see him released soon.

I decided I would not benefit by talking to the others, so I made my way back to the train station.

There's something about riding a train that is conducive to contemplative ponderings. Maybe it's the rhythmic clanging of steel wheels on steel rail. Maybe it's the smooth rocking side to side like a metronome. Maybe it's the blur of the landscape as we zip by, as if they were memories dashing through our consciousness. But something about it tends to lift me to profound ruminations.

On the way back to Hillsville, I relived my familial past, the wonderful life they had given to me, their willingness to let me learn, and earn, my own way. I thought about how much I wish I could have lived the last two years over with my father, and had known that he still loved me. I accepted my yesterdays had been sealed, there was nothing I could do about it now. But I also knew that I could change my tomorrows. I had sufficient means to live a prosperous life in Carroll County. I could continue my writing as a free-lance journalist. Maybe Jeff and I could even start some kind of business if his job at the cotton mill didn't work out. For the first time in two years, I truly felt I had something to live for. And what I had most to live for, was a woman named Nellie Wisler.

I also made a decision. Too much time had been spent investigating this story for only a few articles, or even a major magazine article. This would have to be something bigger. I knew though that I still needed much more information for a book. There were just too many loose ends. News stories are spontaneous, so they did not have to have an ending, a climax. I remembered reading once that either Socrates, Plato, or Aristotle, I could never keep my philosophers straight, had said that every book must have a beginning, middle and end. I had my beginning, was well on my way to a middle, but I needed a lot of help with the end. I needed one great event, one great revelation that would tie this whole mess together. I was determined to find it back in Carroll County.

I thought of two people who could help in this. The first was Cyrus Phibbs, an engineer who had drawn a map and catalogued the location of each of the thirty-eight bullet holes in the walls. The second person I would seek out, after I collected the map, would be Mary Tate.

Upon arriving in Hillsville, I found the engineer in his office Ten minutes later, for the sum of five dollars, I left with a carefully drawn floor plan of the courtroom showing the location of the bullet holes, with the position of the various participants involved in the shoot out marked.

I found Mary Tate sitting on the stone wall in front of the courthouse.

"Are you cleaning today?" I asked.

"Yes sir. I am. Why do you ask?"

"I'm going to make a request of you, but I'll completely understand if you decide to refuse."

"Does it have anything to do with what Mr. Floyd asked you to do?"

"Yes, it does. But if we're caught, it might get you in trouble. I need about thirty, maybe forty-five minutes alone in the court room. Will that be possible?"

"I think so," she said. "There's no court in session. I'll work in the hall outside the door. If anyone comes by wanting in, I'll tell them I've just oiled the floor and it's drying. But if it's someone like Deck Goad or the sheriff, they'll just ignore me and tromp in anyway."

When she opened the door, I noticed a box holding umbrellas and hats of every shape and color. I asked what they were, and was told they were items that had been left behind and were unclaimed. I entered the courtroom with my notes, my map, and about a dozen hats.

The forty year old courtroom was like so many of the others built throughout rural Virginia. It was about 36 feet north to south and forty feet west to east. The two doors on the west end both entered at the top of separate exterior stairs covered by a portico. Inside, a middle door opened to the grand jury room. There were benches along the back wall and three benches about twenty feet long centered after entering the courtroom. I went to the middle of the courtroom to the area where the prosecuting and defense attorneys, and the defendant, had sat. Just to the left and right of this area were two wood-burning stoves. Straight ahead, and to the east, was the Judge's bench, elevated a couple of feet higher than the floor. In front of the bench were about a dozen chairs. To the right, toward the south wall, was a boxed-in area with a swinging door that with a sign that read 'Clerk of the Court'. Just behind the judge's bench were two doors. The door to the left opened into the judge's office and the door on the right into the petit jury room.

I took a seat in what I had assumed to be Floyd Allen's chair. The finish was as slick as oilcloth. I thought to myself, this was probably due to all the squirming that had occurred in the seat over the years. I studied the map I had purchased. I began recalling the hundreds of articles I had studied over the last year and had committed to memory. I mentally separated the room as if it were a clock. Twelve o'clock would be straight ahead of me, to the east. That would be where the judge presided.

Bunched together, in an area that would be between one and two o'clock, I pictured Deck Goad, Bud Edwards, William Foster, sheriff Webb, and Deputies Jett and Fowler. I questioned if it was usual for that many of the court officials to have been present in the court at one time, much less bunched together, instead of dispersed throughout the crowd.

There was one exception. Woodson Quesenberry, the deputy Clerk of the Court, stood at four o'clock, just behind where the Prosecuting Attorney, S. Floyd Landreth, would have sat at three o'clock. He would not have been more than eight feet away.

I began locating where the Allen family had been on that day.

Behind me, just off my left shoulder, at eight o'clock would have been Wesley Edwards. To his right, sharing the bench, would have been Victor Allen ,who on this day was unarmed. This in itself was of interest because Victor was a mailman, and the only people in the courthouse that day that could legally have a gun was the sheriff, his deputies, and mailmen. To my left, sitting against the north wall, at eleven o'clock, would be Sidna and Claude Allen. All the way at the back of the room, sitting on the west steps going into the grand jury room would have been Friel Allen and sitting on the bench to his left would have been Sidna Edwards.

I had to admit, if the Allens had conspired to shoot up the court, they certainly had the positions. I had read accounts though, and Jack Allen reiterated, that the various positions the Allens took on that day was dependent upon what time they arrived, and what seats were left.

Using the floor plan, I began placing hats in the vicinity of the major participants of that day. I scanned my eyes at the five hats representing the court officials and law enforcement officers. It was believed that there were at least eight court officials and law officers who were armed that day, and all had fired direct shots that varied from twelve to twenty five feet. How in the world had Floyd Allen escaped death? There had been the rumor he had been wearing a steel chest protector, but that theory had been mostly debunked.

I had been reading about a new scientific process called mental imaging. Supposedly a person could close his eyes, and tune his mind to imagine an event, and it would appear to him as vivid as an actual event. This would be a good time to use this technique, I thought.

I closed my eyes, blocking out all external distractions. I began taking slow, deep, breaths. I thought back to how Floyd looked, not in his prison garb, but wearing the clothes of that day. The sweater. His long moustache. I found myself becoming Floyd Allen, sitting in the chair, leaned back against the rail.

The jury re-enters. I'm told to stand up. The verdict is read. But it's being read by Deck Goad. He's not supposed to read it. Damn him. Why isn't the foreman reading it?

"Guilty. One year prison."

I hear the silence that followed the verdict. A few nervous coughs. Some people standing to leave. Some seem to be in a hurry.

Guilty? It can't be. It will be ok. I'll win on appeal. My legs weaken. I sink to my chair.

I hear Judge Bolen asking for bail.

What? No bail?

The sheriff is given the direction to take charge of me. I look over at Goad. He's smirking. He's leaving his box to approach me. He has no right to take charge of me.

As I start to stand up, I fumble with the imaginary buttons of a sweater. I'm reaching for the two coins. I smile as I think about the look on Deck Goad's face when I pull them out and begin to flip them between my fingers.

Just when I started to stand up, my chair tips backwards. It hits the wooden railing with a resounding bang.

This jars me back to reality. I'm no longer Floyd Allen. The sound was almost like that of a gunshot. Had Floyd, or someone in their haste to leave the courtroom, tipped over a chair? Was that the sound so many referred to as the first gunshot?

OK, where was I? I close my eyes, again imagining myself as Floyd Allen.

Yes, Deck Goad's approaching me.

He's smirking.

I'm reaching for the coins. That'll wipe that grin off his face.

I see his eyes change before me, a flash of hatred, or maybe fear?

I see Lew Webb pulling his gun, fumbling as he pulls it out. He has no right to do that.

Bang. Bang. I hear a shot from my right. Then another.

I hear shots from the left of me, where Sidna and Claude sit. More shots. I feel burning pain as I'm hit in the hip.

I fall to the floor on top of my attorney, Judge Bolen.

Bang, Bang. Bang. Bang.

I hear shots from all sides around me. I hear shouts all around me.

I try to raise up, but fall back.

Splinters are flying from the wood railings.

Judge Bolen screams at me to get off him before someone shoots him by mistake.

I finally make it back to my feet.

I pull my gun and begin shooting. First at Deck Goad. At anyone who is aiming at me.

It seems the entire right side of the room is firing at me.

All around me, front, rear, left, right, guns are being fired.

Never-ending gunfire, like a Gatling gun.

No one standing still. Running. Shooting. Screaming.

The room fills with smoke, stifling my lungs.

I hear chairs, benches, crash to the floor as people escape.

I hear people scream as they take their last breaths.

I wait to feel the bullet that will end it all for me.

The shooting stops. The room is a strange blue mist. The kerosene lamps glitter like stars buried behind a cloudy night.

Through the smoky haze I see Judge Massie, laying face down. He's bleeding. Too bad. He was a good man. A good Democrat.

I try to leap over the railing, trip over it.

I drag my leg trying to make it to the rear door. Trying to make it to the outside.

I remember I have my horse waiting outside. If I can just make it to my horse.

Wait. Did I send Claude off on my horse?

Claude! Where is he? Is he laying back in the courtroom? In a pool of blood?

I see my brother Sidna, my sons, my nephews running to me. We make it down the steps and out to the street, under darkened gray skies. The skies are gun barrel blue. A thunder storm is on its way. There he comes, Deck Goad. My mind is a blur as we shoot at court officials leaving the building.

A sharp cracking sound jerked my attention back to reality. I heard a key turning in the lock. I looked around, trying to find a place to hide, when Mary popped her head into the door.

"Sorry," she whispered. "I dropped my mop handle."

I opened my eyes, and studied the still room around me. There are no sounds of gunfire, or screams. The thick suffocating smoke of gunpowder has been replaced with ribbons of sunlight gleaming through openings in the thick curtains.

I walked about the room. Many of the bullet holes are evident in the walls. I removed pencils from a box at the clerk's desk and began sticking them into the cavities. Most had been reamed where reportedly citizens had taken souvenirs, an explanation I always questioned. Some of the holes though are more pristine. I stick the end of the pencils into them. I get a rough idea of the trajectory of the bullets.

Most of the holes behind where Sidna and Claude Allen had sat indicated shots from the rear. But two holes would indicate the shots came directly across the room. I scanned across the room where Deck Goad would have been seated. Slightly behind the line of fire would have sat Judge Massie. I walk to the other side of the room, and find similar holes in the wall there. If the judge had leaned forward the slightest, he would have been caught directly in the cross fire. Which person had shot him? Probably more than one person. To my recollection, Sidna was left handed, Dexter Goad was right handed, which meant both would be firing with their hands that were closest to the judge.

If only an autopsy could have been performed to show which bullets were lethal. I knew I needed to question Dr. Nuckolls, who served as the county coroner.

I heard another sound from outside, then muffled voices. Mary had told someone she had just oiled the floor, for them to wait. I ducked behind a bench as the door opened.

"They're going to be back in fifteen minutes," she whispered. You need to skedaddle."

I pulled the pencils from the holes, replaced them in the box, gathered the hats together, returned them to Mary, and then slipped out the door and down the steps, pausing only long enough to view the bullet holes in the steps and wall. Hopefully, no one was the wiser.

I returned to the boarding house. My psyche was spinning from imagining myself in the courtroom during the shootout. I knew my emotions though were miniscule compared to those who were actual participants.

After dinner, I excused myself and told everyone I was going out for a while.

"Tell the Wislers I said hello," Jeff called to me as I walked out the door.

Nellie and her father had seen me coming and met me at the door.

"I am so sorry about your father," she said, as she embraced me.

Her father expressed his sympathy, and then we walked into the parlor. I laid a wrapped package on the table.

"What is that?" Nellie said.

"Open it and you'll see."

Her delicate fingers removed the ribbon, and she opened the wrapping. Her mouth opened into a wide smile.

I had wanted to bring Nellie a gift. I knew it would be improper for me to bring her something like a shawl, or a hat. I knew she would love to travel, so I had bought her a European tour book.

"Oh, Jeremiah, thank you so much," she said as she started leafing through the pages. "It's all the places I've always dreamed of traveling to."

I wanted to fall to my knees right then, beg her to marry me, and promise I'd take her to all those places. I knew I had to be patient though.

We talked until nearly ten. After the pastor yawned twice, I knew I needed to take my leave.

17

Spring, 1914

That spring I received a letter with a Richmond postmark. As soon as I opened it, I immediately looked for the bottom signature, but it was unsigned. The writer informed me that he was a former Baldwin-Felts detective who had been beaten up badly, and could no longer work. He offered to sell me valuable information for $500. By this time I was so desperate for some kind of a connection, I knew it was worth the price. But being a journalist meant I would try to get it cheaper.

The letter had a post office box address I could reply to, so I wrote and advised that I was no longer employed by the newspaper, and that I would be interested in the information for my own purpose. I told him he had to give me some idea of the information he had, and I offered $150.

Ten days later I received a reply. The former detective claimed to possess a list of both Allens, and Allens' sympathizers, that were to be "permanently silenced." He also claimed to have the information that linked several officials to "secret deals" with his former employer, and the name of a person who had maimed and even killed those who had gotten in the way. The writer told me that I would find the information very useful, because it was documentation of "informal agreements between

Baldwin-Felts and high state and county officials. The writer gave me a counteroffer of $250.

I wrote him back and agreed we would meet half way, at the Lynchburg, Train Depot. I informed him I would bring the money, but he must let me examine some of the information. If I thought it was worth the price, I'd pay it.

He responded that he would meet me at the designated location a week from that Tuesday. He told me how he would be dressed, that he would be reading a copy of the Richmond Evening Journal, and that he would answer to the name 'Walter'.

I feared I was setting myself up to get mugged again, so I invited Jeff to go along with me. Also, I thought he might be able to watch from a distance, and possibly identify the informant for me.

That Tuesday morning we left Blair Station and started on our way. Five hours later we pulled into Lynchburg Station. Jeff had brought along an old slouch hat that covered most of his head. With his size, and the hat pulled down over his eyes, he looked like some kind of a bank robber from one of the old cowboy dime novels. He left the train several minutes before me so we wouldn't be seen together, and took his place inside.

I soon followed. There were at least sixty people sitting or standing in the lobby; looking at schedules, dozing, eating at the counter or talking. I soon spotted a man holding a Richmond Evening Journal high in the air. I approached him, and sat down. He looked toward me.

"Walter?" I asked..

"Yes," he answered without lowering the newspaper.

He folded the paper, and handed it to me. I picked it up, unfolded it, and found a few leafs of paper concealed within the newspaper. I began to read a hand-written list of last names, and first initials. Several caught my eye, two particularly.

Allen, J.

Marion, B.

Then there were several that I had not heard of.

"That's not much information for $250." I said.

"Keep reading. One page has a list of people that was suspected of aiding the Allens in their escape. They could also give you information. There's other names I think you'll especially find interesting."

"I think you wasted both of our times. Why should I believe this letter came from Baldwin-Felts? There's no letterheads, or signatures, nothing to link them with these lists. "

"Baldwin-Felts is like an onion," he said.

"You mean they stink?" I said in poor attempt to be humorous.

"No, I mean there are many layers to them. You'll never find much directly from either Mr. Baldwin or Mr. Felts. You'll understand what I mean when I give you the other pages. *After* you give me the money."

I stole a glance across the room. I couldn't tell if Jeff recognized the man or not. I wasn't sure he could even get a good view of him from where he sat.

"And there's more," the man said. "After this, for an additional $250, I'll give you some very interesting information on how the detectives found Sidna and Victor out in Iowa.."

"Every one knows Maude Iroler turned Wesley in for the reward money," I said,hoping to bluff him.

"It goes a lot deeper than just that young girl. You'd be shocked to know who else was involved."

"You mean family?"

"You'll be surprised," he said. "I also have information on what happened to the autopsy report."

I thought I was going to spring out of my chair with this announcement.

"What report? They said there was no report prepared."

"The Carroll County coroner had done autopsies in the past. He even used some of that forensic science stuff in other cases. You think he'd not do them on the biggest case in the country if it was left up to him?"

"How much will that cost me?"

"Let me think about it. It's not going to be cheap though. I'll get in touch with you."

I thought for a few minutes, then took an envelope from my coat pocket. I placed it inside the folded newspaper and handed it back to him. He looked around nervously, before slipping the envelope into his inside coat pocket. He then handed me several pages wrapped inside the Richmond Evening Journal.

"Take the paper with you. I'll be contacting you about the rest of the information."

I waited for him to disappear into the mob of people departing the depot, then I left the bench. I rolled my eyes at Jeff as I walked by indicating for him to follow me to the restroom.

"Let's not talk here," I said once we were inside, "There's a café across the street. Watch me. If I go in, and stay, that means it's clear, and you come over and join me."

Ten minutes later Jeff walked in, spotted me, and came to join me in a back booth.

"So did you know him?"

"Sure did. His name is Win Phaup."

"So did he work for Baldwin?"

"Yep, he worked in Carroll County. Then a couple of months after the trials, he went out to the coal fields. Got the crap beat out of him by some of the miners. They thought they had killed him, but apparently Baldwin-Felts shipped him off to a hospital in Richmond, and he pulled out of it."

"Sounds like being a detective for those guys was detrimental to one's health."

"Sure was. They tried to get me to join them. Glad I didn't though. I'm too handsome to have my face all messed up."

"Do you think he knows as much as he claims?"

"He did seem to be in their inner circle. It surprised me that the agency just dumped him after his injuries. He's probably ratting on them not just for the money, but also for the revenge. He's gotta know that could get him permanently hurt ."

I studied the names on the page, asking Jeff if he knew various names who were not familiar to me. It was complicated by only listing the initial of the first name, as it could mean several different people. I then remembered Phauf telling me I'd find the other page interesting. I turned to it and started down the list.

Cox, A.

Howlett, A

McMillan, G.

Then my heart stopped long enough to jump up into my throat, as I read, not in typed letters, but penciled in, Haynes, J.

Without speaking I showed the name to Jeff.

He studied it for awhile, then turned his head to look out the train window at the passing landscape.

"So how many J. Haynes are there in Carroll County?" I asked.

"Including you, and me, probably three or four. I noticed it had been written in pencil. That's probably just Win jerking your chain. I wouldn't worry about it."

Jeff didn't sound convincing.

I spent the remainder of the trip to Blair Station studying the material I had purchased. It wasn't anything startling, other than seeing on paper the names of people that someone was seeking revenge upon. Had Baldwin-Felts prepared a hit list? I didn't think they had the money to have things like that done, and if so, why were they doing it on their own? Was someone else funding it? Was it a hit list to kill, or just scare off? But my mind kept going back to some of the other information he had proffered. Was he lying, or just boasting over zealously? Could there be an autopsy report floating around out there? And if there were, what would it cost me? Five hundred, maybe a thousand dollars?

I also wondered what I should do with the information I had. I certainly felt no inclination to turn it over to the authorities, as they may have been the ones who had prepared it. I did feel an obligation to warn others on the list though. Besides, this would offer a great opportunity to interview them.

After arriving back at the boarding house, I began circling names on the list that I was sure I knew. I decided I would contact them, the ones I could. I had no doubt that Marion, B was Byrd Marion, who had originally been charged with the Allens. He was the first person I searched out. Jeff said he'd better drive me down to his house.

"Mountain people are different than city folks," Jeff said. "You don't just go barging in on them unexpectedly. You have to prepare them for your arrival."

We pulled up about three hundred yards from the house. Jeff got off the wagon, walked up the road about fifty feet and waved his hands up in the air.

"Hey-oh, Byrd. This is Jeff Haynes."

We waited a few minutes, and a man in his forties came out onto the porch.

"Hello Jeff, what brings you up to this neck of the woods?"

"My cousin here wants to talk to you. OK if we come on up to the porch and sit a spell?"

"Sure," he said as he set the rifle back inside the door.

He started toward us, his hand extended. We met about thirty feet from his house.

"Maybe we should take a walk, out back." Jeff said.

"Yeah, good idea. The wife's been feeling might poor lately," he said. "Let's go down by the creek to talk. Aren't you that reporter feller from Richmond?"

"Yes sir. I am, and I wanted to share something with you," I said after we got out of hearing. "I recently acquired some information from a source. He provided me with a list that he claims are names of men that are, well, in possible danger."

"And I'm sure my name's on that list."

"The name of B. Marion was on it, and Jeff said he thought you were the only B. Marion he knew of."

"I think I am, in these parts," Byrd said, as he skipped a stone across the creek.

I subconsciously counted the skips. One, two, three, four. It surprised me that he appeared so phlegmatic. I decided that I would then begin trying to get his side of the story.

"Can I ask you some questions, Mr. Marion."

"You mean, since you brought me your warning, you now get to ask me questions?"

I was set back, surprised he had so quickly seen through me. It didn't take long for me to realize this man required honesty.

"Yes sir, that is exactly what I did. I hope you won't hold that against me. I'd just like to get your side of the story."

"I don't care you knowing, or you writing in that newspaper of yours, that I was a friend of the Allens. They never did me no wrong. Helped me out of many scrapes, they did."

"Is it true you helped them load their guns?"

He studied me for awhile. I could tell this man was noone's fool. He could judge a man. Mountain people seemed to be able to do that. I hoped he didn't find me lacking.

"Yes. One of them. I was so scared, to this day I can't remember if it was one of those Edwards boys, or one of the Allens. I didn't want to see anybody get killed. I just wanted the Allens to save their own hides. They were about to get shot down in cold blood."

"Mr. Marion, I have to ask you this. Were you part of a conspiracy with the Allens?"

"Hell no, there wasn't no damn conspiracy. If they had planned it, you think they'd have gotten themselves shot up like that?. And do you think for a second I wouldn't have helped?"

"So what about the court? Do you think they had a conspiracy?"

Byrd squatted, picked up an oak branch, and began whipping it about in the stream. After what seemed like a full minute, he answered.

"There's been a lot of tales told. I've had some people tell me people from the court warned them to be carrying a gun."

"You mean like Alph Thomas signing an affidavit that William Foster had advised him to come armed, and if Floyd made any attempt to resist, that if Alph shot him, Foster would get him off?"

"Yeah," Byrd said, "and there were others. I don't know if I believe all of them."

"What about the deputies themselves? They were expected to be armed, but do you think they were told to shoot?"

"Some of them were just boys, like Buddy Edwards. I'm not sure there was really a conspiracy, but I think Deck and Foster hoped something would happen. They were just too damn ready for it"

"Mr. Marion, if that was your name on the list, who do you think is out to get you?"

"I don't rightly know. Some of the Allen's, they think because the court dropped the charges against me, they think I might have told some things on them. But truth is," he said, as he looked me straight in the eye, "is that I know a lot more than I'm a'saying."

"Why aren't' you saying?" I asked.

"Because I've received letters. They tell me if I say anything, they'll kill my wife and family. Now I'm not scared for myself. But I couldn't live with myself if I knew I let something happen to them."

I thanked him for his time, and wished him and his wife well.

When, after three weeks, I hadn't heard from Win Phaup, I wrote a letter, addressed to him, at the last address I showed. I knew he would be surprised that I knew his name. The letter came back marked "undeliverable". There was no doubt in my mind I had been duped. Not only was the information I had already purchased questionable, but it didn't look like I'd be getting the information that would lead to answering the many questions I had.

A month laterJeff came back from town.

"Byrd Marion's been thrown into jail for bootlegging," he said.

"I didn't think anyone got arrested for that anymore," I said.

"I didn't think so either. I guess the sheriff figures he's gonna make an example of him. It's getting close to election time."

I went into town to see Byrd, and found him in a back cell. He was looking about as low as a human could look.

"Mr. Marion, I'm sorry to hear of your troubles. Is there anything I can do?"

He looked at me forlornly.

"No, I don't think anyone can do anything for me. And I didn't do it. Someone made it look like me."

"What do you mean?"

"I have an old home place on my land. I haven't been up to it for might near a year. Somebody stuck a still in it, and then called the sheriff. That still hadn't had a run go through it in years."

"You mean you were framed?"

"If thats means I didn't do it, yeah. I'm not saying that I haven't run a still in my life, but not in the last two years. I just wouldn't do it with my wife the way she is."

"What do you mean?" I said. "How is she?"

"She's dying," he said, his eyes misting over. "I don't thing she'll live to see winter."

Byrd Marion was sentenced in August, 1913 and was sent to the West Virginia State Prison in Moundsville. His prognosis proved correct. His wife died just days after he was transferred. Many prominent people contacted the prison requesting that he be granted furlough to come back for the funeral. The prison warden would only say that he had received information from Carroll County that indicated there was a rescue being planned if Byrd was allowed back. Jeff passed a hat and collected enough money for a burial. He and I both promised Byrd we'd travel to West Virginia in the spring to visit him.

On December 1, 1913, Jeff came into the house.

"I just heard that Byrd Marion died in prison. Of pneumonia. They're bringing his body in on the train."

That evening I went to the Byrd's home. His brother had moved onto the small farm and was living there, helping take care of Byrd's children. The closed coffin sat in a back room, away from the visitors. It didn't surprise me that the casket was a simple pine box. Often the family saved money by not having any extra work done.

After all, save a few family members and closest friends, had left, Byrd's brother came up to me with a strange look on his face.

"I want you to go into the back room," he whispered. "I want to show you something."

Silently, he led me into the room with the coffin. To my surprise, he pulled a wrecking bar from his pocket, and proceeded to pry open the lid of the coffin. I looked down into the face of Byrd Marion. They had done little to "prepare" the body. Splotches of blue covered the face, and several areas looked indented. Something just didn't look right. I eyed the brother questioningly.

"Reach down and rub your hand over his arms, his ribs," he said.

I hesitated, but did so. There were places where the skin was broken. I could feel sharp protrusions.

"His bones have been broken," I said.

"The prison sent us word that they weren't able to do much with the body, and for us to not look in the coffin. That sounded strange to me, so I slipped in here and looked for myself."

"Didn't the prison say he died of pneumonia?"

"That's what they claimed, but my brother was beaten to death. I tried to get the sheriff to come take a look, but he said it was out of his jurisdiction. Any investigation would have had to have been done in West Virginia."

In feeling the breaks, I had moved the corpse's hands. I saw a partially folded paper. I retrieved it from under the stiff fingers. It was a religious tract that read "The Wages of Sin is Death." I showed it to the brother.

"That wasn't there the first time I looked," he said with a puzzled look. "I know I would have seen it."

"How long has the body been alone?"

"Maybe three hours, on and off. Who do you think placed it there?"

I shook my head unknowingly, but I knew the killer had left his calling card.

In January of 1914, I received another letter with a Richmond postmark. The address was from a section of town that I recognized as being near the waterfront area known as Shockoe Slip. Opening the envelope I read. 'Mr. Haynes. I have information I know you will like. Bring me $400 and it is yours. I'll be in a small green boat, tied off the pier, in front of Schooner's Bar on Dock Street. You row us out a ways so we can't be heard, and don't talk until we are out and away. I'll wait there between 6 and 6:30 on the evening of January 12. No later. If you're not there by 6:30, then the information gets sold to someone else.'

I thought for a while. That was a lot of money to pay for information, but if it was as good as Phaup claimed, it might well be worth it. The twelfth was only 2 days away. I'd have to leave immediately. The rest of the day I worked on questions I would ask Phaup if his information didn't give me what I wanted.

I had called the judge, and when I arrived at the Richmond station, he had a driver there waiting for me. I had told him I only wanted to stop by to say hello, but he insisted I spend the night. He took me to my father's old house, and showed me the progress the foundation was making in converting the mansion into a museum. After a dinner of turkey with oyster stuffing, the judge and I sat in his study. I allowed myself a hand rolled cigar from the Republic of Cuba. The judge and I talked well into the night before we both retired.

The next day I did several personal chores and visited the Hotel Jefferson for a late lunch. I remembered a dozen years before when my father had brought me here for lunch for my twelfth birthday. Within a month it had burned to the ground. It was now back to its former glory. Although the original tables had been replaced, I went to the same location, just by the west window, to dine. After lunch I went to my father's grave at Hollywood Cemetery. By five I was getting exceedingly impatient for the appointed hour to arrive. Not wanting to chance missing the appointment, I caught a trolley to Shockoe Bottom.

The area had been one of the first settled due to its favorable location on the James River. My father's bank had loaned hundreds of thousands of dollars to businessmen here, and just to the east in the area known as Tobacco Row. If there hadn't been a James River, or tobacco, there would have never been a Richmond. I could still remember my father taking me with him to meet the men he had loaned money to. My father would extend his hand to a small business owner who would say that he couldn't shake it because his hand was dirty. I can still hear my father saying in his baritone voice, "The sun will never shine upon a day that I don't welcome shaking a man's hand that is dirty with the grime of capitalism." The men would look at him quizzically, then extend their hand. I'm sure they had no idea what he was talking about, because I myself was nearly a teenager before I discovered that capitalism wasn't some kind of a disease.

I felt my heart sink like a lead anchor at the thought I'd never see my father again.

Pulling my watch, I saw it was a quarter before six. I was at least ten blocks away from the Schooner Bar, so I quickened my pace. I arrived at the bar at 6:07. Walking over to the dock, I walked along the edge. In the failing light of dusk, I saw a boat tied off to a ladder that extended down from the dock. It was too dark to tell the color, but there was a man sitting at, or rather leaning against the stern. There were no other boats with occupants, so I was confident this was the one. As instructed, I climbed down the ladder and stepped into the boat without speaking. I untied the rope, and waited for Phaup to begin rowing us out into the river. I waited, but he just sat there, motionless. I then remembered the instructions were that I was to do the rowing.

"I have the money," I whispered, as I bent over to take the oars.

Still, he just sat there, laying lazily against the boat railing, his hat slouched down over his face. In no way did he even acknowledge my presence. I wondered if he was asleep. His eyes appeared to be open, or at least partially. I presumed he was drunk.

It had been ten years since I had rowed a boat, so when I commenced, I got overbalanced, and fell forward into Phaup. He pitched to the side, his torso drooping over the side. I grabbed him, to straighten him up before he fell overboard in his drunken stupor. I felt a syrupy fluid sticking to my fingers. In the obsidian light, I saw blood dripping from my hands. Pulling him to me, I saw the knife sticking between his shoulder blades. His hand had fallen over the side, and a piece of paper floated on the water. I retrieved it, but I knew what it would be. I knew it would read, The Wages of Sin is Death.

I drew the knife out, and leaned my ear against his chest to listen for a heartbeat. I heard none. At that moment I heard a clamor from above. I looked up into the eyes of a Richmond policeman, his gun pointed at me.

"Drop that knife, and don't try anything," he ordered.

Thirty minutes later I found myself handcuffed to a chair in the East Richmond Police Precinct. They had allowed me to phone Judge Valentine, and he said he'd be right down. As of that time, I had been told nothing.

The judge arrived within twenty minutes, and I could hear the conversation outside.

"Are you the arresting officer?" The judge asked.

"Yes Judge, I am."

"So what are you holding him for?"

"For murder. We received a call that a man was seen being stabbed outside the Schooner Bar, and someone was pushing him out into the river in a rowboat. When I got there, the suspect was indeed observed pushing the boat into the river. When ordered to halt, he turned and was observed with a knife in his hand. The knife was covered with blood. I also found over $600 in cash on him."

"This is preposterous," the judge said. "I've known that boy for his entire life. He'd never murder anybody. Where is this so-called witness?"

"He didn't give his name. We checked in the bar, but no one knew anything."

"Did you see the suspect stab the victim?"

"No, but as I said, he was holding the knife, and his hands were covered with blood."

"First of all, the suspect has a name, it is Jeremiah Haynes. Does that name sound familiar?"

"I, I think I've heard of it before. But I had to..."

"He's a nationally renown journalist, and his father was Archibald Haynes, one of the most influential men this city has ever known. People like that do not kill runabouts and dump their bodies in the James River."

"But Sir, I had to..."

"Let me finish. Now you can release Jeremiah in my custody, or I will phone the police chief and get him to come down. I'm sure you know how cranky Branson gets when he gets called back to work on his poker night.."

Five minutes later, I sat in Judge Valentine's car as we drove to his home.

"So what can you tell me?" he asked.

"The dead man is Win Phaup. He was an agent for Baldwin-Felts, and was selling me information on the Hillsville shootout. He told me he'd meet me in a boat tied in front of the Schooner's Bar."

"How did he tell you? By phone?"

"No, it was actually in a letter. But come to think of it, his other letters had been handwritten. But this one had been typed."

"Can you think of who might want to kill him?"

"Yes, I know who the man is, but I don't know his name." I said, then remembered I had placed the tract inside my pocket. I removed it and handed it to the judge. "This was floating in the water. It was left by the killer."

The judge perused the brochure.

"So what does this have to do with anything?"

"This is the killer's calling card. They keep popping up when people who have information about the shootout ends up dead."

"But you don't know him personally?"

"I don't know his name, but I sure know him personally. I'm sure he's the same person whot mugged me and left me for dead when I first got to Hillsville last year."

The judge sat puffing on his pipe. His physical stature had diminished greatly in the last year, but I could tell his mind was still as adroit as ever.

"Jeremiah, you know I love you as a son. And I know you will tell me the truth. Did you have anything to do with the man's death?"

I at first felt anger, but then I knew that the judge merely needed to hear it from my lips. Up to this time, I had not denied doing it.

"Judge, I swear on my parents' graves, I had nothing to do with Win Phaups's death. He was dead when I got there."

"That's all I needed to hear. Is there anything you can tell me?"

I thought for a while. Then I remembered.

"Yes, I remember thinking that the blood that got on my hands wasn't warm. I knew it should be close to body temperature, but instead, it seemed cooler. Also, it was clotting. I mean, it was dried on his coat."

A smile came to Judge Valentine's face. He walked over to the phone and dialed.

"Hello, Branson? Michael Valentine here. Have you heard about Jeremiah Haynes' arrest?"

Pause.

"Yes, I thought you would have. OK, I'd like for you to do me a favor. Call the coroner's office. Tell him to do a thorough forensic investigation of the body. I will guarantee that the victim was killed several hours ago, and Jeremiah Haynes was with me until 4:30 this afternoon."

I looked at him. He had to know I left his home before noon. He just winked at me, and continued his conversation.

"And if you'll do one more thing to humor an old man. Send a couple of detectives down to the docks. Have them ask if anyone was seen carrying a bundle wrapped in canvas, or maybe a blanket. Something like that. Then have them check all the trash sites to see if they can find anything that might have been used to conceal a dead body."

Pause

"Thank you very much. Let me know the minute you hear back from the coroner."

He hung up the phone, walked over to me and placed his hand on my shoulder.

"Don't worry about a thing, son," he said. "We'll get to the bottom of this."

I told the judge I thought I was ready for bed, so he directed me to my bedroom. Only then did I stop to remember. I had stayed overnight at the judge's probably a dozen times as a child, but had never slept in a bed. A few times it was a tent in the back yard, but usually on the sofa in his den.

I don't know if it was from the unbelievably comfortable bed I slept in, or the mental duress I had gone through, but I slept until 9 o'clock the next morning. By that time the judge had arisen and had made coffee and toast with homemade jam. Over breakfast he told me of the events that had gone over in the city since my father's death. At least three times he had to cease in mid-sentence to catch his breath.

About ten o'clock the phone rang, and the judge dismissed himself to go answer it. He came back with a big smile.

"That was Branson Smith, the Chief of Police. The coroner placed the time of death of the victim between noon and four. A detective found a bloody canvas sail in the trash pile behind the bar, and they found a witness who saw a large man carrying the canvas over his shoulder, slightly before five o'clock."

"So what does this mean?" I asked.

"That means it all over for you son. The chief sends his apologies for any inconvenience you may have been caused. He also said to tell you since I sprung you before you got fed last night, he owes you dinner."

I dropped my head into my hands. I stood up, and did something I had never done before. I had always revered this man almost to the point of worship. He had always been next to God in my eyes, and so, I never felt I could be familiar with him. But now this man had gotten me out of two major predicaments in the last year. I put my arms around his now frail body, and hugged him. I felt him twitch, and thought perhaps I had overstepped my boundary. But then I realized he was weeping as he hugged me back. I could feel the pressure on my back. It had none of the strength I felt when he would lift me up into the oak tree in his back yard, or lift me up and over the railing on the porch. The pressure was decrepit, but it nevertheless penetrated my very core.

"I love you Judge," I said softly.

"I love you too, son," he answered.

I took the late train out of Richmond Station with very mixed emotions. First very disappointed that I did not receive the information I had come for that would lead to me writing a best selling crime novel, secondly, relieved that I was not looking at a murder charge, and thirdly, wondering how long it would be before my body would be found with a religious tract lying next to it.

Usually when I took an overnight train, it was so I could get some sleep along the way. Otherwise it seemed my time was wasted. But not this time. My mind raced in a whirlwind, trying to take in and process all the events of the last two years: the shootout, the trials, the captures, the executions, and the number of unexplained deaths. How many of these had a common denominator? The person leaving the religious tracts. It had to be too much of a coincidence that the same type of tract was left, when I was assaulted in Hillsville, Byrd Marion was killed two hundred miles to the north in West Virginia, and Win Phaup two hundred miles to the east in Richmond.

Then a thought came to me. Perhaps this wasn't one man, but rather a whole group, acting as a unit. Maybe a select group of Baldwin-Felts detectives?

Was this a secret calling card? I had heard Thomas Felts was a member of several groups, such as the Masons which I knew nothing of, but had heard reports of groups like these having clandestine sects. I now wish I knew how to contact Elmo Brim and ask him if the religious tract was a part of the Baldwin-Felts Agency fraternity. I knew Thomas Felts was well respected in Galax, and was a member of the church there, but what would it mean to leave tracts stating "The Wages of Sin is Death." Maybe it was to warn others. Maybe it was just a scare tactic.

My thoughts went back to Elmo Brim. He had pretty much disappeared from the face of the earth. Had he been killed also? Or maybe Elmo Brim was the murderer. Maybe he had just given information to me to get a feel for how much I already knew.

No. Probably not. He definitely wasn't the man who mugged me at the stables.

I pulled from my notebook the list of potential informants I had prepared on Jeff's kitchen table that second day I arrived. From the over eighty plus names I had originally listed, almost sixty-five had been scratched out. There were three categories of those that had been deleted.

The first group were ones in which I, on my own or at Jeff's suggestion, had decided to eliminate. There were about eight names and those were mostly the immediate family of the victims of the shootout, the mother of the Edwards' boys and the wives of Floyd and Sidna Allen.

Second were people whom I had contacted and they had absolutely refused to speak to me. I didn't have anything to pressure these individuals, so I wasn't able to coerce them to talk as I had Deck Goad. These were mostly former deputies, members of the prosecution, and most of more than forty jurors who had served on the original trial and then the subsequent murder trials of Floyd and Claude Allen, and lastly, witnesses. I had identified many of these from the review of the transcripts of Floyd's murder trial, newspaper clippings, and reports. The most close-mouthed of all the jurors were the ones from Washington county. Not only did they refuse to talk to me, but several actually claimed they were ordered by a local judge to not discuss the case. I had struck out also with the former Maude Iroler.

The third group were individuals which had, for all practical purposes, disappeared from the area, whether by choice or from reported threats. A good example of this was former deputy Pink Samuels who had been sent to the state line to pick up the Edwards boys. Prior to the original trial he had relocated to North Carolina. In spite of subpoenas to testify, he refused to return to Virginia. In the case of Peter Easter, who had been deputized by Samuels on his way to pick up the Edwards, he stayed until the funerals of Floyd and Claude Allen. Reportedly Jack Allen advised him at that time to "best not let the sun set on your ass in Carroll County."

Peter Easter very quickly loaded his family and relocated to Amelia County to join Pink Samuels who apparently thought Mt. Airy was too close to Fancy Gap.

After circling the people I had already interviewed, I had about six names left. I was determined to meet with them.

18

After reaching Hillsville, I had absolute resolve in two matters.

First I would be incessant in finding who the tract dispensing murderer was, because I knew he could be the key to the entire story.

While I was gone to Richmond, it was as if summer had arrived and the fields and forests had taken on a refreshing new life. I hoped this would be an omen for a refreshing new life for me, as my second resolution was to ask Nellie Wisler to be my wife.

My intuition told me that Elmo Brim was not the murderer, but I did feel like he knew a whole lot more than he had revealed to me. The first day back, I rode into Hillsville and began making inquiries as to the whereabouts of Brim. I was directed to a young man from Galax named Norm Williams who was staying for a period with his uncle in Fancy Gap. Williams had gotten to be friends with Brim after the shooting when he and Brim were the only two out the thirty officers who had been deputized who would go into the Elliott Hotel and arrest Floyd and move him to the jail. I found Williams, but he said he had not heard from Elmo in several months, maybe a year. He did give me Brim's home address in Mt. Airy. I made the trip down the mountain, but everyone said they had not seen him for almost a year. This did not decrease my consideration of him as at least an accomplice to all that had gone on.

I did not arrive at home until nearly midnight, having traveled for four hours only by the light of the moon. This was very distressing to me, as I had hoped to visit Nellie that night.

Sometimes a reporter, if he's in a funk, tries to hit a homerun. Later that week I rode to Blair Station. I found myself in front of Cliffside Farm, the home of Thomas L. Felts. I had seen more impressive homes in Richmond, but this estate certainly would rank as one of the most beautiful working farms I had ever spied. From the road, I counted fourteen horse stalls in a stable that was more elaborate than most homes in the area. The groom had several matching black stallions on the outside cleaning them. I saw silos, and what I assumed was a dairy barn as there were probably fifty head of cattle in the pasture. Scattered about on what had to be at least 400 acres were other small outbuildings, shops, and cabins.

The house itself was huge, three stories high, and was at least 10,000 square feet. A dozen semi-circular concrete steps led up to a semi-circular portico, which in turn led to a sweeping covered porch along the front and both sides of the house. Slate covered dormers and gables with decorative railings adorned the third floor, and at the acme, a large widow's walk that offered a view of the entire estate, and Blair Depot. I had heard that Felts hired men to set atop the widows walk to serve as security guards, and also to document and identify every passenger who got on and off the train at Blair Station.

I had paid the telegraph operator at the depot $25 to wire me the moment Felts returned from the West Virginia coalfields. So I knew he was at home. I took a deep breath, straightened my tie, walked up to the front door, and knocked.

To my surprise, Felts himself opened the door, eating a sandwich. He appeared shocked, as if he had expected someone else to be at the door.

"Mr. Haynes, what bring you to my humble abode?" He said with a pasted grin.

This further shocked me, as to my knowledge, I had never met this man in my life.

I struggled to regain my fortitude.

"I was just hoping I could ask you a few questions, Mr. Felts."

He studied me for a few minutes, as if evaluating me, or better yet, what danger I might offer.

"Certainly, but I regret I can only spare about a quarter of an hour. I have another appointment. Please come in and sit down in the parlor."

I followed him into a room that featured a large chandelier that captured the noon sun and reflected it into a hundred colored rays. Large overstuffed furniture of wood and leather marked this as Thomas Felt's lair. In a distant room I could hear a record playing on a gramophone. The center of the room was dominated by an oval mahogany conference table. Atop it was an open box with expensive cigars and a snifter of brandy with small glasses.

"I will be concise then sir," I said as I followed him into the opulent living room, filled with masculine oversized leather and wood furniture.

"Fire away," he said.

"First of all, Mr. Felts, did you feel at anytime you overstepped your legal authority during the days following the Carroll County Courthouse tragedy?"

"I understand you're a top notch journalist, Mr. Haynes," he said. "I'm sure you know that Governor Mann gave Baldwin-Felts full authority. We were in a pseudo-martial law situation at that time."

"Did that include taking possession of personal property without compensation?"

"Can you give me a specific example of that," Felts said. "I have no knowledge of that ever happening."

I looked through my notes.

"One specific case was when a team of mules were taken by detectives from a local farmer. He claims he wasn't paid for them, and they were never brought back."

"In an operation of this size, there are always some logistics that might escape our attention. If the individual you are speaking of would have contacted us, we would have gladly given him recompense."

He spoke so slowly, I at first thought he might be somewhat dim-witted. Then I realized he was carefully weighing each word. I was confident this man never misspoke.

I knew I wasn't going to trip him up to reveal anything unless perhaps I could anger him.

"Did this include intimidating, even beating citizens in order to gain information."

"At no time have I, or Mr. Baldwin ever ordered physical confrontations with the populace. We pride ourselves in hiring men of the utmost character, many former law enforcement officers."

"Have you ever offered bribes for people to offer false testimony?"

"We have often offered rewards for true, factual information. At no time have we ever asked for, or condoned perjury."

"Have you ever ordered the killing of anyone?" I said.

I was sure I detected a slight twitch in the grin that Felts had kept pasted on his face.

"At no time. No sir. Never."

"Did you know there were reports your agents intercepted mail and read it?"

"That is a federal offense. I would never order it, and my men would know better than to ever do it. Any that ever did it would have acted on their own, and if we had learned of their act, they would have been terminated immediately."

I wanted desperately to ask if he had ever employed Elmo Brim, and if so, if he knew the whereabouts of Brim. I knew if Brim had been honest with me, and the Baldwin-Felts Agency was as ironfisted as he stated, this would put his life in danger though. I then had a sick feeling as to why perhaps no one had heard from him for awhile. Just as I was about to ask another question I noticed Felts reach underneath his desk as if reaching for something. I continued with my interview.

"I know the Allens were convicted of conspiracy. Have you uncovered any evidence that any of the court officials, Dexter Goad, or William Foster, had also conspired?"

"No. We found absolutely no evidence that there was any type of collusion between any officials of the court."

"Do you have any knowledge of what happened to the autopsy report?"

"Mr. Haynes, once again you seem to be confused. There *was* no autopsy report.

He seemed very confident of his answer, that I really felt there probably was never a report; that Phaup had merely implied this for the money. I continued though.

"If not then, do you have any knowledge of who might have ordered for no autopsies to have been performed? I mean, a case of this importance, I can't believe an autopsy would not have been performed."

I thought I saw the slight hint of a twitch from Felts. He licked his lips, and appeared ready to speak when someone knocked on the door facing. A man who looked like he could pick up and toss some of the cows I saw in the pasture stood in the doorway. He was nearly as tall, and broad-shouldered, as the opening.

"Excuse me, Mr. Felts," he said, eying me sternly, "I didn't know you had company. Mr. Baldwin is here for your scheduled meeting."

"Thank you Jason, tell him I'll meet him in the office," Felts said, as he stood up and extended his hand to me. "I guess I'll need to cut our discussion short, the Big Man is here."

I extended my hand half-heartedly.

"When might I schedule another meeting?" I said. "I have just a few more questions."

He began turning pages on a calendar on his desk.

"Oh, I'm sorry, Mr. Haynes, but I'm booked solid for the next month or so. Between banking business, the farm, the unpleasantries up in West Virginia, the Masons…"

"Speaking of the Masons, Mr. Felts, do you recognize this brochure? Is it something the Masons, or your detective agency might distribute?"

I laid a copy of the Wages of Hell tracts on his desk. For a moment, I thought Thomas Felt's had lost his ability to speak, but he quickly gathered his composure.

"No, I've never seen one of those in my life. I do have to run, but one more thing. I'm in need of a special person, someone to handle the public relations of our agency. I think you'd be excellent for it. It would pay $3,000 a year. Think about it and let me know."

"No sir, Mr. Felts, I don't think I'm interested," I said, as I picked up my brochure and left.

That evening I visited Nellie, hoping my second resolution might prove more obtainable than that day had been to my first resolution. I used as a guise that I had found a painting of Venice that I thought would look wonderful in the Wisler's parlor. We spent two blissful hours on the front porch swing before Pastor Wisler came out.

He came to the edge of the porch, and looked up at the dark sky.

"It's very cloudy tonight, and not a sign of a moon," he said, then turned to Nellie. "Perhaps you'd better let Mr. Haynes start before it gets too dark to find his way."

I smiled understandingly at her, while she just shook her head. I told the two of them good night and started toward my horse.

"Tomorrow night we are having fried chicken, Mr. Haynes," the pastor said, "would you like to join us?"

"Fried chicken's my favorite, I'll see you then." I quickly accepted.

One of those nagging questions that had twisted like a knife in my gut was why Dr. Chester B. Nuckolls, a well-educated physician who served as the county coroner, had reportedly deemed it unnecessary to perform autopsies on any of the victims. Even the mere removal and identification of bullets would have given almost inconclusive evidence of what guns, or at least which side, had fired lethal shots. My first inclination had been that, unlike our coroners in Richmond, with their unlimited knowledge of forensic science, Dr. Nuckolls had simply lacked these skills.

After Win Phaup had referred to the Carroll County Coroner's previous experience, I had researched the matter and discover that indeed, a decade before, Nuckolls had in fact used modern forensic science techniques in performing an autopsy on Jefferson Dixie Bolt who had been found dead. He had removed the top of the victim's skull and matched a fireplace skillet leg to the hole present in the skull. By doing so, he identified the murder weapon that led to the arrest and conviction of two local men as the murderers.

But yet, with the most celebrated crime of its time, he had performed no investigation. I wasn't sure if Win Phaup had insinuated that the coroner had decided on his own not to do the investigation, or if he had received orders from higher up. I guess now I would never know which he meant.

I decided to visit the good doctor himself.

I had inquired, and found that he took lunch every week day at precisely noon, and he always ordered the daily special from the Elliot Hotel. When he started out of his office that day, I was sitting in the waiting room.

"I'm sorry," he said, "I'm out to lunch right now. I'll be back about one if you want to come back then."

"I apologize for disturbing you, but I'm going to save you some time. I've got the Thursday special right here. I was hoping we could sit in your office, and I could ask you a few questions while you eat."

He studied me for a few seconds, then a vexed look swept across his face.

"You're that reporter from Richmond, aren't you?" he said.

"I'm Jeremiah Haynes, but I no longer work for a specific newspaper. I now work with the Associated Press, which, as you know, is national."

It was only a small white lie. David Laurence worked for the AP, and I submitted articles to him.

"I really haven't the time, Mr. Haynes. I have a very busy schedule. I usually read professional papers during my lunch time."

"Dr. Nuckolls, I'm nearly finished with my story for the Associated Press. I'd just like to clarify a few things with you before I submit it. If you simply don't have the time, I'll just have to report my findings, and state that you were asked to verify or deny, but you declined."

He looked at me with a hardened glare, then I could tell he forced himself to smile.

"Of course, Mr. Haynes. I'll answer whatever I can."

We returned to his inner office. I handed him the bag. He opened it and began placing the food upon his desk. I opened up my notepad, took out my pen, and began my questioning.

"Dr. Nuckolls, are you familiar with the term 'forensic science'?"

"Yes, I've written a few treatises on it for the Virginia Medical Society."

"Yes sir, I've actually read those. They were excellently written. Did you write them yourself?"

"Sure did. Every word."

"I think I also read you also used forensic science in the solving of a case, about ten years ago."

He again grew cautious. I regretted I hadn't continued to soften him up.

"Yes, I did." He answered.

I could tell I had blown it, so I went for the jugular.

"Dr. Nuckolls, as the County Coroner, why didn't you do an autopsy on any of the victims of the Courthouse tragedy?"

The doctor's mouth looked as if he had accidentally swallowed salt water. After three quick swallows, two swipes around his mouth with his tongue, and a sucking in of his lips, he answered.

"It's not an automatic decision. My first consideration is if it's ordered by the governor, or the attorney general. In this case it wasn't."

"But you can also make that decision yourself?"

"Yes, but you must realize, there was so much confusion those first few day. Also, I got direct requests from the families that they wanted this handled as quickly as possible. As you know, an autopsy would have taken several extra days."

"Did the families make this request in writing, and if so, may I see the requests."

"I think that would be unethical to show you the letters. They're personal. And I'm not sure they were kept."

"Sir, did anyone other that the family instruct you to not do an autopsy, or to even identify the bullets?"

He laid the fork down and stood up. Walking to the window, he looked out upon the street.

"You don't know how it was. Like I said, there was so much confusion. We didn't know when the Allens were going to come back in, and commence shooting up the whole town. There simply wasn't enough time."

"Did the governor order you to not do an autopsy? Did Dexter Goad?"

"No," he said. "It was my decision. Based upon the evidence I had at that time., I feel it was the correct choice."

"How long would it have taken to just remove the bullets, and to identify them, and catalogue who they came from?"

He continued to stare out the window, refusing to face me. His voice changed to a monotone, as if he was reciting an oft used poem.

"There was no need. We could tell from the angle of entry they had come from the Allens' side of the courthouse."

"Dr. Nuckolls, I've read the transcripts from the trials. I think they showed there was a strong likelihood that there could have been serious misinterpretations of the directions of the entry wounds."

The doctor turned to me, his face ashen.

"Mr. Haynes, there's not a day goes by that I don't wish I had make a different decision. I was just so shocked, I just wanted it all to be over. Nothing you write could make me feel worse than I already do."

I saw before me a man tormented, but I have no doubt, a good man. An honest man.

"Dr. Nuckolls, I'm sorry I bothered you. Thank you for your time."

That evening I enjoyed a fried chicken dinner that rivaled anything I had ever eaten at the finest Richmond restaurants. Afterwards, Nellie and I went to what had become a regular meeting place for us, the porch swing. From our seat, we could see the stars, and Nellie would often point out the constellations to me. I, in return, would point out and offer her my constellation names for her. She would laugh at my monikers. Especially my identification of the fly swatter, which she insisted was the Big Dipper.

I had never been a person who felt comfortable for long lengths of time with one person, even my wife. But with Nellie Wisler, it never seemed we had enough time together. I knew it would soon be time for me to leave, so I summoned up my nerve and spit out the words, in one breath.

"There's a matinee showing of David Copperfield Saturday at the Galax movie house. Would you like to go with me?"

"David Copperfield? Oh, Dickens is my favorite author. You know, I've never been to a picture show before."

"I was hoping you hadn't. I was wanting to do something special for you," I said.

"How long will it take us?"

I explained that we would have plenty of time. We'd need to leave by nine that morning, and would be home by dark, so the date was made.

I became increasingly frustrated that I could not find the last piece of my puzzle. Perhaps I had missed something. I reviewed all my notes. They seemed complete, or as complete as they could be considering the participants' resistance to speak to me. The ones willing to be interviewed always seemed to be holding something back. I could never tell if it was due to fear, or to protect themselves. Perhaps it was a combination of the two. There was certainly plenty of guilt to go around when it came to the tragedy.

An exception to my frustration was my time I spent with Nellie. That summer had been glorious. With school out, I was able to see her several times a week. I was even beginning to enjoy spending time with her siblings, who had accepted me as a part of their life, and no longer felt they had to compete to be the one to steal time with me away from their older sister.

I spent the time prior to each of our dates contemplating if this should be the time I should ask her to marry me. I told myself I was trying to find the perfect time, but I knew it was really because I was simply scared to ask her.

I just kept thinking there had to be something in the trial manuscripts that I had missed the first time. Additionally I had spent all my previous time in Wytheville reviewing Floyd Allen's trial. Due to my time constraint, I had totally ignored anything related to Claude's trial. I decided to travel to Wytheville for the next few days to read the court transcripts first of Claude's trial, then to re-read Floyd's. I would return to Hillsville on Friday, and we would go to the picture show on Saturday. Perhaps somewhere in the middle of David Copperfield, and on the ride home, I would find the perfect time to ask Nellie to be my wife.

19

As soon as I entered the Wythe County Circuit Court building, I was met by a recently installed plaque honoring the victims of the Carroll County courthouse tragedy who had been 'assassinated'. It was obvious where the sentiments of Wythe County laid.

I began reviewing the transcripts for Claude's trial. They seemed to mirror the ones I had previously reviewed for Floyd. I got the books for both trials and compared them . At first appearance, it was as if the transcript for both men's trials had been copied, nearly word for word, with the exception of the jurists chosen. Both carried the motion the defense counsel had made to dismiss charges due to the clerk's office losing the judge's original list of potential jurors, but in each case, Judge Staples overruled.

Nearly the exact witnesses were chosen for both trials, and once again there seemed to be several commonalities. The prosecution had twice as many witnesses as the defense. The prosecution witnesses were shown, under defense cross, to have substantiated vendettas toward the Allens. The bulk of the evidence was more toward proving conspiracy to commit murder, than the act itself. Much of the testimony of the prosecution witnesses seemed very similar, almost to the point of being practiced. The prosecution had contradictions between their own witnesses, especially when it came to testimony as to which court officials had guns, and who had fired theirs. Once again, although a letter from Dexter Goad to the

Roanoke Times stated that sheriff Webb drew his gun and approached the convicted Floyd Allen, the Clerk of the Court repeatedly stated he misspoke to the newspaper. I saw a pattern of Judge Staples over-ruling many key defense objections.

This made it even more surprising that the evidence in both cases could have been so homogenous, but yet Floyd's jury found the evidence of conspiracy compelling, and found him guilty for the first degree murder of Judge Massie and Foster carrying the death penalty. Presented with the same evidence, Claude's jury did not accept the conspiracy charge and found him guilty of the second degree murder of Judge Massie, with a 15 year sentence. In the second case charging Claude with the conspiracy of murdering Foster, the jury could not reach a verdict.

For the third trial, a jury was selected from nearby Washington county. I again read a clone of the second trial, with the exception of the jury. It was amazing that the same evidence could be presented to three different juries, the first jury finds no conspiracy, and returns a second degree murder conviction with a sentence of fifteen years. The second jury was unable to reach a verdict, but the third Washington County jury, presented the same evidence, returned a first degree murder charge with a death sentence.

I could not get past the seemingly biased judgeship of Judge Waller R. Staples throughout all the trials. I worried that I was losing my objectivity, something a journalist should never do. I knew I had to overcome the bias that I knew I had built in favor of the Allens.

After two eight-hour days of being bent over the trial transcripts, I had found nothing significant. I did have a new appreciation for the defense counsel though. It was clear they fought overwhelming odds in defending Floyd and Allen. It did make one thing clear, I had to make a second attempt to speak to one of the defense lawyers.

Since Floyd had had all his property seized, he and Claude were left destitute. Therefore the courts had appointed attorneys. I had contacted all five of the principal defenders. Both Judge Hairston and Judge Oglesby of Bristol had relocated after the trials. Attorneys Coxe and Cocke of Roanoke had emphatically informed me they had put this part of their life aside, and never wanted to relive it again. Of the five, only R. Hoilman Willis of Roanoke had offered any hope. He had informed me previously that he had an extremely busy caseload at the time, but perhaps he could meet with me in the future. At the time I thought it was his polite way of refusing an interview, but now I felt I had to contact him again.

As soon as I reached Hillsville, Friday evening, I phoned Mr. Willis. I received the best news of the week, or at least the second best after Nellie accepting my movie offer. Willis had a case in Hillsville the following Wednesday. He made me a deal I couldn't refuse.

"Meet me at Blair Station at ten o'clock that morning with a buggy," he said. "And I will promise you my undivided attention for the next two hours to answer your questions."

After my phone call, I went by Tom Barnett's stable, where I rented a surrey and a black gelding from the livery stable for the weekend. The next morning I arrived at Nellie's a quarter before nine. She was waiting on the porch wearing a sky blue dress that brought out the color of her eyes. Unlike when she attended church, her hair hung down over her shoulder.

"That is one beautiful buggy and horse," she said as I helped her into the seat. "I feel almost like Cinderella going to the ball."

To me, she was Cinderella.

The trip to the Galax Movie Theater took a little over two hours. It was a little brisk for a late summer morning, which was fine with me because it meant Nellie rode close by my side. Along the way she would see friends, or students from her class, at whom she would cheerfully wave.

I had attended several shows in Richmond. The Galax Theater was naturally much smaller, but I was surprised at the quality of the movie, and the piano player who accompanied the words on the screen was most proficient.

Nellie was as excited as a little girl getting her first baby doll on Christmas morning. Several times I would hear her weeping, and would hand her my handkerchief. Perhaps it was the sentimentality of the movie, or the darkness of the theater, but when I placed my hand upon hers, she wrapped her fingers around mine.

All too soon, the movie ended, and we had to leave. Once outside, Nellie tiptoed to kiss me on the cheek. I could feel her cheeks, still moist with tears.

"Thank you for the most wonderful day of my life," she said.

We were more relaxed on our way home today than on the trip we had taken to Pilot Mountain. I had been wanting to ask her questions about the tragedy, but I had put it off. I hoped she was ready to talk to me, not as a journalist, but as a close friend. A close friend, who wanted to be ever so much more.

"Nellie, would you be comfortable telling me about you and Claude?"

She was quiet for awhile. I was afraid I had ruined our otherwise perfect day. But she began telling me her story.

"Claude and I knew each other growing up. I think he flirted with me, but I was too young. He asked me out once, but I told him I couldn't. He then left to go to school down in North Carolina to be an office worker."

"But he had to come back because his mother got sick?" I asked, remembering the story.

"Yes. That's right. When he came back, I wanted him to ask me out, because I was sure Daddy would let me go out then. He finally did."

I looked over to see her smiling, her eyes sparkling.

"What was your first date?"

"Our first dates were him just sitting with me in church," she said. "Kinda like you and me."

"So you think those times I went to church with you were dates," I said mockingly. "Young lady, I'll have you to know I only went there to hear your daddy's preaching. I barely knew you were even there. But please continue."

She elbowed me in the ribs playfully.

"Then we went to some church things, you know, ice cream socials, dinner on the ground."

"When did he ask you to marry him?"

"He asked my daddy the first week of March. When my daddy said yes, he told me he was going to buy me a ring."

Nellie got very quiet. I looked over at her. She was looking down. I could tell she was crying.

"That's ok, we can stop talking about it now," I said.

"No. I've needed to talk to someone. I've not had anyone before," she said, then turned to me. "He bought the ring the day before the court sentencing. He was going to give it to me as soon as he got home from the trial."

I could feel her body trembling next to me. I knew it wasn't from the air, but I pulled my suit coat off and wrapped it around her. She turned and looked at me, her eyes lost in a pool of despair. She pulled a necklace from the bodice of her dress. On it hung a gold wedding band.

"He gave it to me the first time they let me visit him in jail," she said softly, then her voice hardened. "If they had planned on the shootout, do you think for a moment he would have bought me a ring?"

"No. I don't think he would have," I said. I knew I meant it. No man would have willingly done anything to have sacrificed his life with her.

We didn't talk much the rest of the trip to her home. She slid close to me, and laid her head against me. I knew this was not the time to propose. My hopes were restored though when we reached her home. As I was walking her to the door she turned to me.

"Next week is our annual church dinner on the grounds," she said. "May I impose upon you to escort me?"

"I would be most delighted to," I answered.

Before disappearing into the doorway, she looked back at me and said, with a smile, "They're auctioning off box lunches, so be sure you bring lots of money."

She then rushed into her house.

That Wednesday I was waiting at the station when the train pulled in. I watched the passengers exit until I saw a gentleman whot had all the looks of a lawyer. He wore a three piece suit and carried a thick leather satchel. I approached him to discover it was indeed Mr. Willis.

It would have been very difficult to have asked questions, and take down notes, while driving the buggy, and I certainly did not want to impose upon him to drive, so I had asked Jeff to come along as a driver. After introductions, the three of us climbed aboard. Before Jeff even got the horse up to a trot, I had begun my questions. I wanted to take full advantage of the lawyer's undivided attention.

"Mr. Willis, to begin with," I said, "let me state that I know you were court appointed since the Allens were destitute after their land was seized, and that you personally borrowed the money to mount a defense, and you received no compensation for your work."

"Yes," he said, eying me curiously. "Do I sense a 'but' coming up?"

"It's just that I know you worked with very limited funds that put you at a great disadvantage to the prosecution., I don't want you to think the questions I ask are challenging your, and the other attorneys', competence. I'm just trying to get a grasp of what happened."

"Oh, don't worry Jeremiah. My proficiency has been challenged by better men than you," he laughed. "Continue."

"Could you tell me some of the hardships you did suffer because of the lack of funds?"

"Getting our witnesses to trial was difficult and costly. Wytheville is very progressive, on a major rail line, with good streets, electricity and phone service, but they may as well have been two hundred miles from Hillsville."

"Is this why you had half the witnesses the prosecution did?"

"Exactly." He answered. "The prosecution had a seemingly bottomless bucket for paying the costs for witnesses. We had very limited funds, and many defense witnesses could not pay their own expenses, regardless of how vital their testimony might have been."

"What effect did that have upon the trial?"

"Evidence is like a pyramid. You have to build layer, after layer, until you reach the top, the apex of irrefutable evidence. With our funds, we could only afford to bring a primary witness in to testify, but could not bring in a secondary and tertiary witness to substantiate the primary testimony."

"So the jury may have interpreted that the evidence presented could not be supported by others."

"Yes," he said. "That's it exactly."

"Were there other problems with getting witnesses?" I said.

I had heard reports, but I wanted to hear him say it. I think he knew what I was referring to.

"I know for a certainty that some potential witnesses refused to testify due to direct or implied threats."

"From court officials or from Baldwin-Felts agents."

"Probably both, but I think mostly from the agents," he said. "Some of the detectives even bragged to newspapers how they had roughed up people. The court just seemed to turn a blind eye to these events though. Then of course, there was also the problem with the crime scene."

"What was that problem?"

"No one took charge," he said. "The integrity of the scene was totally compromised. The governor was notified almost immediately. He should have ordered the entire courthouse and yard secured. He didn't, so we have citizens digging the bullets out of the walls and taking the guns as souvenirs."

"An area that disconcerted me," I said, "was that the evidence against Clyde was nearly exactly the same for all three trials. The first trial led to a second degree conviction, with fifteen years for the murder of Judge Massie. The second trial, in the murder of Foster, hung. The same evidence was presented to the third jury, the Washington County jury, found him guilty in the first degree, with a death sentence. Why do you think that?"

"No two juries will ever rule the same, but there's no doubt in my mind the Washington county jury was tainted."

"What do you mean, tainted?" I asked.

"Two of my co-counsels were from Bristol. They have it upon good authority that Judge Staples and a prominent Washington County judge were both contending for an appointment to the Supreme Court of Appeals of Virginia."

I leaned forward. This was getting interesting.

"So what happened?" I asked.

"The Washington County judge openly professed that he would personally ensure that swift justice would be brought to the Allens. I have no doubt the venire, that's the list of potential jurors that we are given, had not only been handpicked, but had been prepped with the answers to give us during jury selection."

"Did you expect anything? During jury selection I mean?"

"It did seem that there were some excellent defense biased jurors that we selected but were sure the prosecution would strike, but they never did. We were very optimistic going into the trial."

"I know that you have to be careful what you say," I said, "and I'll not name you as my source, but how do you rate the judgeship of Staples during all the trials."

Willis didn't answer for ever so long, and I was afraid I had lost him. I looked over, and realize he had turned extremely red. He swallowed, setting his lips tensely. Twice he almost said something, but it was as if he were waiting for the right words to come to him.

"There were some extreme irregularities during the trials," he said. "In my opinion."

"Such as?" I said.

"Usually, a judge has a lot of give and take. He'll over rule an objection you think is valid, but later he'll give you a ruling you never dreamed he would. Judge Staples gave us very little, but the prosecution was given a lot."

"In reading the transcripts, it appeared the commonwealth was given some questionable lee-way in scheduling trials."

"You mean like when we showed up the first of July to defend Claude against the murder charge of Lew Webb, but then at the last minute it was changed to the charge of murdering William Foster?"

"Yes, that's what I mean."

"Actually it didn't surprise us that much, because we had gotten reports that the prosecution had absolutely no evidence of Claude shooting at the sheriff. So that didn't surprise us. What absolutely floored us though was that Judge Staples would not grant us a continuance."

"Wasn't there another similar incident?"

"Yes. We showed up, I think it was on July 17, ready to defend Friel Allen. Ten minutes before trial was to begin, the commonwealth decided to try Claude instead. Again we requested a continuance, but it was denied."

"Do you think this was Judge Staples acting on his own?" I asked.

"No, I think it came from much higher. Governor Mann enjoyed his reputation as a law and order governor. He believed all the stories about the Allens, and wanted to make an example of lawlessness. I have no doubt he was pushing the buttons on this case."

"I'm sure there were times you regretted having been placed in the position of defending the Allens," I said.

"I admit, at times I asked myself why I was doing it, but then I'd look over and see Nellie Wisler. She always took a seat as near to Claude as she could. They would exchange looks, and she would always give me a big smile. That was my regret. Not that I had let Floyd down. Not that I had let Claude down. But that I had let her down."

"At Claude's last trial, it seemed to me Judge Staples spent a lot of time addressing the jury."

"I've seen closing arguments take a fourth the time that Judge Staple's instructions took," he said, as he opened his satchel, thumbed through it, and pulled out several sheets. "Let's see, I wanted to make sure I was correct. Yes, he presented 21 instructions."

"And that's unusual?"

"Most unusual. Usually there will be only five or six. But worse, it's what he said, or at least the subtext of what he was saying."

"For example?" I asked.

"He informed the jury that the deputies had the full right of the law to pull their weapons if Floyd showed any sign of resistance, which I totally agree. But he summarily dismissed all the evidence that had been presented that both Goad and Foster also pulled theirs, which they had no legal right doing."

"You feel the evidence was there?"

"There? Goad admitted to it. But it just seemed the court officials had total amnesty from any wrongdoing. Probably the worse, the most damaging instruction though was," he hesitated, moving his finger down the page, "was number 16."

"What does it say?"

"It instructs that in order for a person to claim self-defense, he must be totally inculpable of any crime. Well, Floyd and Claude had already confessed to shooting at the others. That instruction sealed the Allens' fate."

"Would I be correct in surmising that you were surprised at the verdicts, the first degree verdicts I mean?" I asked.

"We were truly shocked. We knew there was no way we could avoid a second degree conviction. But even with our limited testimony, we established that there could not have been an conspiracy. We felt we had showed if there had been a confederacy, it was between the court officials and the sheriff."

"What do you feel was the best evidence the Allens did not conspire?"

"For one thing, the Allens had showed no preparation. Sidna had deposited nearly $500 into the bank the day before, and had only pocket change on him. They had their horses locked up at the stables instead of having them held outside the courthouse. Medicine had been ordered at the drug store to be picked up that evening."

"On the other hand, what do you think showed the possibility the court and sheriff had conspired?"

"Oh, let me count the ways," he said, as he began counting off on his fingers. "You have a sheriff who had never been known to carry a gun show up with a borrowed gun. You have a clerk of the court buying a new automatic just weeks before, then he and the commonwealth attorney take target practice the day before the trial."

"That does sound contrived," I said, then added. "Not to mention the additional ammunition they had stored in their pockets and offices. So, Mr. Willis, did you think there was any way you could have gotten a favorable Supreme Court ruling?"

"No. Not after all that had transpired. I did find it interesting that one of the reasons the appeal was struck down was because it had not been filed within a timely manner, but then the justices recommended that legislation be passed in order to prevent that from being a problem in the future."

"Did it surprise you that the thousands, I've heard nearly a hundred thousand, of people who signed petitions did not sway the governor?"

"Not at all," Willis said, "knowing his track record for not commuting sentences in the past. I am proud to say that some of the very first petitions originated at the University of Virginia Law School and at Washington and Lee."

By this time, we were almost to Hillsville, and I knew my interview would soon be ending.

"Mr. Willis, is there anything you wish you had done different with the trial?"

He fell silent. I'm sure he had asked himself this same question a hundred times in the last two years. He had a pained look on his face.

"I think I would have been more outspoken in my belief that we did not receive fair rulings, even if it meant being charged with contempt of the court. Serving a few nights in jail would have been preferable to the consequence."

"You mean of the Allens dying in the electric chair?"

"No, I mean the consequence of seeing the look on Nellie Wisler's face when they sentenced Claude to death. I will take that look to my grave."

20

I spent the rest of the week going over all the notes I had taken on the buggy ride from Blair Station to Hillsville. I had to phone Mr. Willis to clarify a couple of notes due to the difficulty in writing legibly while being jostled in a buggy.

I only had a few names left on my original list without a circle or a mark through them. I still had not decided if I wanted to talk to Floyd's brothers Garland, who had been leading the church service that the fight started at, or to Jack's son Barnett. Both were very peaceful men, and I'm not sure how much they would be able to contribute. Alverta Edwards Mundy, whose two sons were still in prison, had been a witness in the courtroom, but from all reports, had spent her time trying to keep her sons from participating and probably could not contribute anything worthwhile. George "Bud" Edwards was the deputy who had been in the courthouse, who had been one of the participants in the church service fight, and who had been appointed acting sheriff after the shoot out. I had asked him once to talk to me, but he had refused. I was thinking of asking him again with the hopes he had changed his mind. It was looking doubtful I was ever going to find the person who would lead me to the tract distributing murderer, or to provide the final link to finding the truth.

In spite of these doubts though, by Saturday I found myself especially blissful. The next day I would be spending first in church with Nellie and afterwards on the grounds, after I outbid every other man for the privilege of sharing her picnic lunch. It would take Thomas Felts or George Lafayette Carter to outbid me for that opportunity, and I was pretty certain those two would not be there.

I squirmed through the service the next day, the roll of five dollar bills nearly burning a hole in my pocket. After the benediction, we filed out of the church. Saw- horses and timbers had been converted into tables. The ladies and their baskets were asked to form a line. A local auctioneer-wanna-be started the sale.

"OK, what am I offered for this delicious basket of food, and a chance to share it with Michelle Jones. Do I hear a dollar? A dollar? A dollar there from Eli Bishop, do I hear two? Do I hear two? OK Eli, no fair waving your pocket knife around in the air at other bidders. Going once, going twice. OK, sold to Eli Bishop."

Nellie and her basket was the sixth to step forward. She was holding it with both hands. The bidding opened.

Before I could raise my hand, a gentleman, who looked as if he had been too old to have fought in the War, hollered "One dollar! Someone else can eat the food 'cause I left my teeth at home, but I just want to set with Miss Wisler."

This brought laughter from everyone.

Either word had gotten out that the journalist from Richmond had sold all his earthly possessions to purchase the basket, or others were afraid of any of Claude's family or friends, because no one else spoke up. Before the auctioneer could start his count down, and just after Nellie cast me a pleading glance, I called out, "Ten dollars."

Everyone turned to look at me. Until that time no basket had brought more than three dollars. I glanced at Nellie, and she showed relief that the octogenarian had been outbid.

"Ten dollars from the gentleman in the back. I think he's that city-slicker from up Richmond way. So I've got ten, do I hear eleven? Eleven? Didn't think so. Going once, going twice..."

Before I could stop myself, I called out, "Thirty dollars."

This brought a hush from the crowd. I did not dare look at Nellie.

"Sir, you do realize you had the high bid of ten dollars? You didn't need to bid again."

"Yes, I realize that, but well, it is a big basket."

"Maybe that's the way they do things in Richmond," he said. "OK, do I hear forty dollars? Forty dollars? Sir, are you sure you don't want to bid forty?"

I smiled and shook my head.

"OK then," he said. "Going once, going twice, SOLD to that very peculiar bidder in the back."

As I expected, Nellie was extremely red-faced as she approached me. She was smiling though, so I felt some relief.

"Well, Mr. Haynes, that was quite a spectacle you made of yourself," she said. "You just broke the all-time record for the most paid for a picnic basket, by, I'd say, about twenty-five dollars."

"Well, Miss Wisler, as I said, it IS a big basket. And you know how much I can eat. Besides, it's going for a good cause."

"Yes it is," she said. "And you single handedly paid for the new roof."

I took the basket. It was very heavy, I was surprised she had been able to carry it. As we walked off, I sensed people watching, perhaps glaring. I knew this was the first time most had seen Nellie with someone in public since Claude had gone to jail.

She led me toward the back of the church.

"You know we are about to stir a scandal, don't you?" she asked. "Leaving the church grounds. But there's something I want to share with you."

We reached the edge of the forest behind the church, and walked into the woods a short distance. She stopped at a thicket. A few dense rhododendron bushes blocked our way. Their yellow, pink and purple blossoms were nearly as big as a basketball. She looked behind her, saw no one watching, then pushed through the foliage. I followed, expecting to fight a heavy undergrowth, but instead found myself in a clearing of about ten feet square. The rhododendron formed one side of the box; the other three sides by dogwoods, poplars and maples whose limbs arched overhead to form a topiary cathedral. There was just enough room beneath the lowest limbs to stand. The sun, filtered through the leaves of the trees, cast a celestial aura. The bouquet of fragrances from the various flora and fauna was pure ambrosia. This was, perhaps, the closest to Eden I'd ever been. The ground was as soft as a feather tick. Small rocks, covered with moss like green velvet, randomly penetrated the forest floor.

"Do you like it?" she asked.

"It's perhaps the singularly most beautiful place I've ever been," I said. "How did you find it?"

"When I was about thirteen, I was trying to catch a stray cat. She ran through the bushes, and I followed her into here."

She took the basket from me, laid it on the ground and opening the top, removed a blanket and laid it on the ground. She sat down, and motioned for me to join her.

The bodice of her dress opened just enough that I noticed she was not wearing the necklace with the ring. I felt my hopes soaring.

"You're the only person I've ever brought here," she said, a distant look in her eyes. "It's always been my inner sanctum."

"The first?" I said.

"Yes, the first," she said, knowing what I was asking.

"Why me then?"

"Because I know God sent you to me, to ease my sorrow. I don't know if I could have made it this last year without you."

I took her hand. Perhaps she did feel the way I did.

"Nellie, I love you. You do know that, don't you?"

She looked at me. Even in the dimness, I could see the moisture in her eyes. The tears on her cheeks.

"I had hoped you did. I need someone to love me. I think I love you too."

Reaching in my pocket, I pulled out the box and placed in on the blanket in front of her. Her expression changed in a way that nearly made me pick it back up. I knew I had to continue though.

"I guess I should talk to your father first, but I wanted you to know."

She opened the box, and removed the gold band. She turned it over in her fingers, as if trying to absorb strength from it. She wrapped her hand around it and held her fist to her chest. I waited. Her eyes closed. Her lips moved. I think she was praying. After what seemed like minutes, she opened her eyes. She extended her hand, and dropped the ring back into my hand.

"I'm sorry Jeremiah, I can't." She said hoarsely. "I just can't."

I always knew there was a chance that she would say no. But hearing the words, feeling her fingertips as they opened up against the palm of my hand, and feeling the band dropped back into my hand, left me numb.

"I saw you weren't wearing the necklace. I thought that meant..."

"Oh Jeremiah," she said, grabbing my hand. "It broke. It's being repaired."

Suddenly the ring felt as if it was a branding iron burning its mark into my hand. I threw it to the blanket.

I stood up, and without looking back, pushed my way out of the thicket, and out of Nellie's life. Her sobs were my last memory of her.

Once I reached my horse, I galloped away from the church grounds. A mile away I reigned up the horse. I reached into the saddlebag and found the bottle that I knew Jeff kept hid from Annie. I just needed a small drink to settle my nerves before I returned to Jeff and packed my bags. I took a long drink. It didn't settle my nerves, but it did intensify my numbness. I realized that is what I needed. To be numb. To forget. I drank. Ten minutes later, I smashed the empty bottle into a tree. By nightfall I had left the boarding house, left Carroll County, and left Nellie Wisler.

21

The month following my return to Richmond will forever be lost in the obscurity of an alcoholic stupor. I think I would have drunk myself into oblivion if I had not received a visitor at my door on the fifth week. I was told that Judge Valentine was on his deathbed, and had asked to see me. The driver said he would wait in the car.

I went to the washroom. I was repulsed by the person that stared back at me from the mirror. The month growth of beard that covered my wasted face hung like moss from its skeletal orb. The two dark, sunken cavities that stared back at me were as void, as lifeless, as any corpse I had ever viewed. I wept at the thought that not only was I now losing the only remaining person who even remotely presented a familial image, but also his last thoughts of me was going to be like this. I went back to the driver, and told him to come back in two hours.

I took a steamy bath, probably the first I had taken in the five weeks, and shaved. The skin beneath the beard looked almost translucent, broken only by the blue spider-web veins. My hair sprung Medusaic, and all the hair tonic in the world would not make it lie down. I pulled the scissors from the drawer and began to snip away the wildest sprigs. My hand shook so badly, I nearly cut off an ear. I went downstairs and fixed myself a strong pot of coffee. While it was percolating, I fixed some bacon and eggs. Once the coffee was ready, I poured a cup, and fixed a second serving of eggs and bacon. I had to use both hands to prevent spilling the cup of coffee on me.

God, why did I let myself slip into this. After I'd gone through this before.

I guess I must have dozed off because the next sound I heard was a knock at the door. It was the driver returning. He looked at me, still in my robe.

"Sir, you really must come now. The doctor says there's not much time left."

I rushed back upstairs to dress. I pulled on the only clean pair of pants I could find. They sagged off my hips. I tried using the belt I normally used, but it was too large. I quickly made a new hole with my pocket knife. I looked into the cabinet and saw a jar of Vaseline petroleum jelly. I took a dollop from the bottle, held my hands over the lamp and warmed the thick goo. As it began to melt, I rubbed my hands together, and rubbed the thick mixture into my hair. It was so thick my comb wouldn't penetrate it, so I used the brush to force my hair down into a viscous mat.

I filled the twenty minute drive to the Judge's mansion deciding how to explain why I had not been to see him since returning to Richmond; how to explain my appearance.

But I need not have worried. Once I arrived, the doctor was leaving the room. He just shook his head, without saying a word, and I knew I had waited too long to say good-bye.

Once again, my weakness to accept adversity had cost me time with a person I cherished, time that been lost for eternity.

Judge Valentine had no immediate family, just distant nephews and nieces who had grown up in distant cities and knew this man of integrity and respect only in name, or from family portraits. A couple of them made their way to Richmond for the funeral. None were invited back to the mansion for the reading of the will.

I was.

Much like my father, Judge Valentine left the bulk of his wealth, estimated to be in excess of one million dollars, to various charities and foundations. He left me his mansion, his automobile, and a lifetime annual stipend of $10,000. This made me feel even worse considering that I had allowed him to die alone.

At this stage in my life I had no idea what I would do with a house of this magnitude, or the car. The estate lawyer must have sensed this, for as soon as the reading of the will was finished he advised that if I did not wish to move into the house immediately, he knew of a newly appointed judge who would be willing to rent the former home of Judge Michael Valentine while his new home was being built. I readily agreed, with the condition that the car could remain in the garage.

I feared greatly if I did not find a purpose for my life, or at least a safe harbor to find solace from drifting in my sea of despair, I would find myself wallowing in a wasted life of dipsomania. I had lost all desire to write the book on the courthouse tragedy, although I knew I had been so close. I could never return to Hillsville. To Nellie.

I phoned the Richmond Associated Press office, and found out that David Lawrence would be there on the following Thursday. I left a message asking him to phone me when he arrived. He did, and I met him at the office.

"Good to see you Jeremiah," David said as he stood up to shake my hand. His face stiffened as if he were looking down at a cadaver.

"I've been good, just a little under the weather," I lied. "I think the mountain air gave me the grippe. I was hoping you might have some work for me, or at least help me find something."

"Oh, have you finished your book? I'll be excited to read it."

"No. I've laid it aside for awhile. I didn't find the information I needed to complete it. So do you know of anything?"

"Well, actually I do. I don't know if you'd be interested though. I know I would be, if I wasn't tied to that damn D.C. office."

"What is it?"

"I know you've been keeping up with what's going on in Europe. You know England will be jumping into the mess any day now."

"Yes, I think you're right," I said, not letting on that I had been oblivious to any events of the last month. "They can't ignore the inevitable much longer."

"Well, a friend of mine that I know from Harvard is putting together a volunteer group of ambulance drivers to work in the war..."

"Ambulance Driver? Why would I want a job as an ambulance driver?"

"Because," he said, "they're not about to let a journalist come to the front lines to report what's truly going on there."

He gave me an insidious grin. I wasn't quite sure what he was getting at. Then it came to me. Of course. If I were there as an ambulance driver, I'd be right in the thick of things and could file reports that might be read across the nation, or even around the world.

"How long do I have to decide?"

"Richard said they are training drivers now in London. They hope to send the first group to France by November. It's to be called the American Volunteer Motor Ambulance Corps. But he said there's already a large number of enlistees. I think you need to decide quickly if you want to go."

It required little consideration. If I remained in Richmond, it was a good chance I'd continue drinking. Instead, I could go to Europe, serve a good cause, and perhaps gain national recognition as a journalist. The money wasn't even important, as I now had enough to live a comfortable life, and in one of the most beautiful houses in Richmond. Perhaps this might be the opportunity to become a man that my father, and Judge Valentine, would be proud of.

"Call your friend and tell him he's got the best ambulance driver in Richmond," I said with a laugh.

"Great. I'll call him today. Come by the office tomorrow, I'll let you know what he wants you to do, and I'll tell you about the type of stories we are going to be looking for."

So in October, 1944, I found myself in the city of my favorite author, Charles Dickens, walking the streets I had read about on the pages of the first edition copies in Judge Valentine's library.

Richard Norton, the forty-year old founder of the American Volunteer Motor Ambulance Corps, was a nice enough old chap, to use the British vernacular. Apparently he had been living in England and with his aristocratic air of confidence, and the use of a monocle, he appeared every bit the English Gentleman instead of an American.

He had witnessed the horrors of how soldiers were coming back from the front after riding for hours in the back of a horse-drawn cart. That is when he decided motor vehicles could get casualties back to hospitals much quicker, thus saving lives.

The first drivers had departed for the front lines the day I arrived for training. Naturally, our primary job was driving the ambulance, although some of the volunteers had never driven a vehicle in their life, having always been driven by the family chauffeur. We were also taught extensive first aid procedures.

On January 5th, 1915, I shipped out to the front lines. The France I found was far removed from the idyllic country I had read about. The long months of war had already turned its people into what reminded me of a beaten dog, once proud, but now whimpering, slipping off with cowered head and tail tucked between its legs. It made me angry that a foreign invader had done this to the country that had produced such great soldiers as Lafayette and Napoleon.

Anyone who had thought their life of an ambulance driver would be glamorous was sorely mistaken. Days and weeks were spent with little or no action. Most drivers filled this slack time by seeking out the company of local peasant girls, and drinking until the rooster crowed, then sleeping throughout the day. I chose to do neither of these. Sir Norton, as we called him, was kind enough to loan me books from his extensive library. I devoured action books by authors such as Mark Twain and Jack London. I would read until I fell asleep at night. Then my dreams would be haunted by Nellie Wisler.

The last major engagement had been the Battle of the Marne back in September before I arrived. There appeared to be an increase in skirmishes though, as both sides positioned themselves for strategic locations in what would become trench warfare. As a consequence, my reports back to David Laurence and the Associated Press related more to the civilian hardships and sacrifices than actual battle reports. They were well received though by the American people starving for news of what was happening nearly half way around the world.

On March 2nd we were instructed to load up our gear and we were relocated a little more to the north to a small farming village called La Bassee. We were restricted to the base hospital we worked out of, so we knew a battle was eminent. The scuttlebutt was that the First Army was hoping to drive the Germans from the town of Aubers and Lille.

We were awakened on the morning of March 10th to cannon fire that sounded as if it was within a mile distance, but was in reality about fifteen. We were immediately rousted from bed and told to 'make ready'. The first ambulances were dispatched around noon.

I didn't go out the first day as the British troops under General Haig made surprisingly easy progress. On the second day, it was apparent things had escalated. I was dispatched about 9 AM. I made five trips carrying British casualties, along with Indian casualties who were fighting along with the Brits. We did not get to bed until after midnight, and were told to be ready to roll out by daylight.

I arose around six the next morning. Little did I know that my life would be changed dramatically over the events of the next four hours.

I had made three pickups and was almost back to the field hospital when the left front wheel of my ambulance dipped as if I had run into a rut. The car came to a screeching halt. I got out to find the front axle broken. An ambulance following pushed mine to the side; we doubled up our casualties, and I rode back to the hospital. There were no other units available, but we were running low on medics, so I was told to go out on the next ambulance as a medic.

We picked up one casualty, but I could tell he wouldn't make it as his pulse was already barely detectable. Then an officer approached us. Two medics bore a German soldier on a stretcher.

"Get this man back to the hospital, and get him patched up." The officer said. "We suspect he's intelligence, and we hope to get some vital information from him."

I climbed into the back with the already dead soldier, and the German, who appeared to only have superficial wounds. When I removed his jacket to begin dressing his injuries, I saw the blood staining his shirt just below his left rib cage. Protruding was a piece of shrapnel.

"Am I injured badly?" The German said.

I looked at him in surprise.

"Not too bad," I said "Just shrapnel. But you'll have to remain still until we get you back to the hospital. Why do you speak such perfect English."

"I graduated from the Massachusetts Institute of Technology in Boston as a Mechanical Engineer."

"Oh I see," I said.

"Where did you go to school? You are American, am I correct?"

"Yes, I am American." I answered, then remembered that the officer might be intelligence. I considered, then answered, "I graduated from Richmond College. In Virginia."

"Ah, a beautiful state. Very historical."

I just nodded.

"Are you married?" he asked.

"My wife...," I said, then added, "no, I'm not."

"I am," he said. "Here permit me to show you a photo of my wife and child."

He pulled a folded picture from his shirt pocket. He attempted to hand it to me, but it dropped to the floor.

"I am so clumsy," he said. "Please be so kind as to pick it up for me."

I bent to pick up the picture. I saw a lovely woman, holding a child, standing in front of a modest house. I turned to hand it to him.

"She is very..." I started to say, just before I saw the thick glass medical bottle, being swung toward my head. It was the last thing I would remember for weeks.

For the second time in my life, I found myself opening my eyes to an angel. After a few attempts at focusing, I realized it was actually a nurse but in the brilliant light shining through the window, she had taken on a divine aura. She had her back turned to me, tending to someone in the adjacent bed.

"May I have a drink of water?" I asked

She whirled around, stared at me wild eyed, and dashed out of the room. I could only imagine that I had a horrific disfiguring of my face. Within minutes a doctor rushed through the door with the nurse behind him. He immediately began shining a light into my eyes. He finally spoke.

"Mr. Haynes, do you know where you are?"

"I assume I'm in a field hospital."

"Actually you're at the Southern General Hospital in Birmingham. Can you remember anything that happened?"

I squeezed my eyes, trying to draw from the dark recesses of my memory.

"I can remember making it to the front.," I answered slowly. "We picked up a casualty. I then remember us being told to bring a German officer back."

That was when things began getting fuzzy. It was like I was just remembering flashes of events. Then it came to me.

"I remember him dropping something," I said. "Yes, it was a picture. A picture of his family. I bent to pick it up."

"Do you remember what happened then?" The doctor asked.

"I remember turning back toward him. He was sitting partially up on the stretcher. I remember he was swinging a heavy glass bottle toward me. Then, well, that's all I remember."

The doctor smiled.

"Well, there was quite a bit that happened following that, but I'm going to leave the telling of that story to Richard Norton. I'll call and let him know you're awake."

"Richard Norton? What does he have to do with it?"

"You might say you own your life to him," the doctor answered.

Later that day Richard Norton came to the hospital. After having the doctor examine me once again and finding me well enough to talk, Richard Norton started his story.

"Now what I'm telling you, old chap," he said, "is a compilation of what other's observed and what I have been able to find out. There are a lot of details that may not ever be truly known. Do you remember the German officer?"

"Yes, but barely."

"His papers showed his name to be Otto Schmidt, but there were some suspicions that he might have been intelligence, so his papers may have been fake. But irregardless, apparently he managed to knock you out. He then proceeded to change uniforms with you, including taking your identification."

"So he escaped? Dressed like me?"

"Well, I guess it just wasn't his day. He apparently jumped from the rear of the ambulance, right into the path of another ambulance, which immediately ran him down. Tore his body up quite a bit, it did."

"So he at least didn't get away."

"But you're forgetting he was wearing your uniform, and had your papers, so it was believed that *you* had fallen from the ambulance by accident, and had died."

"So, what happened to him, or me, or whoever was lying in the ambulance?"

"When they discovered you in the back of the ambulance, dressed in the German's uniform, unconscious with a serious head wound, it was just naturally thought that you were the German. You had his paperwork on you, and you weren't talking, so there was nothing that would make them think otherwise."

"So the German is dead, but thought to be me. So he's not talking. I'm unconscious, and thought to be the German. And I'm not talking. Am I getting this correct?"

"Yes. So they took you back to the field hospital. Now here is where it gets a little controversial. The doctors said that to operate on your brain injury would have meant certain death, but it's just quite possible that, intelligence officer or not, the doctors just weren't interested in saving the life of a kraut."

"So they just left him, or me, lying there?"

"Yes, I think they would have left you there till you died."

"But the doctor said I owned you my life."

"I guess this is where fate smiled upon you.. I had come to the hospital, as I often do, to check on the troops. I saw you lying there, and I immediately recognized you. I had somewhat a difficult time explaining how I knew you were an American, and not a German. But then it came down to one thing."

"And what was that one thing?"

"You and the German were almost the identical size, other than shoe size. The German's foot was 3 sizes larger than yours, so he was not able to change boots with you. I made them locate the boots you had been wearing when they brought you in. Sure enough, they were the boots you were issued when you joined the ambulance corps. Had your name stenciled on them."

"But how did I end up here?"

"I'm sure the field doctors were correct. If they operated on you, in that field hospital, you probably would have died. So I brought you back to Birmingham. They did surgery to relieve the pressure on your brain, and now, a week later, you are back among the living."

"So I do owe you my life," I said.

"No, not at all," he said, patting me on my shoulder and laughing. "I haven't lost a single driver since I started the corps. I wasn't about to have you break my streak."

"So what's now?" I asked.

"Well, old chap, I'm afraid your driving days are over. You'll have about three weeks of recovery, then I'm shipping you back to the US of A."

22

On the 21st of April, 1915, I celebrated my birthday back in Richmond. After spending two days getting caught up with sleep in my own bed, I went to the AP office hoping to find David Lawrence. He wasn't there, but they phoned the DC office and let me talk to him.

"Great to hear your voice, Jeremiah," he said. "I was overjoyed when I heard you hadn't been killed, that it had all been a big mix up."

"I guess I didn't know that you had been notified."

"Oh yes. Richard phoned me, since I had recommended you. I knew you didn't have any immediate family, so the only other person I told was your old editor, William Archer. I've never gotten back to him though. You should go by and let him see the good news himself."

"I'm sorry I wasn't able to get any good stories to you."

"What do you mean? The ones you sent were great human interest stories. You have a job anytime you want it. Besides, you're sitting on a great story. Take a few days and write down what happened to you. That will make a great article."

I thanked him and decided to immediately head down to see my old boss. I couldn't wait to see his reaction.

It was an hour before press time when I reached the office Everyone was so busy I walked into Mr. Archer's office unnoticed. He was bent over a layout, marking and editing as he wildly chewed on his cigar.

"I understand you're looking to hire a *'ghost writer.'* I said from the doorway.

"Who the hell told you..." he blurted as he whirled around, irate that he would be interrupted from his last minute editing. His cigar dropped to the floor.

"Good to see you Mr. Archer," I said with a chuckle.

The old man did something I never thought I'd live to see. He ran across the floor, grabbed me in a bear hug and lifted me completely off the floor, not an easy feat as he stood half a foot shorter than me. I swear I believe I heard him crying.

The editor then did a second thing I never thought I'd live to see him do. He went to the door, told his secretary to not let anyone disturb us, and then just came into the office, sat down with me on his sofa, and listened to my story.

When I finished, he just sat there shaking his head.

"That is an amazing story," he said. "You are going to let us have the exclusive, aren't you.?

I remembered the interest David Lawrence had expressed, and knew the AP would probably pay four times more than the Journal could pay, but I still couldn't say no to the crotchety old man.

"Yes, sir, as soon as I can get to it. For now though, I need to get word back down in Hillsville to let my relatives know that, as Mark Twain said, the rumors of my death are greatly exaggerated."

"There's one other person who will be very excited to see you. Nellie Wisler."

"Nellie? Why do you say that?"

"About a week after you left for Europe, she came by my office. I had talked to David Lawrence, so I knew about your 'adventure'. She was extremely upset when she found out you had left for the war."

"That surprises me," I said. "Things hadn't ended well when I left the mountains."

"I gathered that. As I said, she got extremely emotional, and kept telling me she had made a grave mistake, and had hoped to come to Richmond to beg you to forgive her."

I had promised myself the year before that I would never return to Hillsville, but after hearing that Nellie had followed me to Richmond, I felt perhaps there was still hope.

I contemplated if I should send advance notice, perhaps a telegram, but felt it was something best done in person. I knew I should have been ecstatic while riding to Hillsville, but for some reason I felt a perplexing sense of dread. I considered it to be merely anxiety as to what would be my first words to Nellie.

I saw no one I knew at Blair Station or on my ride to Hillsville. The first person who recognized me was Mary Tate. She was just crossing the street to go from her cleaning job at the hotel to the Courthouse. I smiled at her with my best, 'No, I'm not a ghost, I'm still alive' grin.

"Hello, Mary. It's good to see you."

She showed only slight suprrise, just smiled for a few seconds, and said.

"I told Jeff you weren't dead."

"How did you know that?" I asked.

"I just knowed it. Jeff's over at the mercantile. I know he'll be mightly glad to see you."

I walked down the street to the mercantile and entered. Jeff stood at the counter, arguing the price of something like he always did. The young kid behind the counter looked up and eyed me as if trying to think where he knew me from, then a startled look spread over his face. By this time I was standing directly behind him. I placed my hand on his shoulder.

"Hey cousin," I said. "Seen any ghosts recently?"

Jeff whirled around so fast he knocked a box of cigars from the counter. His mouth dropped open as he saw me.

"I'll be damned. Mary was right."

He then grabbed me in a bear hug that nearly broke three ribs.

"Are you headed to the boarding house?" I asked.

"Yeah, but Annie and me don't live there no more. We live over in Fries now in one of the new company houses. They're a mite small compared to the boarding house, but it's all ours. I still come over on weekends to help Ma with supplies."

On the ride, I related to Jeff the story of how I was mistaken for dead. After I had finished the story, I asked what I had been thinking about for the last twenty-four hours.

"So how's Nellie doing?" I asked.

Jeff never took his eye off the road. I could see his jaw twitching as he seemed to be attempting to swallow an apple whole. He finally turned to me.

"Jeremiah, I'm sorry to tell you. She married a fellow and they live up in Bluefield now."

I truly felt as if my heart had dropped down to my belt buckle. I didn't know what to say, and Jeff didn't know how to respond.

"She followed me to Richmond, but I had already left," I finally said. "I just thought that meant..."

"She thought you had died. She took it hard. Real hard. She grieved for weeks. I really think she just needed to leave the area, so she married and moved to West Virginia."

I nodded. Neither of us spoke the rest of the journey. When we pulled into the yard, Annie sat on the porch, holding a baby in her arms. Mrs. Guynn sat in her rocking chair darning. For a moment, I thought I actually saw a smile break the old woman's stoic face. Annie jumped up and rushed to the porch.

"I guess we'll learn to listen to my sister," she said, then held the baby out. "Say hello to your new cousin Sarah."

I don't know if Annie had seen the emptiness in my eyes, and had guessed the reason, but holding baby Sarah helped take my mind off my heartache. The beautiful little girl, now about four months old, cooed as she smiled at me. I held her for the next hour until dinner was prepared. We took our pie and coffee back out on the front porch.

"So what else has happened since I left?" I asked.

"I guess the biggest news," Jeff said, "is that Jack Allen was shot and killed down at the foot of the mountain."

"You're kidding? What happened?"

"The official story is that he had stopped for the night at a so-called road house, but it's more than that. They claim that Jack and a young fellow named Willie McGraw started arguing over the courthouse shootout, and to boot McGraw was acting kinda frisky around a young filly named Hattie Houseman that Jack had taken a liking to."

"Willie McGraw, that name sounds familiar," I said.

"Yeah, he was in the courthouse the day of the shootout. But I heard some rumors that just don't add up."

"Really? Such as?"

"I think it might be a good idea for you to go speak to the young girl, Hattie Houseman. I understand if you take her a gift, she'll give you all the information you want."

The next day I went into town, purchased a dollar bottle of perfume that bore a French name, and started my trip down to the foot of Fancy Gap Mountain. I soon found the roadhouse Jeff had told me about. Sitting barefooted outside on the steps was a young girl of about eighteen wearing a well-worn dress of floral print. She watched me with wide eyes as I got off my horse and started toward the steps.

"Hello," I said. "Are you Hattie Houseman?"

"Yes sir, that's me." she answered, smiling to reveal a beautiful set of white teeth. Even dressed plainly, her hair barely brushed, it was clear why men would be attracted to her.

"Hattie, my name is Jeremiah Haynes. I'd like to ask you some questions about the night Jack Allen was shot."

She held her hand up over her eyes to shade them from the mid-day sun.

"Are you a police man? I've already told them all I know about it. I don't like to talk about it."

"No, I'm a writer," I said, then handing the bag to you. "By the way, I brought you a present from town."

She leaped from the steps, and within ten seconds had jerked the bag from my hands, opened the bottle, and was smelling the perfume.

"I've never talked to a writer before. This smells real good."

Then her face took the look of a little girl playing dress-up. She poured it into her hand and splashed it on like a man would cologne. The overwhelming scent assaulted my nostrils.

"This present only means we talk, right? Some people tells stories about me, but I'm a good girl. I don't do bad things."

I joined her on the steps. She turned the bottle of perfume up again, and dabbed some on several spots of her neck and behind her ears. She leaned over to let me smell, letting her neck brush against my lips. Her top two buttons were unfastened, and I could see she wore nothing underneath. I couldn't tell if she was naïve, or was perfectly adept at being coquettish, but it became very clear to me how some of these mountain men could lose their heads and kill each other for the attention of Hattie Houseman.

"Yes, Hattie, we will only talk. We can do it right here on the porch if you'd like. How much can you remember about that night?"

She leaned back with a nervous giggle, but then her eyes took on an almost hurt look.

"I remember a lot. Mr. Jack, he was a nice man. Every time he went to Mt. Airy, or to Greensboro, he'd bring me a present. I never did anything with him though. I just talked, and brought him something to eat and drink."

"The night it happened, how many men were here inside?"

"Oh, I'd say on and off, about eight for the whole night. Most of them left, but Mr. Jack, he sometimes spent the night. He was going to that night."

"Was Willie McGraw spending the night?"

"No, Willie didn't have the money to spend the night. He was just here drinking."

"So what did the two of them get into an argument over?"

"I think Mr. Jack thought Willie was spending too much time with me, so I think that started it. Do you think I'm pretty?" She said, as she began playfully smacking her knee against my leg. Her dress inched its way up her thigh.

"Yes Hattie, you're very pretty," I said, then turned so my knee distanced her from me. "So go on with your story."

"Then Willie kept bringing up things about the shootout at the courthouse. Saying if it had been him and his family, they'd've shot up the whole town. He made it sound like some of the Allens had been cowards. That's when they really got mean with each other."

"What happened then?"

"I don't rightly know, because I could tell they were real mad, so I went upstairs to bed. I heard a lot of racket. Then I heard at least one shot, but I think it was more.

I went running down stairs, and there laid Mr. Jack sprawled out on the floor."

"So do you think Willie shot him?"

"I thought he had. But Willie claimed they was wrestling together, face to face, and the gun went off. But Mr. Jack, he was bleeding out of his back. I don't see how Willie could have shot him in the back, and why the bullet didn't come through and hit him."

"Anything else you can tell me?"

"Well, the window got shot out someway."

"Was the glass from the window on the inside of the room, or the outside?"

"It was a whole lot on the inside. I know because I stepped on a piece and cut my foot. See," she said, lifting her foot up to rest on my lap. "Right here on the side."

That was exactly what I had hoped to hear. If the glass was on the inside, that meant the shot had to come from the outside of the house.

"Hattie, this is important. I want you to think back real hard. Was Willie McGraw doing anything strange that night? Anything he doesn't usually do here?"

"Willie, he don't come here. This was the first time I'd seen him. He don't usually have money, but he did that night."

"I see. Anything else you can think of?" I said.

"Willie, he acted real nervous. He kept going and looking out the window. I asked him who he was looking for, but he never answered. And then, when I came down stairs, after I heard the shots, he was standing there again, looking out the window."

"Did you ever see anyone outside that night?"

"No sir, but I have a feeling someone was out there."

"Hattie, did you ever find anything around after the shooting?" I said. "Maybe a religious tract?"

"I don't know what that is," she said. "But I did find a piece of paper folded up. I don't read good, so I don't know what it said."

"Do you still have it?" I asked.

"Oh no. It scared me because it had a picture of hell on it, so I threw it way."

I thanked the young girl for her time. She invited me to come back and see her anytime. She said she really liked the perfume, and she also liked chocolate candy. I said I would, but I knew I wouldn't.

Over the next several days I wrote an accounting of what happened in France, and sent it off to The Evening Journal. Several times I thought about boarding a train to Bluefield, just to let Nellie know I was alive. But I felt it would only keep the ache in my heart alive. I did decide to spend a few extra days with Jeff, Annie, and especially Baby Sarah in the new cotton mill town of Fries.

23

The next week, on a Saturday afternoon, I was sitting on the porch of the boarding house when I saw Jeff climb from his horse. He wore a dismayed look.

"I thought you'd want to know," he said. "I just saw Nellie Wisler leaving the train station. Preacher Wisler is dying."

"Yes. I do want to know. I'm going over there. I'll be back... well, I don't know when I'll be back."

I rode the five miles, taking time to think what I would say to Nellie, or to her husband if he was there. I wasn't afraid of him. In other circumstances, I'd almost wish him to start something. I think I would get some kind of satisfaction from smashing my fist into his face. To watch the blood flow freely from his mouth, his nose. To show him I was the better man. To show Nellie I was the better man. But I knew this was not the time, nor the circumstance.

But I never had to practice my self-constraint. When I rode into the yard, there sat Pastor Wisler, rocking in a chair. He had aged greatly since I had last seen him, but he was very much alive. He eyed me quizzically, I wasn't sure whether it was because he did not recognize me, or because I had such a shocked expression on my face.

"Sir, it's Jeremiah Haynes. Is Nellie here?"

"Son, I thought you were dead. Praise God you're not."

"No sir, it was a case of mistaken identification," I said, not wanting to go into details. "But Nellie's not here?"

"No son, she's not here. You do know she's a married woman now, living with her husband in Bluefield. She thought you were dead, but that doesn't matter now. She's married, so you need to leave her alone."

"I know that, but something strange is happening. I just talked to Jeff. He saw Nellie not two hours ago at the train station. He said she was very upset, that you were dying, and she was coming home to visit you."

The pastor stood up and taking his cane, walked to the edge of the porch.

"I've been ailing, but certainly not dying. That is strange. I wonder if the buggy has anything to do with it."

"What about the buggy?"

"I went to the barn this morning, and my horse and buggy is missing. Often Pastor Hamn borrows it, because he knows I never use it anymore, but he always leaves me a note when he'll have it back."

My thoughts went back to the times Nellie had told me that she often felt like she was being watched, and that at times she found strange notes in her room, and just thought someone was playing jokes on her. I looked at Pastor Wisler. He was wobbling on his cane, his face pale. I could tell he was very upset.

"Pastor Wisler, I hope I haven't upset you. I evidently misunderstood Jeff," I said "The next time you see your daughter, please give her my warmest regards. And tell her I hope she has a wonderful marriage."

I turned my horse and left the yard without hearing the pastor's reply. A chill swept from my neck, down my back into my legs. Nellie was in danger, I had no doubt of that fact. I knew that I had to find her.

My first thought was to ride back to Jeff's, and get him to get a search party together. The day was about to turn into evening, and the woods on both sides of the road were already dark. Just as I got near the road that led to the hunter's cabin that Nellie and I had waited out the thunderstorm nearly two years before, I saw a piece of paper fluttering in the wind, caught in a blackberry bush. I rode by, but something deep inside me urged me to go back. Returning, I leaned over in my saddle, and retrieved the pamphlet. I read the heading *The Wages of Sin is Death.* Flipping the paper over, I saw, written in pencil, today's date, the time 12:35 PM, and Blair Station. A heart was drawn around the name, Miss Nellie.

I got off and tied my horse to a bush. It was then I saw the wagon tracks in the mud. It had rained this morning, so the tracks had to have been left since then. I reached into the saddle bag, but the .32 Jeff usually carried was not there. A hunting knife was, so I took it. I crept up the path to the cabin. I was still 50 feet away when I recognized the pastor's buggy, his horse tied off to an apple tree. I swung in an arc to flank the horse so as to not spook him, and came in from the rear of the cabin. When I got to within twenty five feet I could hear the muffled voices. By the time I got to within ten feet, I recognized the voice of the man from three years previous in the stable. Then, I heard the unmistakable voice of Nellie Wisler Boyd.

"So I wasn't dreaming," she said. "That was you that came into my room that night when I was a child."

"Now when I passed by thee," he said in a sing-song tone, "and looked upon thee, behold, thy time was the time of love; and I spread my coat over thee, and covered thy nakedness: yea, I swear unto thee, and entered into a covenant with the Lord GOD, and thou becamest mine."

"Your words are embarrassing. You're scaring me."

"But they are from the Bible; they are God's word. He gave them to me. All I want to do Miss Nellie is to say sweet words to you each morning when we wake up, and each night before we go to bed. Pleasant words are as a honeycomb, sweet to the soul."

I heard Nellie wail, not with the weeping of a woman grieving, but almost hysterically, as if she were on the verge of panic.

"But I was just a child, I couldn't be your wife."

"You were the age of the Virgin Mother," he said. "God promised you to me ten years ago. I've never stopped loving you. Everything I did, I did for you. To give you beautiful things. No one else deserved you but me."

"They said you died," she said.

"Sometimes a person is better off if he's thought to be dead. He can carry out God's work better."

My first thought was to storm the cabin, but I knew I needed to be more prudent. I'm sure he was armed, and my knife would prove a poor equal. Easing myself to the window, I peeked through. No more than three feet away sat Nellie, tied to a chair. In front of her stood a man I knew had been my attacker, and now knew it was the man called Preacher Lucas."

"Mister Lucas, if you are a true man of God you must recognize the fact that I am married, and I can't marry you because divorce is a sin."

"You are not married in the eyes of God, because He promised me that you would be my bride. As long as you live with this other man, you are committing adultery. And besides, I can easily make you a widow. There is no sin against a widow re-marrying. And Miss Nellie, I promise you. If I can't have you, no one else will. Ever."

I watched him approach her, his eyes smoldered like men I had seen in the mental asylum in Richmond who were addicted to opiates. He knelt in front of her, and took her face in his hands. She twisted, repulsed by his touch. I immediately saw his shooting finger was missing. I could see Nellie's body shuddering. I knew I had to do something quickly, because this man had no concept of right or wrong.

I quickly retraced my steps to my horse, torturing my brain to come up with a plan. I remembered seeing Lucas's horse munching apples from the tree he was tied off to. Searching the saddle bag, I took a bottle of Sloan's Rubbing Liniment. I slowly approached the horse so as to not spook him. I removed from the horse's reach all but four apples. Taking two of those, I halved them with the hunting knife, and poured a generous dose of liniment on each half, then laid them back among the others. I then untied the horse from the tree. As I started back to the rear of the cabin, I saw the horse begin eating the tainted apples. Before I was barely by the porch, the horse began snorting, then neighing loudly. As hoped, he jerked free from the tree, desperate to find water to wash the scorching taste from his mouth. I was barely past the front door when Preacher Lucas came storming out. By that time the horse was thrashing through the brush. I ran to the back, raised the window and climbed through.

"Jeremiah!. she gasped. her eyes flooding with tears. "How... ?"

"Shh, we don't have time to talk," I said as I pulled my knife, and cut the ropes. "Lucas won't be gone long. We need to get out of here. I have a horse tied off down by the road, but we'll need to work our way around the ridge so he can't see us."

I cut the ropes, and drove the knife into the window sill. I had just started lifting her through the window when I heard footsteps on the front porch. I pushed her through the opening, hearing her crash to the ground, praying she wasn't injured. I whirled around just as Preacher Lucas started through the front door."

"Miss Nellie, I think it's time..." he said, and then saw me.

I rushed him. He drew his gun, and had it nearly leveled when I threw my body into him. I heard the blast, and felt the burning slash of pain as the shot skimmed my hip. We crashed through the open door onto the porch. My momentum carried me over top of him, and into the yard. His gun was knocked loose. He turned to grab it. I dived on top of him just as his hand reached it. He overmatched me in size and strength, and he finally gained control of the gun. He swung it across my head. I remember my last thoughts being, "he's cracked my head again."

When I opened my eyes, I realized I had been tied in the same chair that had held Nellie. My hands were free, but my arms tied back, tight enough so I had little movement. In front of me, sitting on the bed was Preacher Lucas.

"Reporter man, you just don't learn, do you? I thought I had killed you in the stable, but I'm going to make sure I do this time."

"Can you at least answer a few questions for me before you do? You owe me that much," I said, hoping I could at least buy some time.

Maybe Nellie would be able to bring help. I knew I had to do something. I wasn't afraid of dying, but I knew if I died, this psychopath would go on killing. I had to find a way not only to live, but to stop him. I saw his lips twitch, and a little sparkle appeared in his normally void eyes, but quickly disappeared. I could tell I had him hooked.

"I guess that will be ok. Dead men don't talk. What do you want to know?"

"Well, speaking of dead men. Why did you let people think you were dead?" I asked.

"There are some people who wanted me dead. If they thought I was, that would leave me to finish God's work."

"And what is God's work?"

"To bring power to the righteous, and to send the wicked to the deepest depths of hell."

"I thought the Bible tells us to "judge not, lest we be judged," I said, grateful for the Bible scripture quizzes Miss Zarfous and Miss Hess used to give me during vacation Bible school.

I saw a cloud sweep over his eyes, and for a moment, I was sure he was going to shoot me. I tried to hide my overwhelming fear from him. By this time it had turned to darkness outside

"I don't judge! I am His Avenging angel. I only bring vengeance upon those that are deserving."

"So God tells you who these people are? The ones that you need to seek revenge upon?"

"God. And others."

"Others? You mean other people? Maybe other people like Thomas Felts."

"Mr. Felts is a righteous man. He has the wisdom of Solomon. Many people possess knowledge, but wisdom must come from God."

"How many people have you killed?" I asked.

He looked at me, weighing his words.

"Several."

"What about Byrd Marion?"

"Byrd Marion died in prison," he said giggling.

"Byrd died in prison, but he was beaten to death." I said.

I saw an evil smirk twist Lucas' mouth.

"Yeah, it's amazing how easy it is to get jobs as a guard in those West Virginia prisons."

"What about Win Phaup?"

Another smirk.

"I thought I was going to be able to kill two birds with one stone on that one."

"You mean me and Phaup?"

"You always had that judge fellow in Richmond getting you out of scrapes. Like in Richmond, then when I planted that pea shooter on you."

"It was you that slipped that derringer in my pocket at the courthouse?"

He erupted with a demonic laugh that sounded like the bad notes from a fiddle.

"That was pretty slick, wasn't it? He said. "Pretending I was some drunk. Slipping that gun into your pocket."

"How much did Deck Goad pay you to do that?" I asked.

His eyes hardened.

"Mr. Goad didn't know nothing about it. I did it for him."

"Why did you do it, if he didn't tell you to?"

"Cause you have tried to overthrow the righteous from their place of authority, for their just punishment of wicked men," he said. "You needed to be stopped."

"Why did you kill Jack Allen?"

"Jack Allen was a liar, and he corrupted young innocent women."

"How many more did you kill?"

"There were a few in West Virginia. In the coal fields. They have nothing to do with you."

"So why do you think God wants you to kill me?"

By this time, the evening had turned to night. I could barely make out his image. He lit the kerosene lamp on the table, and brought it over to me. He squatted down and raised the light to my face.

"You have done everything in your power to bring disgrace to those that have tried to bring justice to a Godless land. Nothing you can do will make sheep out of those Allen wolves."

"And God thinks I should die for that?"

"That, and because you have tried to defile Miss Nellie."

"Defile her? What do you mean? I've never had anything but respect for her."

"I've seen how you look at her. The carnal lust in your eyes. I should have killed you the day you were here in this cabin. If I had thought you had forced yourself on her, I would have. But I knew she would never do it without being forced."

"You were here?"

"I was here then, and I was in the woods when you and Jeff Haynes returned from the funeral. I was even in your room once. I could have killed you the day you left for Richmond, but that would have been too easy."

"Why don't you let me be the last person you kill. Leave Nellie out of this. If you truly love her, you won't bring her any more sorrow."

"You can't be the last. With Claude gone, with you gone, and soon, with her husband gone, she will then know that it is God's will for her to be with me."

"You really know a lot about the entire shootout, don't you?" I said.

"Yes, I do, and I have it all down on paper. In my saddlebag. I'm going to write a book and then I'll have more money than Sidna Allen, or Mr. Felts, or George Lafayette Carter all put together. She'll want to marry me then."

I knew I had little time left; that something had to be done now. I again tested the ropes holding my arms to the chair. My legs were free. How could I use them? Then I saw his eyes turn as black as a moonless midnight, and I watched as he pulled his gun from its holster.

Not knowing what else to do, in one motion I pushed the chair backward, kicking outward with my feet. My left foot kicked the gun just as he leveled it. My right foot hit the table, flipping the oil lamp. I heard a blast, and waited to feel the searing pain of a bullet. Instead, I saw him simultaneously drop the gun and grab his side. I heard a crash as the oil lamp hit the floor. My chair tipped backwards, stopping against the window sill.

I saw the broken lamp leak its fuel onto the hard wood floor. An instant later, it burst into a flickering blaze.

Preacher Lucas, laid there against the bed, the blood oozing between his splayed fingers. The fire lashed along the path of spilled kerosene onto his pants leg. His pants became a fireball. Then his shirt. He looked at me, his eyes now cloudy with incomprehension. The melody of the ravenous flames devouring cloth was broken by his low guttural whimpering. It came not as a prolonged scream. More a random huffing. Almost like the sound of a diesel locomotive just starting up.

He dropped to the floor, and began slapping at the flames as if it were a swarm of bees. He grabbed a wool blanket from the bed. Wrapping it around him, he succeeded in partially extinguishing the flames. He threw the fiery blanket back onto the bed, catching the feather tick on fire. Raising himself to a knee, he stood before me, clothing hanging like strips blowing on a clothes line, his body blackened. The smell reminded me of a time once, when I was a child and visited my Uncle Garn's farm, he had killed a hog and scalded it in a huge vat of water.

Preacher Lucas reached down, his hands shrouded with blood, and picked up the gun. He aimed at my head.

"With her enticing speech… She caused him to yield," he said in a labored, sing-song voice. With each phrase, he appeared to gush smoke. "With her flattering lips… She seduced him… He went after her like… An ox goes to his slaughter… Like fool… To stockade… Till arrow strikes… His liver… As bird… Hastens… To the snare… He did not… Know it would… Cost… His life."

I looked into the nefarious eyes of the Prince of Darkness himself, sprung from the very depths of Hell. I took a deep breath. My last breath. At least I knew Nellie would never have to worry. I closed my eyes, not to escape the inevitable, but so my final memory would not be of evil.

I heard an explosion. I grimaced. Then I heard a second, a third, a series. I opened my eyes to see the entire bed an inferno of flames, fueled by bottles of blockade liquor stored beneath the cot. The silhouette of Preacher Lucas stood before me, a feral lamentation drawn out in a banshee howl, before he crumbled into the pits of Hell.

I scanned the bed, engulfed in flames. I knew within minutes, so would the rest of the cabin, including me. Even if I could push my chair across the floor, access to the door was totally blocked by a curtain of fire. My only escape would be through the window. I knew there was no way I could raise the chair up enough to push myself through it. I leaned my head back to escape the heat. I felt something press against my shoulder. It was the hunting knife I had brought from the wagon and had stuck into the window sill. Raising on my toes, I hoisted my body up enough to begin rubbing the ropes against the knife blade. Up and down. Up and down. The heat now overwhelming. I knew I only had minutes. I felt a loosening of my arms and realized that some of the ropes had been cut through. I furiously pushed up and down. Only a few more left at the very top. I tried to shift the chair to cut the upper ropes. I felt the knife shift, and suddenly, it fell to the floor.

I watched as the flames leaped from the feather tick to the wooden posts. I knew I only had one last hope. I stood up enough to spin the chair around, then I pushed it back against the bed post. The flames flickered up the post, as I tilted the chair back. I could feel the heat through my jacket. I knew my hair would catch fire any second, but I could smell the ropes burning. I shrugged my shoulders up and down. I was almost free. I smelled the singeing of my hair, and felt the heat burning through my coat. I was on fire.

With one last thrust, I jerked my arms forward, and felt the final rope give way. I jumped to my feet, and threw myself through the open window. My coat and hair were ablazed. I ripped the coat off. I smacked at the hair. I rolled on the ground until the fire was finally extinguished. I turned in time to watch the roof come crashing down, sending tiny fireballs forty feet into the air.

I ran to a safe distance, then fell to the ground, spent. Lying there in the grass, the burns threatening to put me into shock, I remembered what Preacher Lucas had said about his notes. I stumbled to his buggy. Sure enough, beneath the seat laid a black couriers satchel with the inscription B-F Detective Agency embossed upon the flap.

I opened it to find a dozen of the "Wages of Sin is Hell" tracts. I pulled what had to be a hundred pages of handwritten notes, along with some typewritten pages that appeared to have been ripped from a binder. The moon and the fire to my back offered sufficient illumination to read. I flipped to the final page, with the last week's date shown at the top. I began to read the handwritten notes;

Sent telegraph to Nellie today. Know she'll return to me if she thinks her father is dying.

Nellie arriving on tomorrow morning's train. Need to steal Pastor Wisler's horse and wagon tonight. This will be her last chance. If she doesn't accept God's will, it will be His will for all of them to die. Her and her family today. Then go to Bluefield to kill her husband. I won't quit until I find the reporter. It's all his fault.

Leaving to pick up Nellie today. God told me last night that she would be mine before the end of today.

That was the last entry. I turned to the first page, which was dated nearly ten years earlier.

God has told me that I must have Nellie Wisler as my life if I'm expected to do His Work. I will go to her tonight, and like the angel Gabriel that visited the virgin mother, I will bring the virgin Nellie tidings of great joy.

His next entry read;

Nellie did not have a chance to accept my proposal. Her father came in. But I will not stop until she is mine.

I then began leafing through the loose pages, scanning them to find familiar names. The first ten pages detailed attempts he made to contact Nellie Wisler. Notes and flowers he had left for her, unsigned letters he had mailed. Then on the eleventh page, I read.

Those infidels Allens shot up the courthouse today. I'll make sure Nellie's pretty boy Claude will die.

A later entry read;

Got job with Baldwin-Felts Detective Agency. God has promised that I will be an instrument of His vengeance upon the wicked of this county.

A re-occurring theme throughout the pages were Bible scriptures that were written to justify each deed he performed, or planned on performing.

As the flames licked the night sky, I read page after page detailing his actions; threats, beatings, anything to turn up any information on the whereabouts of the Allens and Edwards still at large.

I then read an entry that sickened me. It read;

Jeff Haynes $50: Allen and Edward hiding out at Devil's Den.

I re-read a second time. I could only hope that Jeff, like so many others, fed false information to the detectives to give Sidna and his nephew time to escape. It nevertheless made me wonder what would happen to Jeff if this word got out.

I turned the pages, continuing to read random entries.

Iroler paid $200 for information on Edwards and Allen. I asked to go to Iowa to get them, but Mr. F. told me I had more important work to do here.

Took train to Moundsville.

Got job today as security guard at West Virginia State prison.

Marion will not talk again. $100

Found out Phaup is telling things.

Took train to Richmond.

Took care of Phaup $100

Heard reporter got off. I'll take care of him.

I continued to scan the page, finding familiar names, both of high officials and of Allen supporters. Some typewritten pages that had appeared to have been ripped from a notebook listed initials, money paid, and what the recipients were expected to do for the money. The faster I leafed through the pages, the faster my heart raced. There were dates, locations and names that connected various Baldwin-Felts agents and officials with high ranking local and state officers. One of the directives suggested by the detective agency, and agreed to by a local official ordered all the guns that had been used in the shootout be 'seized by whatever means necessary, and disposed of in a permanent manner'.

I felt as giddy as a young boy on Christmas morning. Names began jumping out at me. A pyramid of information was being built. At that moment, I knew the missing links to my chain of information had been supplied. My book could be written. I dreamed of the literary honors that would await me.

I heard horses approaching in a gallop. Suddenly, I felt solicitous. I knew I had to make a decision. A very tough decision. One that would change what I had dared envisioned my future to be. I had waited my whole life to write something that would make me famous. I literally held that opportunity in my hand.

Sure it bothered me that people I knew, and had grown close to, might suffer repercussions. Even physical. Maybe even death. Although some of the actions may have been innocent, taken here, out of context, I was sure that a lot of people, both good and bad, stood to suffer irreparable harm from these notes. Just then I saw the name of Joel Victor Bowman, the man Nellie had married. My blood chilled at what I then read.

But wouldn't the good, outweigh the bad? After all, I had to respect Floyd Allen's final wish, didn't I?

Then, it was as if the whole world stopped turning. There was total silence. With complete lucidity, I heard a voice. A familiar voice. A voice I had spent hours listening to in a jail cell on death row in Richmond,

Virginia. As clear as if he were standing beside me, I heard Floyd Allen's voice say, "You've found the truth. It was only for you, and no one else."

At that moment I knew I did not have to have fame to find fulfillment in my life. I walked to the inferno before me, and threw the satchel and its contents inside.

I watched as the flames reached for the stars. The pages of notes were soon but mere ashes, borne upon Gossamer wings to all points of this mountain that Floyd, Claude, and now Jack Allen had loved so much. In their eyes, they had died defending this mountain, and their way of life.

Jeff and Nellie were the first to arrive. Nellie had gone immediately to my cousin's, and the two had rushed back, not sure of what they would find. She rushed up to me.

"Are you alright? She said, as she hugged me. "Preacher Lucas, is he ... ?"

"I'm fine, just a few burns," I said. "Preacher Lucas, he'll never be a threat to you again."

"You saved me from him. You saved all of us," she said, then she took my face in her hands. "You're alive. Thank God. But I heard you were dead."

I spent the next ten minutes rehashing my mistaken demise.

"Mr. Archer said you had come to Richmond," I said, "to tell me you were sorry."

"Yes. I did love you. Believe me. But I just felt I would betray Claude if I ever married. But after three months of not seeing you, I knew just how much I did love you."

"So what happened?"

"I went to Claude's grave," she said. "I prayed by his tombstone. Suddenly it was so clear to me that he would want me to be happy. I knew he'd want me to be with you, because his father had liked you so."

"That's when you came to Richmond?"

"Yes, just a few weeks later. I found out you had left. I promised myself I'd wait for you to come back. But then, we got the word you had died. Oh Jeremiah, I thought I'd die. I had only loved two men in my life, and both were taken from me."

"Well, as you can see, I'm ok," I said, trying to console her. "So you're married now?" I said, the words leaving me numb.

"Just before I heard you had died, my daddy remarried, and we all moved to Bluefield. Joel attended our church there. He asked me out several times, but I kept saying no. But after I heard you had died, I needed someone. He is very kind, and is a wonderful husband."

"I'm glad you're happy," I said, choking back my emotions.

She pulled a necklace from her dress. On it hung a crude crucifix.

"After I heard you died, I slipped the wedding band you left onto the necklace with the band Claude gave me. When I got married, I knew that would not be proper, so I had a goldsmith in Bluefield melt down both rings, and make them into a cross. I always have it here, near my heart. I hope that was ok."

"That's wonderful," I said. "I hope it will always help you remember me."

She smiled, that smile that I always wanted to spend the rest of my life looking at, the smile I wanted to wake up to, and grow old with. She kissed me on the cheek.

"I promise I always will."

Within the next half-hour, more than a dozen people had come, including Sheriff Edwards. Nellie and I said our goodbyes there at the cabin, the place I had first kissed her. The place I had first lost my heart to her. In a way, as she and I stood, staring into the glowing embers, it was the closure we both needed to a chapter of our lives that I think we both would remember, but we both knew had come to an end.

24

The next morning, as I had promised, Jeff and I rode into town.

I explained the circumstances to sheriff Edwards. I had never asked again for the interview with the former deputy and witness to the shoot-out. I did not think this was the time to ask now. Deck Goad sat in the corner. I did not tell them what Preacher Lucas had told me, other than he had meant to either marry Nellie Wisler, or kill everyone in her family. I did not tell them the confessions Preacher Lucas had made to me, or of his notes I had burned. I had to keep some of my dignity. After hearing this, and with the promise that I would never print any future articles, and would never return to Carroll County, they decided that I had acted in self-defense, and all charges would be dropped.

On the way out of town, I saw Mary Tate sitting on the courthouse wall eating an apple. She motioned me to come closer, then she whispered.

"Mr. Floyd came to me last night. He said you did good. You found the truth about them, and the truth about you."

I returned to Richmond and worked once again at the *Evening Journal.* William Archer retired, and convinced the owners to hire me as editor at the ripe old age of 28. I served as editor until the paper folded, then I went on to purchase five newspapers throughout central and northern Virginia. I married, and had four children, two daughters, and two sons.

Preacher Lucas' notes had burned in that cabin fire many years ago, but the memory of my investigation had indelibly burned itself into my mind. I kept my promise to Carroll County. I never printed another article on the Hillsville Courthouse Tragedy of 1912.

What I did do though was to write a manuscript which will become a family heirloom. Instead of a true accounting though, it is a fiction. Some truths just should not be reported. This way, I can honor those I wish, but leave the punishment of mountain injustice to a power greater than I.

I promised the courts I would not return to the county, but I never promised my story wouldn't. My hope is that one day, maybe a hundred years after the tragedy, one of my heirs will decide the time has come to publish my book. That is my dream, that one day a grandson, or a great-grandson, will stand on the steps of that very same courthouse, if it is still standing, and reveal my story.

I never saw Nellie Wisler after that night at the cabin, but I never stopped loving her, for she had restored me.

Prologue

Dexter Goad jerked upright in bed. His heart pounded so rapidly, so intensely, that he thought his ear drums were going to rupture. Breathing came fast and heavy, like the exhaust of one of the old Norfolk and Southern steam engines. Was he having a heart attack? His mind swam through the murky waters of semi-wakeness until he began to crawl out onto the shore of consciousness. He blinked his eyes, trying to focus on what had stirred him. The darkness of the night revealed no intruders.

This was not unusual. The former Carroll County Clerk of the Court had not had a week of good sleep since the Courthouse shootout in 1912, some 27 years before. But tonight was different. Although it was a sweltering July night, Dexter felt chilled, the same kind of damp, bone numbing iciness he felt when, as a child, he would go into the spring house to get milk. The smell was also similar; musty, fetid, like decaying leaves or dirt, that always seemed present in the dairy. He threw off the light sheet, and swung his legs to the side of the bed to shut the opened window.

An unseen hand, or rather force, slammed him back to the bed.

"Who the hell's there?" he snapped.

A breeze rippled the curtains away from the window. They then fluttered back into place.

"I said who the hell's there? You'd best tell me or I'll, ..."

A voice, no, not really a voice, more of a mono-syllable tenor note, riding a putrid gust into the room, barely perceptible, but distinct, weakened Dexter.

"Floyd", was the chilling answer.

The single word plunged an icicle into Dexter's heart. He again tried to rise, but the unseen presence now pinned him to the bed.

"The only Floyd I've ever known was Floyd Allen," he answered in a wilting voice, "and he's six-feet under down at Wisler's Cemetery. You'd best tell me who you are if you don't want a hole blown through your chest."

"Floyd Allen," the voice spat.

Dexter felt a familiar pressure on his chest that brought back a memory. He was 14 years old and had gotten jumped by Floyd Allen. The older boy had knocked him to the ground, then jumped on him, digging his knees into Dexter's chest. Floyd had claimed he had stolen two half-dollars from his younger brother Sidna. That's not how he remembered it though. Now, nearly a half century later, he again felt those gaunt knees pressing him to the bed. He instinctively covered his face, awaiting the fists he had felt that day a lifetime ago. Instead, he heard the sound of metal clanging against metal, and then a clasp, or a hinge, of some kind being opened. He swung his left arm the best he could to strike out at the specter. Something snapped tightly around his wrist, jerking his hand back to the bed. With a clank, he felt his wrist secured to the bottom rail of the old cast iron head board. When he struck out with his right, he heard the same sound, and instantly his right hand was tightly fastened to the opposite side. He struggled against the manacles, but only felt the pain of metal bands biting into his wrists. He wrested until he felt blood dripping from his hands.

Just when he thought he was going to lose consciousness from the weight on his chest, the pressure abated. Dexter immediately tried to swing his legs to the side of the bed, but it was too late. His left ankle was jerked down, feeling as if his knee joint would be separated. The cinching of a shackle around his foot made him scream. Within seconds, the other leg had been splayed, and Dexter found himself drawn between the four corners of the bed. The only part of his body that could be raised was his head.

"Why are you doing this?" he pleaded.

"Revenge," was the answer.

"Revenge? For what," he whimpered.

"Revenge, because you caused it all." came the distant intonation.

"But I wasn't the first to fire, I swear to God I wasn't, it was..."

"But you was the cause," the voice interrupted.

The sound of a chain first striking the side of the headboard, and then being dragged toward the opened window echoed throughout the room.

"This can't be happening. You died in the electric chair, in Richmond nearly thirty years ago. I've gotta be dreaming."

Dexter felt a skeletal hand wrap around his throat, halting his breathing for a moment.

"And so did my son. You killed us both as sure as if you'd thrown the switch."

The hand uncoiled from the man's throat.

Dexter smelled that undeniable scent so prevalent during the summer time. One that you first smell, then you get that coppery taste on the tip of your tongue, and then eventually, you have the first sighting, far in the distance, of lightning. It first came as a flickering light, like a lamp about to run out of oil. Then seconds later, the light appeared again, closer, brighter. Then the rumbling sound of thunder rolled into the bedroom. A clammy mist, denser than any fog he had ever witnessed on Fancy Gap Mountain, boiled through the window. Within seconds his body was drenched.

"Why have you come back now?" Dexter said.

"So I can rest. An eye for an eye," the ghostly voice answered.

A lightning bolt flashed just outside the window, illuminating the room. Dexter Goad saw an image of a man, his eyes wide but sunken, his black moustache accentuated against a cadaverous face, his suit charred, silhouetted against the night sky. One skeletal finger slowly raised and pointed at the man shaking uncontrollably in his bed, while in the other hand, he dangled a logging chain out the window. Turning his head, Dexter saw the other end of the chain attached to the iron headboard.

Another lightning bolt struck the chain. Dexter Goad felt his heart pounding, barely able to breathe because in that moment he realized what was about to happen. He knew his last sight would be of Floyd Allen. Suddenly Dexter's eyes erupted as if a million lightning bugs had taken flight. His body felt as if it were a throw rug, being shaken to free itself of dirt and grime. His arid mouth gasped for just one more breath. His palpitating heart felt swollen as large as a head of cabbage. His moribund thoughts were of a hawk taking flight, its wings starting slowly, and then speeding as it soared. As his final heartbeats sped to a continuous rhythm, Dexter Goad plummeted into a dark abyss, filled with spent gun powder, screams, and gunshots. Then, there was nothing, except a dispassionate voice whispering in an imperceptible voice that grew faint, disappearing into the night.

Mary Tate woke from her bed. The lightning flashed outside the raised window. In the midst of a bolt, she saw a gaunt figure. Although it had been nearly 30 years, she recognized the stern, but admirable countenance, and heard the soft voice saying, "Lil' Mary, it's time to finish it."

"Where you off to in the middle of the night?" Mary's husband asked as she swung herself from the bed.

"I expect I need to go meet Dr. Branscome."

The response did not surprise Lee. Over the last twenty-five years, at least a hundred times he had heard similar words. It was usually to birth a baby on her own. But when it was something to do with Dr. Branscome, Mary always knew before the doctor even arrived at their house. He had been skeptical of her gift of sight when they first met, but he had witnessed it enough to accept it, not as something evil, but rather divine. She never used it for her personal gain.

She quickly dressed, then opened up the drawer of the hall buffet, and removed an old snap purse. She checked the contents, then placed it into her smock. Usually the doctor drove his Model-A to pick her up, but she was sure he had not been notified yet. He didn't really need her help on this night, but she did have things she needed to do. She threw a blanket over the riding horse and slipped a bridle over his head. Gathering her dress in front, she jumped up, throwing her stomach across the horse, then swung her leg over.

"Come on Old Floyd," she clucked as she snapped the reins, "It's time we finish this."

An hour later she was in front of Dexter Goad's house. She could see the headlights of the Model-A bouncing up the street. The Model-A chugged to a halt, and the old doctor got out.

"What are you doing here Mary, this isn't a birthing?"

"I know Doc, I just needed to be here is all."

Doc Branscome learned years ago not to question Mary, for she knew things that he would never understand. He was a man of science, but she was a woman who defied science. Since he had trained her 25 years earlier to be a midwife, she had delivered nearly as many babies as he had. The only time he ever had to help her, were those times that Mary had seen there was going to be a problem, For those, she assisted Doc Branscome. It was better to let the still births be handled by a doctor. Just then the sheriff opened the door, and motioned for them to come in.

Old Doc Branscome knelt by the bedside, lifting his stethoscope from Dexter Goad's chest.

"I guess his heart just gave out," the doctor said. "I don't understand it though, because I gave him a check-up not two weeks ago, and he was fit as a fiddle."

"Why is he laying all spread-eagle on the bed, almost like he was tied to the headboard and footboard?" the sheriff asked. "I've seen a few corpses, but none like that."

"Sometimes when people die, their body convulses, although that's usually not the case with a heart attack. That's mostly after something more traumatic, like electrocution. He must have had the night sweats too, just look at how his clothes are soaked."

"What about those bruises around his wrists, and ankles?"

"I've heard that sometimes during very violent heart attacks, the capillaries rupture at pressure points," the doctor said, although he didn't believe his words.

"Is there anyway to get his eyes closed, before his daughter sees him? He looks like he was scared to death."

"I tried, but I guess rigor mortis has set in. We'll cover him up and let the funeral home take care of that."

"I'll take care of it," Mary said, stepping forward from the darkness of the room.

The doctor and sheriff just nodded, and turned to leave.

She waited until they had left. She took the purse from her smock, and removed two 1878-S half dollars. She looked down into the dark, secret abyss of Dexter Goad's eyes, and there, like the negative image on an old tintype, was the undeniable image of Floyd Allen. She pressed the coins into the sockets. Turning, she started for the door. Reaching the door, she stopped and turned back to look back over her shoulder at the corpse.

"It's done," she whispered, and then sighed with relief as she left the room.

WA